The Last, Long Journey

By the same author
The Windows of Heaven

The Last, Long Journey

ROGER CLEEVE

CHARLES SCRIBNER'S SONS · NEW YORK

Printed in the United States of America

Library of Congress Catalog Card Number 76-85265

For my mother and father

The Last, Long Journey

Mountains

Ernie Maher stepped off the train and the heavy stink of the
River struck him in the face like a blow. Then he was borne
backwards with the tide. The platform squatters, whistled
from sleep among the cooking pots and Ali Baba trunks and
hobbled pairs of chickens, were surging at the doors. Red-
turbanned porters fought at their heels, holding the luggage
high on their skinny arms. A bearded one had his case tipped
from his head in the fight; Ernie grabbed his arm and showed
him a rupee. The man stared : the coin had the three Asoka
lions on it; he had only had ten years to accustom himself
to the new coinage. He hesitated; then, accepting destiny,
he pulled Ernie's suitcase from the rack and pressed backwards to the gate.

As Ernie followed, keeping men off with his elbows, he
smelled the River again . . . and he saw it was really the
people he smelled. They had all come from the Ghats, their
clothes still damp from the brown water, the red and yellow
flowers full-blown in their fists. They carried little pots of the
River under their arms. His people! He walked down the
ramp to the waiting tongas.

'George Hotel, sahib?'

It was as immutable as caste. He was as dark as an Indian;
he wore the accepted gurrah cloth of the middling ranks of
civil service. But somehow they recognized the sahib, they
always knew. And he was despatched to the city's best hotel.

He sat holding the sides of the tonga as the driver forced
the shabby pony to a trot; this was his first visit to Benares,
and he had ten hours till the departure of the Delhi train.
The houses were tall, with shops on the ground floor and

odours of dal and curry drifting from the compounds behind. The streets were slow with people moving on the broken pavements, sitting outside the bare restaurants with their glasses of milky tea and sweetmeats, bicycling with clamouring bells on the wrong side of the road. Hawkers with their betel leaves, cigarettes, chapatties and bottles of warm Cocacola caused islands of hesitation in the current.

A small boy was running beside him waving a garland. He heard the claim 'No money!', smelled a gust of cheap perfume, then the boy was dropping back with the other hand appealing for baksheesh, the contradiction unnoticed among the worshippers of ritual cleanliness in a city of filth.

He mopped his face in an unconscious European gesture and stared almost furtively at the small brass water pots, the shaven heads, the clothes damp and steaming in the hot sun. He had once believed in this. Memory tugged at his attention and he leaned forward and said in Hindi:

'Take me down to the Ghats.'

The tonga pulled to a stop and the driver turned to stare, amazed.

'Ghats, sahib?'

'Yes, take me to the Ghats. Any of them.'

It had been a mistake of course; the driver sat unhappily on his box, turning the whip in his hands.

'Hurry and take me to the Ghats.'

The man picked up the reins, then let them slack again. 'Not George Hotel?'

'No. Now I wish to see the Ghats.' Already the Indian frustration caused his anger to rise like a sickness.

The driver was trying very hard to accommodate himself to the changed idea. 'George Hotel?' he tried once more. Behind him a small crowd had quickly collected to offer advice and the boy with perfumed flowers was pushing towards him again, for baksheesh or a sale.

'Ghats first. Hotel afterwards. First you take me to Ghats and then—Oh God, never mind!'

But understanding brightened the driver's face. He turned the horse's head to the left and now its hooves slipped dangerously on the steep cobbles as he lashed skilfully at the sore places on its back. At the bottom of the slope lay a market of fruit and flower stalls, and beyond it lay the Ganges. The heavy odour of sewage and warmth, the sweet stink of India, came to him from the stalls of rotting fruit. He felt a remembered sadness settling upon him though he saw it now for the first time. He had never been to Benares before, though he had lived for years first in Delhi and then in Calcutta. They are each only a thousand miles away; not a great distance for an Indian, for a Hindu. But he was not a Hindu; he wasn't anything.

He told the tonga-wallah to wait and stood for a moment at the top of the steps, watching the heavy water ooze slowly by like the bowels of the continent, disposing of everything thrust into it. Some late worshippers watched him curiously from under their chattris. Not long ago you could tell a man from his bearing and his colour, whether he was rich, or twice-born, from Bengal or the Plains or the south. But they had become a republic; there had been Partition. There were many strangers now. Not that anything had changed: the opposite ideas easily juxtaposed like the mendicant salesman and people urinating into the water they worshipped.

He walked slowly down the steps, wondering why he had come. It was years since he had given up this sort of thing, carrying his search for identity into their homes and secret places. It belonged to childhood, before he learned that no one wanted to be changed, that the less they had the more fiercely they eschewed improvement.

He was drawn to watch the group on his left, the three men and the fourth man, and the smouldering heap of ash on which he lay. Two of the thin-legged youths stood resting on their shovels as the third youth, stripped to his dhoti, hurled

bucketsful of ash on top of the corpse. The steep pile of ash
ran in a steady stream back to his feet, to be hurled up again.

Lack of wood, the usual problem. It was costly to die with
dignity. There was no alternative to the Brahmin's fee, but
afterwards it was still possible to acquire merit with a little
wood and some clever handling of the hot ash. Living or not,
flesh drops away easily enough, though once a man is a skele-
ton he is a hard thing to destroy. As Ernie watched, the heat
played a gruesome trick on the rubble of bones. A charred arm
contracted slowly at the elbow to point to the sky. But the
man with the shovel knocked it down and covered it
with ash, working with unemotional haste as if clearing a
drain.

One of his friends in Oxford had been studying Indian
anthropology. He was interested in comparative religions, and
had talked convincingly of the psychological relationship between fire and water. Now here it was applied to human
beings, as the Oxford scholar would never see it, though he
was probably a Doctor by now, but still not understanding
or caring that whatever the academics and politicians could
achieve, measured out and distributed over the devouring continent, would not add up to an anna's worth of extra wood
for that fire.

Gandhi, whom he had tried to love, tried to respect, had
achieved nothing. A few rich Indians had taken over the
white men's jobs. But the poor, the 400 million of India,
what had they gained? Not the toe-nail of one more buffalo;
not a cup of milk in a year. And he was past caring, the final
humiliation. That was what India did to you.

In the evening he went on to Delhi. The night service was
fast and he arrived at New Delhi railway station at nine in
the morning. His appointment with Ram Lal was for eleven
o'clock. He was pleased to be back after ten years in Calcutta.
Perhaps Lal was going to offer him promotion, a new job in
Delhi. Or abroad? But he retreated immediately, sudden hope
drowned by the fear of disappointment. However much

accepted on the surface, it was unlikely they would allow foreign eyes witness their need of *him*.

He went to a hotel on Connaught Circus to wash and change. Connaught was as always, the circle of pillared, flat-fronted shops, the ugliness of huge-lettered Hindi advertisements, and in the centre the amber grass and flame-of-the-forest trees and the beggars asleep under them. An ox-cart obstructed thirty yards of traffic on Janpath; a policeman screamed orders but the driver was asleep and the bullock was from Jaipur, he spoke a different language, and pressed back obstinately in the clumsy shafts.

He would have taken a taxi to the office on Rajpat but it was a matter of diplomacy; he must not appear too proud to be seen on a scooter. Always one dragged oneself down to the commonest level, which itself sank a little lower each year. The bullock driver had awakened now and was using his goad in the animal's rectum, but a small boy was idly throwing dust in its eyes. How much could he accept of the ignorance and cruelty of India? As much, he had once thought, as he felt capable of changing. But you could change nothing: least of all yourself, he heard echoed inevitably in an old memory.

When he reached Ram Lal's office he was annoyed to find it empty; his effort with the uncomfortable scooter had been wasted. But Lal came hurrying in a moment later with a bunch of dusty files under his arm; Ernie noticed that they still bore the old British registry numbers. Lal had put on weight round the stomach and neck but was still very smooth-skinned and looked more like a lizard than ever. . . .

'Ernestiji! My brother!' He clapped his hands together in namaste and slid forward to clasp Ernie warmly. 'I have not seen you for five years, but I am hearing plenty. You have been a great credit to me in Calcutta.'

Ernie Maher smiled. 'Take no notice of my miserable efforts,' he quoted.

'No no, you have done brilliantly—but you are teasing me, aren't you? He paused, and regarded his protégé proudly;

he had chosen Ernie from an unlikely background. 'They told me you would not be right for the new India, but no one has worked harder than you. But that is what a republic means, eh? We are not Hindus and Sikhs and Muslims now. We are Indians. Even the Anglo-Indian—'

Ernie said quickly: 'I hope so, Inspector-sahib.'

A shadow flickered across Ram Lal's pale skin; he was fairer than Ernie. Then he chuckled.

'Ernest, I love you like my brother. You prefer to be known as an Indian, don't you? That is true, is it not, you promised me—?'

'And how are you,' Ernie asked him suddenly. 'Your health was not good when we last met.'

Ram Lal smiled happily: recurrent ulcers from hunger strikes and forced feeding. He began to describe his symptoms, then he glanced at his watch.

'Oh tut! There is no time. Come, you must meet the Minister.'

Ernie stared. 'I am to meet the Minister?'

'You did not know? I thought you had been informed. Anyway, you may rest assured, this business is important.'

He ushered Ernie out of the office and started down the dim corridor, the white-turbanned chaprassies popping up to salute and down again as they passed by.

'Ram Lal, one moment. Am I to meet the Minister, really? What does he want me for? Is it a job abroad?'

'You have special commission,' Ram Lal said. His pace did not slacken: they hurried along the passage, passing across the cool gusts of air where water was being sluiced on to the window screens. 'You may rest assured,' Ram Lal said, 'I am certain of you. This is my very personal recommendation. Perhaps you may not like what I have let you in for, but it shows how I trust you. It is your great chance—to show which side your soul is on.'

He stopped in front of a door and gathered himself. Only now did Ernie notice the moustache, which had not been there five years before. It too was pale, and drooped like its owner's eyelids. But he had managed it at last. The space on Ram's lip had always been able to remind him of the angry crowd at the racecourse, the flight on his bicycle, Ram's pale desperate face watching the guns and dogs go by, in the days when there was still hope. But achievement dissipates hope as love consumes desire. Ram Lal raised a small fist and was about to tap on the door when it opened silently inwards and left his hand knocking the air.

The Minister was a small, neatly-dressed Sikh with delicate manners. He did namaste, and Ernie bowed stiffly in response. The office was full of brown leather furniture, and pictures of the Mahatma and Jawaharlal Nehru hung either side of the tall window. The noise of an air-conditioner droned annoyingly into the room, seeming to push forward heat in front of it.

'Will you excuse us, Ram Lal? I know you wish to attend to your many duties.'

They exchanged a secret look between them, and Ram Lal smiled nervously; then he bowed and hurried away. Ernie started the courtesies. 'Your Excellency,' he murmured.

The Minister waved a careless hand. 'You need not say those things.'

'I don't think I—'

'No, no. I am correct, I think. You are more British than Indian.'

He protested quickly. 'No Sir—'

'It does not matter. We are all British to a certain extent. Here, let us shake hands. Jolly fine. I was at Oxford too, you know. I was also in British jail. I think that gives me some advantage.' But he skated over this distinction, which earned him automatic respect from most of his colleagues; his information on Ernie Maher was better than Ram Lal's.

He waited till Ernie was seated and had refused a cigarette; he took one himself from a box inlaid with a picture of a beefeater and three ravens.

'Mr Maher, I have been searching into your background, and was most diverted apropos some particulars. There is a certain, er, venture to be undertaken, and I think you are the man best able to accomplish it. First of all . . .' He hesitated, and toyed with the gold metal strap of his watch. 'You see, I am shy of telling you. Perhaps this job you may refuse.'

I will refuse nothing, Ernie thought. He was ready to accept any responsibility which would put obstacles between him and the boredom of Calcutta.

'You are aware, of course, of the troubles in Kashmir? In Sheikh Abdullah they have lost a leader, but are still agitating for secession?'

'Yes.'

'Since the confrontation in 1947 there have been continuous efforts from Pakistan to effect disturbances in Kashmir. There have been incursions into our sovereign territory.' The Minister was a prison graduate, reared under British wardens on a diet of dictionaries. *How to Write Good Letters* was one of the books he kept always on the shelf behind his desk.

'Behind the ceasefire lines. . . .' He turned to a large wall-map and pointed to an area east of the border, which on the enemy's maps was marked 'Indian-occupied territory of Pakistan'. His index finger moved vaguely; the border had shifted a few times that winter. 'Somewhere behind this line Pakistani soldiers are training Kashmiri guerillas. Infiltration is being effected under our very noses—into the Vale itself.'

Ernie thought he was expected to say something.

'How is that possible?'

'They just do it,' the man said despairingly. He wiped his face with a handkerchief thoroughly, as if trying to rub off the shadow of debt. An unaligned country fighting a war. It was simpler for Home Affairs, they just let people die, carrying problems with them.

'Have you been to Kashmir, Mr Maher?'

'Once,' Ernie said. 'When I was fourteen. I rode from Sialkot to the Lake. With—' but it made him twinge, like the first hint of toothache.

'Well.' The little Sikh went to the window and fiddled with the air-conditioner to reduce the noise. He wore a tie which Ernie vaguely recognized: Pembroke perhaps, or St. John's, Cambridge.

'The training of these guerillas, and their weapons, are primitive. But it is an issue of morale. Here they are, these poor fellows, with political convictions of the flimsiest kind—and while India is necessarily policing them, Pakistan is training them to engage in military operations and an Englishman is supplying guns, er,' he searched for a longer word, 'weaponry into the heart of Kashmir.'

'An Englishman?'

'That is correct.'

Ernie stared.

'It is a clever idea. It lends dignity to the cause. These ignorant fellows don't understand mercenaries. If an Englishman fights, England is on their side. And the weaponry is American. So America, Britain and Pakistan are all fighting on behalf of the Muslims in Kashmir. The guns themselves, they are a nuisance of course, but not enough to make any difference—yet. There's plenty left over from forty-seven, and some of those fellows can make their own. But it's the moral uplift they are getting which is dangerous.'

'How do we know it is an Englishman?' Ernie said. He felt the twinge again, a little stronger than the first time.

'There is no doubt of that. Many people have seen him. He is the very caricature of the English upper class—blond, blue eyes, Oxford, son of an Indian army man. Awfully good at cricket.' The Minister paused and a little smile spread slowly over the bottom half of his face, leaving the eyes alone. 'He comes of awfully good family—unsullied,' he said oddly, but was able to giggle at the flush of anger and alarm on his visitor's face.

'I imagine he has not been identified?' Ernie stammered but

the pain went thud thud in his memory and brought him back again.

'Oh yes! He has definitely been tabulated. And he must be apprehended and brought to Delhi. But we are between the devil and the shallow water.' He hesitated, glancing towards his bookshelf, but Ernie's complete silence reassured him and he went on: 'There must be no dramatic arrests or headlined trials. He is a petty criminal not a martyr. This is honestly a terribly dangerous situation. But we feel that if someone can get close enough to him, some trusted friend, perhaps, or an old colleague—'

Ernie sat with memory blocks banging back like doors leading to his past: Srinagar; Oxford; Delhi Cantonment.

'—someone who could perhaps identify themselves with his motives, and think ahead of him, that's who we need. He works alone, they say, without accomplices. It shouldn't be difficult,' the Minister said, and with a gesture waved away the problem like he waved away Goa and the Chinese and all the files the expatriate civil service men kept sending in to him marked 'Immediate'. It was his job to define problems, not solve them, he was not a professional man; it had been much more fun in the days when their only problem was the British Raj.

'Ram Lal informs me that you might be able to help us in this respect. You were—er—close to—'

'Yes, Your Excellency. I know him.'

Wiltshire; Great Russell Street; the banyan tree. There were no secrets in India. Out on the Rajpat a bullock cart was creaking up towards Lok Sabha and beyond to the north, heaving its high load of rice sacks to Ambala. They had probably come from there only a week ago by train but a deal had taken place, a move in the Indian economy. The two soft-faced creatures stepped in apathetic unison; the driver was already asleep, the reins looped round his neck. At that speed the journey would take about two weeks, consuming half the profits of the rice, but Ernie did not doubt it would get there; the vast will of India was amorphous but never diverted. Kharma watched over his people while they multiplied their problems in their beds.

'Will you accept this task for us, Mr Maher?'

It was his kharma. Ram Lal had talked, but the Minister would have known anyway; it was inevitable. As an educated man he did not believe in superstition but there was something about India that turned myth to reality. After the events of Wiltshire, no one knew that better than himself.

There is a bus which runs from Pathankot northwards to Jammu, and then through hills of pine forests to the Kashmiri capital of Srinagar. From there it is not far to the Muslim town of Baramula; but first you have to get to Pathankot.

Ernie travelled in a second-class compartment overnight through the wide, watered plains of the Punjab. The moonlight relieved the land of its flatness, casting strange shadows to make valleys of darkness amongst hills of luminous light. He did not manage to sleep; whenever his eyes closed against his troubled thoughts another station drew up and stopped noisily outside the window. There was the hurry to alight, the frenzy to get on, the luggage passing to and fro on upstretched arms like wrecks above the tide. Pan-vendors cried and thumped at the windows; the red-faced chapatti-wallahs smacked and twirled and puffed up their frenzied offerings on braziers which they wheeled cursing between the heavy, sleeping forms and bundles. A boy crawled about his legs with a dustpan and brush. Even when the train drew out there was no relief, for the beggars and vendors stayed on, plying their trades. They had no home away from the trains, and measured their lives in annas and naye paisas.

Pathankot was already hot at eight in the morning. It hadn't changed much after sixteen years. He sampled the false luxury of a shower in the first-class waiting room, then went out to the bus station to buy his ticket. He had an hour's wait for the bus. The station restaurant served breakfasts of eggs and bacon at one window, vegetarian meals at the other. From a nearby table he was watched curiously by the family who had shared his compartment on the train. He could see them peering over their teacups, remembering how he had spread out his own bed on the bunk, instead of calling a porter.

Outside, Ernie saw his luggage stacked on top of the bus, then leaned back heavily in the seat and half closed his eyes. Was it revenge he was being offered at last? It was too late for anything else, certainly. Years of bitter humiliation could not be wiped out at a blow. The gangrene could be arrested but you had still lost the limb. Now it was all too long ago and he didn't know what he wanted. He had outgrown his memory and felt only the dull pain of the amputation.

The bus ran noisily through the avenues of the town and started to climb on a good road through scrub country; but they were stopped at the Jammu and Kashmir border. Everyone climbed out of the bus while two customs men clambered among the bundles on the roof. Ernie announced his business as tourist; the Minister had warned him to trust no one, though he was still in the predominantly Hindu part of the state.

The bus crossed one large river and several small ones. At midday it climbed steeply to enter the town of Jammu. Most of the passengers had brought their own food in cloth-wrapped bundles and sat in the shade of the tourist centre to eat it, but Ernie walked across the road to the town's good restaurant, once a favourite among the British tourists making for Srinagar, now deserted but for tables and mis-spelled menus and fans moving too turgidly to shake the dust off their blades. He ordered 'omlett and slice' and ate it slowly and thoughtfully, staring at the wall, preparing for all the sores that would be reopened on this journey he had done before. They had refused to let him fly, too conspicuous.

'Coppee, sahib?' suggested the proprietor. He had a dirty white coat and too much hair oil.

Ernie nodded.

'Nes-coppee?' the man said hopefully.

'No, Staines.'

It steamed slowly in front of him until it was cold. The bus
hooted outside, but he did not hear it. The driver came in to
tell him the bus stood at the door; if he had not been an
obviously important man it would not have waited.

The sunlight surprised his eyes and he sat perspiring until
the bus was away from the town, bouncing now on an un-
metalled road, racing with the bright-painted lorries to avoid
their dust. A fleet, disturbing thought flicked through his
mind, of a man's sad face at the end of a rifle. He watched
with apprehension the pine trees beginning to appear on the
steep, rock-strewn hillsides, the small streams flowing across
the road. It was the torture all over again. Instead he applied
his mind to other things . . . there were the small brick homes
in Delhi with veranda and postage-stamp lawn and extrava-
gant iron gates, the dry, stinging odour of the sweeper village
opposite, the sliding of the pye-dogs back into their yards as
the bicycles moved by through the dust, the disturbing beauty
of the dark-faced women walking with bucket from the well,
the slow, black, blue-tongued buffaloes stretching nose forward down to the pool to sigh and settle into the cool morning with the water sending up great green bubbles for half
an hour after its disturbance.

They came to a wide, shallow river with boulders butting
at the white flow. The bus ran along beside it for a mile until
it came to a girdered bridge, with planks that rattled beneath
the wheels as it crossed. A notice at either end prohibited
photography; a sentry with a rifle stood self-consciously in his
doorway. The road was steep on the other side and the dust
had coated the pines for ten feet up their trunks.

He thought determinedly of the slow, walking-pace train
moving down behind Jor Bagh every morning, piled with
white-clad figures on running board and roof; the children
mounting, and leaping off at the level crossing. Traffic had

always waited in two struggling lines pressed tight against the crossing gates on either side, and it took ages to open them against the crowd when the train had gone by. The bicyclists would sit astride and jangle their bells or lift their bikes over the gate and carry them across the track; and there was the harnessed cow circling and turning its crushing stone with the cane juice spilling into the wooden bowl; the Sikh fortune-teller at the corner of the market; and the expectancy of the coming monsoon, the greyness in the sky one morning, the shivery wind, the first great drops striking people's faces as they ran out to look at the sky and drink it in.

But sadder thoughts kept flicking at his memory; hockey on a field in Oxford; the greenhouse by the river; her in a raincoat; a photograph carefully torn down one side . . . memory is opposed to the effort of will and like desire brings pain not of its own choosing.

At Banihal another bus had arrived before them; the serai was full, no one knew what could be done. The wind was chill and there was a smell of charcoal and food from the little bazar down the road. After twenty minutes a bearer hurried out, and led the party by torchlight down a hillside path between the rice terraces. Half a dozen wooden, windowless huts stood by themselves in the dark. The bearer tried several keys, then pushed open the door with his shoulder. His torch flickered among the waiting passengers.

He pointed to Ernie. 'Your place, sahib.'

Ernie indicated some of the waiting women. 'They can go in first,' he said. Whispering broke out behind him; immediately he knew he had made a mistake, it was hopeless, he would have to obey.

'No, sahib, this is the best place. Other huts have no electrical light.'

A bearer made up his bed. He had the three-roomed hut to himself, while a dozen people slept out in the cold. He ate rice and mutton curry at the guesthouse, then walked down the hill again by himself in the moonlight. The terraces of

rice fields sloped down and away into the last big valley before
the highest range. On the other side of the hard line of hills
lay the Vale of Kashmir. The pines stood all about and reminded him. He was flirting with his memories, seeing how
far he could go. One part of the sky was still not quite dark;
an orange glow silhouetted the last line of hills. A night bird
was calling from the opposite hillside, but the intervals grew
longer between each note. A faint noise of the bazar floated
down to him, and again he smelled the acridness from the smoke
of dung-fires. The bird had stopped calling now. He waited a
long time but it did not sound again. The next day he abandoned the futile effort at blocking his memories. It was all too
much like it had been before. The tall wooden houses stood in
clusters of willow groves and little streams were dashing by
on an apparently dead flat land. The road was lined on both
sides with slender poplars and he could watch other poplar-
lined avenues joining it miles ahead. The people were fair-
skinned, much lighter than he, their carts were sturdy, the
ponies trotted as if involved in the energy of their drivers. The
mustard fields were bordered with low herb-covered mounds
and the narrow ditches channelled water briskly far out into
the purple-flowered meadows. Grass grew on the mud-packed
roofs of the houses, with straw and rice and potatoes stored
in the top open-fronted storeys. Fat donkeys waddled beside
the dusty white road, weighted and balanced with heavy straw
panniers, and the tall poplar trees, purposeful, equidistant,
went on and on across the brown plain.

Plains

It was called the 'green' by the people who lived round three of its four sides. . . . At one end was a broken see-saw erected by an I.C.S. man returned years ago to Scotland; and at the other end, as if in some attempt at symmetry, a wooden bench warped by the sun.

During the monsoon some shafts of grass managed to force a way up to the muddy surface. But all effort was futile; they were instantly beaten flat by the rain, like the squatters by the railway track on the 'green's' fourth side when they tried to challenge nature by briefly raising themselves above the common level.

For the other nine months of the year the ground was baked as hard as the concrete road and the boys who played football on it came home with grazes on their elbows and knees. Ernie envied them. He sat with his face at the window of one of the square's smaller houses and stared out with angry longing, his hands clutching the window bars like a cage.

He was small for his age, thin, with black hair and a skin darker than either of his parents, which had made Victor Maher weep with rage that night ten years ago when his wife had whispered the shameful news. Even now Victor would sometimes notice, reflected in his boy's black eyes, his own furtive shame at the memory of his grandmother's darkness, the guilty secret he had kept even from his wife. Now the woman was dead, and it made no immediate difference, but you couldn't escape her shadow. It was as if the power which visits iniquities unto the children's children, in what should be a smooth progression, punished for its own mistakes as well as ours.

Ernie shifted reluctantly, but with relief too, from the window.

'It is time for my lesson in the English.'

Victor thought about it but decided not to correct him. He had learned not to press too hard. And the boy might have said it deliberately. But: 'Don't hang about with the Indian boys afterwards,' he said. He couldn't take chances with that.

'No, I won't. I have geography homework and I desire to achieve top marks like I did last week.'

'Well done,' Victor said. 'English is more important, of course, but top in Geography is very good indeed.' Conversation was always a tussle between them, but like a sparring practice where they hit lightly and left openings.

'One day you will go to British School. I saw the adjutant again today, who is a very good friend of mine. He was very impressed with your essay. Your present school is no good.'

'I like it,' Ernie said.

'I saw John Lemos playing with the adjutant's son this morning,' Victor began, but there, he had immediately broken the rules and hooked too hard: the defence was thrown up immediately.

'I don't want to play with those stupid pigs,' and Ernie's glance towards the window was too swift even for Victor to notice it. 'They're all stupid and stuck up.'

'You mustn't talk of British boys as "they",' Victor said lightly; 'but of course I understand what you mean. They stick together far too much. They don't mix with other— other British people.'

'We're not British,' Ernie said. He had the ten-year-old's aggressive courage towards dangers he had not experienced. 'They call us cheechees.'

Victor decided he had not heard the remark. In his job as civilian quartermaster at the cantonment he was respected by all the officers' families (his assistant attended the N.C.O.s

and soldiers) who certainly were never rude enough to refer
to him as an Anglo, let alone a cheechee. They treated him,
and all his kind, as inferiors but that was only proper. Sometimes he thought of himself as having a sergeant's rank before
the officers; and if the other ranks also treated him with condescension that was probably because they were from England and he was not. But to use words like cheechee and eight-
anna with their hateful suggestion of native skin and habits
. . . well it would simply not be true. At the age of forty he
had little more knowledge of India than the army wives who
ventured outside the compound gates only two or three times
a year. He had never been into the villages and seen the high
walls round the mud huts, the smoke curling up from the
dung fires, the small dusty fields of yellow rice among the
water channels. He had not watched the women strolling to
the well with slovenly grace, the brass pots on their heads,
or sitting in the courtyards picking their children's fleas or
combing out their long hair with clarified butter. Being a
Christian he had never made the pilgrimage to Benares or
Allahabad, washing with two million countrymen in the
Ganges water, travelling back home in the crowded train
asleep on the luggage rack, and he had never driven the shiny
black buffalo down to the muddy pond in the cool mornings
with the bare-arsed children playing on their backs. Even the
grubby life of the squatter colony he had observed only with
a neighbour's indifference: the scavenging cows on the rub-
bish dump; the children running with dysentery. His protection was not strength but distance.

But sometimes the horror veered too close and he caught a
glimpse of all the darkness that formed the background of
their twilight world. And at this moment the important thing
was to get his son to the English lesson.

'You don't find it too difficult, keeping up with the others?'
he suggested, and the transparency of the remark would have
been evident even to a ten-year-old if this one could ever resist
a challenge to his school prowess.

'I'm better than all the others,' he said sharply, knowing it was true. And began to gather his books for battle.

Coming back from the lessons at the British wife's house he practised the sentences with eager facility. The boy was very FAIR. Have no FEAR said the man. The house is very FAR away. Even Victor carried the revealing lilt in his voice, like a Welshman, which Ernie had learned to subdue. He emphasized the vowels in the well-formed lips of his mind, with the English lady's smile bent towards him. He loved competition. But then he turned the corner of the green where the boys were still playing and the shutters of his pride snapped down.

The big blond boy was there as usual. He was tall even for a British boy and already, at twelve years old, very handsome; his face was formed into the strength of a man's. When Robert King appeared at the game there was never any question about who was leader. He chose the sides, played always for the weaker team to balance the contest, was the final appeal in all disputes. If ever he failed to come out on to the green the game was an undisciplined scramble, everyone playing for himself as if it was not a game at all but involved the earnestness of real life.

A few times, more than a year ago, Ernie had tried to join in the game. He would come out of his house and sit on the bench at the edge of the green, behind the goalposts marked by cricket stumps hammered into the hard crust with a mallet. When the ball came near him he would rise, balance carefully and kick it back. But no one ever accepted this mute invitation; from a few yards' distance he really did look Indian, with the dark sad eyes and the slender body. And Victor's careful English slang, the pith helmet and the starched shorts, emphasized what they hid, like the painted smile of a clown.

Shyly, he sat on the bench to watch the game. He could have played better than most of them.

Suddenly the ball bounced and rolled towards his feet; he stared at it stupidly.

'Quick, you—throw it here.' The blond boy was running towards him.

He stood and tossed the ball awkwardly into the imperious arms. 'I don't mind standing in goal for you . . . ' but immediately he winced as the boy looked at him with uplifted eyebrows.

'What, a wog? How would you know how to play?'

'I'm not a wog. And anyway,' he said defiantly, 'you've got Imam Talib playing.'

'That's different. He's a Muslim.'

'But why can't I join in?'

'You're a cheechee,' the boy said, looking at him closer. It was enough explanation; he ran back on to the field, bouncing the ball authoritatively. 'We'll have a goal kick, that went in off Wilson's foot. Take it, Imam. Right up the field now.' He ran off, leaving angry tears pricking Ernie's large brown eyes.

But as soon as he had sat down, the boy was walking back. 'Still want a game?'

Ernie's heart jumped. 'Yes please, King.'

'I might let you in tomorrow.'

A wave of gratitude rolled out from him towards the English boy. His throat felt thick as he said: 'Thank you, King.'

'You'll have to play well or I'll make you linesman.'

'Oh, I wouldn't let you down. I'm jolly excellent at school games.'

The boy smiled and turned away. His legs in the white shorts were strong and big-muscled, a man's legs. Already he looked about fifteen years old.

Ernie watched from the window next evening until Robert King appeared. Then hurried out, swallowing the last of his tea.

'Oh, you. I promised you a game, didn't I?'

Ernie's blood was hammering. 'Yes, please, King.' He hated him, and he despised the others, and he desperately wanted to play them at football.

'I don't know if there's a place for you after all.' But in fact there were several places. At King's orders Ernie went to the left wing, excited and tense. It was his chance: he knew he could run fast.

The first time the ball came to him Ernie sped away, thin legs pounding, the dust spurting under his sandals. Arriving all too soon at the end of the foreshortened pitch he looked round for King and pushed the ball fast across the ground towards him. The British boy hit it once and the ball bounced between the flimsy posts and hit a passing cow on the road, making it sheer away in alarm.

Ernie was exultant; it was he who had made that goal! He looked for King's eyes as he walked back, but met nothing.

It happened twice more that evening, Ernie running up the left wing and passing swiftly inside for King to score. He thought: We're a team. We go together. Victor greeted him on the veranda with shining eyes.

'You are doing splendidly well. Football is a jolly excellent English game. Have you made any friends yet?'

Next evening the Ernie/King partnership scored four goals, Ernie always passing at the end of his run for King to score. He wasn't good at finishing off, he knew. He was the runner; King was the kicker. The other boys didn't like it; Ernie knew it was by King's independence only, an exercise in authority, that he was there on the field. But he threw everything into this chance. When it became too dark to carry on Robert King nodded to him and said, 'You're all right for an Anglo.' Praise from . . . the qualification didn't matter, he was accepted.

But the next evening Robert shocked him by choosing the sides, placing Ernie on the wing, then with a smile walking over to join the other side. He felt deserted. He fumbled the ball and didn't play well. Once Robert ran across and tackled him so hard he fell down winded. He thought: I've done something wrong; he doesn't like me any more. At the end of the game he was walking miserably away when he looked up to see King standing in front of him, a curious smile on his face. It didn't look friendly; King was scrutinizing him, staring through his eyes and soul. Once his gaze travelled down Ernie's body and up again. Then he nodded grimly twice, like dubbing with a sword, and turned away without speaking.

But next day Robert picked the sides, chose Ernie first, and said, 'Let's show 'em.' They scored so many goals that everyone lost count. And afterwards Robert said to him, 'We must always work together.'

He was accepted; he didn't ask for happiness. He never understood the reason for the brutal changes of mood loosed upon him, but he responded with a dog's capacity for self-denigration, the fondled ear compensating for a kick. Over the next few weeks they would greet each other cheerfully, go cycling or playing together, and return to sit on the veranda until Ernie was called in to bed. The harmony would be created; then Robert would cut straight across it: 'You're a cheechee, what do you know about it?' And laugh; but he wouldn't go then. He continued to lounge on the step, enjoying his possession of it, and watching Ernie's struggle to walk in and leave him. He was so sure of his victory that he would not always stay to observe it.

One day Ernie asked him: 'You remember that first day you said I couldn't play football—"

'You can't properly—'

'You said it was O.K. for Muslims. Why is it O.K. for—?'

'Muslims are better than Hindus. They're stronger and they work harder and they've got more guts. My father said so,' said Robert with finality. He was to learn that Robert and his father had many views in common.

'But you don't think I'm a Hindu, do you?'

'You're half a one.'

'I'm half Indian. But I'm a Christian.'

'Not like I'm a Christian,' Robert said. 'You're not as good as us.' Any road served for his destination, and Ernie bore him there on his thin shoulders.

'I jolly well am as—'

'If you say you're as good as me we don't play together any more,' and Robert smiled at the sudden silence. But a moment later bought two cakes from a passing tricyclist with his BUNDS AND PESTRIES painted on the red sides of the basket, and they sat quietly munching with differences subdued.

Victor's delight at Ernie's new friend was balanced by the fear of losing him. Boys' relationships were so ephemeral; a word could break them. But it was hard to hold back; determined on conversation, he had appeared at the front door once, wearing his pith helmet newly blancoed, nodding courteously to the British boy as he marched across the veranda. But the boy had ignored him; he had been forced to continue uneasily past and down the steps and along the street with no destination.

He had even stopped Major King on the Kotwali Road once, and tried to establish the new relationship reflected in their sons' friendship but the major had been vague; after satisfying himself that Robert had not been misbehaving he walked on, smiling diffidently. Victor was irritated but not for long. His countrymen were strange; but Ernie had broken through and stood poised for freedom. No more loitering with the Indian boys and coming home with their mysterious words like sores on his mouth . . . Urdu, Hindi, Punjabi even. He never could understand how the boy picked them up so easily; by the time he made up his mind to put a stop to it Ernie had three languages in his rough grasp, three secret worlds of his own. The British boy would put a stop to that.

In the early summer Major King took his family to Dehra Dun in the hills. Robert was full of the adventure when he said goodbye to Ernie.

'We're staying in a hut by a river. There's mountains and

snow and lakes. My father says it's better than Switzerland. We'll go riding every day and my father's going to teach me to shoot. We'll go swimming every day in the river.'

'When will you be back?'

'Not for three months. We'll miss the heat and the monsoon. You'll be sweltering like pigs back here.'

'I do not care if I do.'

'Ho, yes you do. Sour grapes. We'll go riding. I'm a very good rider.'

'So can I ride.'

'Only those little Indian things. I've ridden steeplechasers at home. And they have lovely horses at Dehra Dun, Arab horses my father says. We'll go riding every day.'

'I wish I could come with you,' he at last admitted.

They wrote one letter each, formal stilted phrases exactly alike. After the middle of May the football games ceased and all the British families disappeared up into the hill stations of Dehra Dun, Ranipur and Simla. Now the nights brought no welcoming coolness and the punkawallahs were kept flapping at the cloths till dawn.

One day Victor asked: 'What about your English friend, the adjutant's son? If he hasn't replied to you then you must write again.'

'I don't think we're friends any more.'

'But that is nonsense.' (He had known it would happen; it was terrible.) 'He wrote to you. You have played games of football. When he returns you will play football again. He will not want to do without you, his star winger.'

'I don't want to,' Ernie said, and went to get his bicycle from his downstairs bedroom. He begged a picnic lunch from his aunt, then lifted the bike over the thin hedge and cycled away up the road. He didn't care about Robert King anyway. After ten minutes he saw where his mood was taking him and a shudder of anxious pleasure caused the bicycle to wobble over the road. If Victor knew; but sometimes Victor's potency to hurt was blunted, and there are things the body will do even in anticipation of the consequent shame. He went on past the Red Fort and over the Jamuna Bridge and on into the villages and the guilt never left him, nor the pleasure. It was the first time for months. He pedalled slowly past village after village, with the smoke of dung fires drifting across the bright yellows and reds and mauves of the women as they chattered at the well or punished their clothes at the pond's edge. Every few hundred yards he came to another village, filling his eyes with the wonder and excitement of it as he went past. He cycled further than ever before. When at last he felt how tired his legs were he stopped, and stood nervously at the edge of the last village straddling the crossbar and munching his sandwiches in large, anxious bites.

He could feel the familiar dry Indian smell stinging his nostrils. Sometimes a few children would creep forward wide-eyed, and dart away when he turned. Some young women were watching him from a courtyard where they were cooking rice. A low mud wall ran round three sides of the compound and as they squatted at the fire they could just peep over the top of the wall, and be doing something else if he noticed. Were they sisters, neighbours?—they lived in such closeness. Behind them, behind the smoky fire, was the doorway of their home. He could see nothing beyond it but darkness.

Now there was a woman walking up the road towards him. She came with an easy, indolent stride, carrying a small boy straddled on her hip. As she came closer he saw she was hugely pregnant, her stomach jutting aggressively through the dirty yellow dress. She stared frankly into his face not bothering to use the veil and he dropped his eyes shyly. Then looked again quickly; she had gone to sit with the other women stirring the ricepots and the baby was crawling experimentally around her legs.

'Namaste!'

He jumped nervously. 'Namaste!' Should he flee? A man of startling thinness stood beside him, his brown face lined like an old map. At Ernie's spontaneous reply he grinned with delight: it seemed to cut his body in two for an instant, before being re-established in its twisted age.

'Would you like water?' the man enquired.

He had never spoken to the villagers before. His Hindi had been learned from the boys at school and it was a shock to hear the phrase out of context. He hesitated; the women were peeping at him over the low wall.

'Thank you,' he said at last, and the man turned and stepped with faltering elegance between the huts to the well. A wooden bucket hung at the end of a thick old rope, knotted in many places; the muddy earth round the winch bore an accummulation of footprints like the strata of generations. The old man let the bucket down with a splash and drew it up brimming. He went into the nearest house and returned with a cup, which he rinsed in the bucket, wiping round the inside with his thumb. The water had a faint greenish tinge; Ernie swallowed it down and was about to refill the cup for the old man when his hand was knocked roughly away. The cup splashed into the mud. The man had to hold on to the winch as he knelt to pick it up for his legs were not only thin but the joints were stiff; he moved around on them like stilts.

'It was for you,' Ernie cried. 'I was filling it for you.'

A sudden anger brightened the man's eyes; then it died, and he threw the cup away and drank with his hands. 'You do not understand,' he said, wiping his mouth. 'I am Brahmin.'

He pointed to the water in the dirty bottom of the well. 'I can draw water for you. But it is not permitted that I accept it from—' He stared curiously at Ernie. 'It is our way, sahib.'

'If you won't drink from my cup,' Ernie stammered, 'why do you call me sahib?' It was like groping with your hand down a dark hole for whatever you might find. But the man smiled vaguely; he did not understand. Caste was not rank.

'Would you rest with me in the shade, sahib.' He pointed

his skinny arm. The hand looked as if it might snap right off
with its dead weight.

'No,' Ernie said. 'I want to go now.' He looked round for
his bicycle; two children darted away from it.

'What honourable name do you bear?' The man had a
keen desire to learn, and opportunity did not often come
bicycling into his village.

'I am Ernie, son of Sahib Maher at the Cantonment.'

'Is he a soldier?'

'He is agent for the barracks.'

'How much do they pay him?'

'I don't know,' Ernie said. The reminder of his father made
him think of the trouble he would meet if Victor found out.
'Excuse me, I definitely desire to go.'

'You are always welcome,' the old Brahmin said as Ernie
pedalled away; but he knew it wasn't true. The man would
now go to wash his hands (they had touched) and have the
cup ritually cleansed after its contact with an untouchable.
He passed the pregnant girl again; she was hardly older than
himself but did not bother to cover her face any more than
the last time. In her eyes he didn't count. Perhaps his father
was right and there was nothing Indian in him. But Robert
had said there was nothing English in him. And as he cycled
home the whole fragility of his existence came upon him, suddenly but then prolonged, like the groping after identity on
waking from a dream in a strange place; and as in a dream,
when the murderer's gun that you have been fleeing for
minutes breaks on your ears at the precise moment as the
real sound that wakes you, time moved backwards in anticipation of horror. And when Robert returned to the green and
never came to call at the house he was not surprised, he had
seen it as he cycled away from the village, and perhaps even
beforehand in the single letter he had received: ' . . . lots of
Muslims up here, fine fellows. Went riding this morning with

Ali Mohammed, the owner of our cabin. He is quite decent for a native and does not attempt to cheat us. Our cabin is very clean. Indian houses always pong slightly, don't you think? It doesn't seem as if we're in India at all. My father told me they are good fighters and their religion is almost the same as ours, for they will not worship idols. . . .'

Robert came home and Ernie looked out one evening and saw him playing football on the green. He would have hurried out, hailed him with the propriety of friendship, but again time compressed: he saw himself spurned or ignored, he could not bear the coolness of searching for a renewed familiarity. He couldn't offer himself again. And Robert didn't come to him. After the second evening had passed he knew it was too late for either of them to change their minds.

They spent the following weeks avoiding each other, and because of this the British boy had been gone from the district for several weeks before Ernie learned of it; and by then it had lost its power to hurt.

The next time he saw Robert he had to face the punishment for his three months of independence. Robert stood like a captain in front of his schoolboy army, with Ernie come like an envoy to ask terms. A brisk wind scattered the dead leaves about. 'What are you then?' asked Robert, drawing on fresh reserves of hostility from the ranks behind him. 'Are you a sweeper or a Brahmin?'

'We are both untouchables,' Ernie replied. It was a defiance of Victor as much as anyone. He had been with his friend Naresh Tandan to the Diwali festivities on the bank of the Jamuna. He had never been before; but this time he risked it. He contrived an evening at the house of a friend unknown to Victor, with elaborate hints of a draughts game, tea, music on the gramophone: they had decided which tunes he would be whistling as he returned. Then they stole away to the Ring Road and caught a bus to the Red Fort. The fireworks and the giant effigies, the excited swirl of the great crowd in the darkness, carried the hours too easily along. Suddenly it was nearly midnight, and Victor stood rigid with anger in the doorway of the house.

The electric light behind him threw out his long accusing shadow down the path on to the road.

'Where have you been?'

Ernie hesitated. The pride that prevented him telling direct lies wavered; he could not go forward or back.

'Before you answer me I have seen Mr Moraes.'

Ernie went cold. He remembered seeing the Moraes' bearer at the Red Fort.

Suddenly Victor stepped forward and smacked him stunningly across the face.

'You little swine. You disgrace me before everybody, the whole neighbourhood. How dare you—'

He hit him again. Ernie could feel the five separate fingers burning a path on his cheek. And he could feel something else, a slow and gathering darkness behind the eyes. 'I—you—'

His aunt was waiting in the dark corners of the room. She moved forward. 'Victor—' But he was beyond her. He could not reach her yet; he could not reach out to anything.

'Supposing the officers discovered. What would they think of me, you wretch?' He brought his hand up again but his sister moved forward. 'No—'

'He must be punished,' Victor shouted. 'He is not an Indian boy to be petted and spoiled. He must learn the responsibility to his class.'

It was more and more difficult to hear what his father was saying. His vision moved curiously in twilight. As if from a distant room he heard his father saying: 'Today I hear that at last he may join British School. After my years of pleading. All the money I must pay for him to be educated like a proper Englishman and then he disgraces me before all Delhi.'

'The British School,' whispered Ernie wonderingly. 'Am I to change my school?'

Victor turned on him. 'I will think about it again. You are

not fit for decent school. You are fit only to sweep other men's houses and live like a pig with Indians.'

He gave up the struggle. 'We are Indians!' he screamed, and then the darkness came down and rested like a tombstone across his eyes. Victor and his aunt and the room beyond were pictured fleetingly in his mind, like the scorched impression after lightning, and then there was nothing but darkness and noise. He fell across a chair. When his eyelids parted he saw the adults staring at him in startled horror.

'What is the matter with you? What are you doing?'

The light was now glaring in the room. He moved his limbs uncertainly.

'It's the heat,' he heard his aunt saying.

He accepted that, for he didn't know what else it could be. He trembled as his father regarded him darkly; suspicion interlocked with guilt. We are Indians, he had said. The accusing eyes had more than anger in them.

He was lifted into a chair. 'What was the matter, dearest? Was it the heat? Victor, I'm sure it was the heat.'

But it happened several more times before he learned the proper word for it. Separation hung between him and every identity; there was no alternative to being alone.

The wind was blowing up the dust on the first morning of school. When the bus came for him, splitting the air with its electric horn, the Anglo neighbours twitched their curtains aside to follow his progress to the gate. He knew they were hoping for his failure at the British School, and their dislike of him would increase as he outgrew their own children in British ways and British knowledge. The English boys stared at him as he took his self-conscious seat; he could feel their antagonism pricking the back of his neck. The Sikh driver grinned at him: irony; sympathy?—he avoided the association, and avoided his aunt also, who he knew would be watching from the veranda. He stared straight ahead.

The bus took ten minutes to reach the gates and turn towards the brick school building behind the domestic lines. He stepped nervously off the bus and saw the boys all waiting for him. The news had travelled ahead.

There was an edge off the playing and laughter, and a gradual hush as he entered the compound. The boys who had come with him on the bus moved hastily aside, avoiding association, but a defiant courage kept him moving steadily forward. He looked round at all the white faces, seeking any familiarity at all; the boys stood in groups arrested by the bus's arrival, and in one of the largest a boy moved his head and it was Robert. He looked at Ernie firmly and without expression. A wave of longing went through Ernie's thin body for this boy's protection, who made him so dissatisfied with his own company. He walked fearfully towards him; it was a gamble; he invited rejection. But did Robert look a little less contained? Well: he took a deep breath, as if to plunge into the cold Jamuna; and they both started on the long return.

Mountains

A half-dozen apathetic figures lounged in the courtyard of Srinagar's new tourist centre, among the pools of diesel oil and pony droppings. A huge-lettered message from Nehru extended a welcome to no other visitor than himself. There hadn't been much tourism these last few years, and the clerk at the desk was inefficient but interested.

'Houseboat? There are many of course. These fellows outside are all houseboat owners but they will rob you. I am getting tonga, you find houseboat for yourself. You get A class houseboat for twelve rupees a day. No, I think it is twenty . . . pay half what they ask.'

'I've been here before,' Ernie said.

'You must get houseboat with piped water, yes, and flush toilet. From what place are you coming?'

'Calcutta,' Ernie said. 'I'm on leave. I've been here before.'

'Make sure it is piped water or they are getting it from the lake. Ask for reference from British. Are you Government or private sector?'

'Government. But now I'm on leave. I am here as a tourist.'

'What are you earning each month?'

'I may be here only a few days,' Ernie said. 'My leave is precious to me and I didn't come here to be cross-examined.' It was silly to get angry at the familiar question. He said, 'I would like to go riding in the hills if possible,' for he couldn't start too early to establish the reasons for his future movements.

'There is a golf course at Guhlmarg, that is the best place. Make sure you are asking for flush toilets. We will cheat you if possible, we are not honest people.'

'I said where can I get horses?'

'You will not need horses,' the clerk said. 'Unless you wish to go riding.'

'I do wish to go—'

'Then you are needing a guide, and cook, and bearer. But we are dishonest,' he sighed happily. 'We are poor people, we have no moral fibre.'

Ernie went out to the courtyard for a tonga. Suddenly the apathy was whipped away like a curtain as he entered in his role of tourist, and they all rushed at him.

'Houseboat! Best rates, sahib, I swear! I have three A class houseboats, very near town, own shikara. You come with me, yes.'

He pushed his way roughly through them, following the clerk. 'I have already made arrangements.'

'No, no, not true. This fellow takes you to friend of his, dishonest, you get dysentery. Special rate for you. . . .'

At the end of a wide avenue with a golf course on one side and a once-British hotel on the other a bridge took the road over a fast, muddy river that flowed down from the bund. On one side of the road, wooden shops leaned against the sheer face of rock where the base of a hill had been cut away for the road. The Muslim owners sat outside, tall and sallow-skinned, Persian-looking in their karakul hats and cotton trousers. The shops displayed a curious mixture hopefully catering for the return of the British tourist families who had left Srinagar poor with their departure. There had been few visitors since Partition, but in anticipation of their return the shops stocked an optimistic one of everything that the tourist considered essential for living: cutlery, torch batteries, sun-hats, toothbrushes.

On the left-hand side of the road the river widened to a black ditch of mud, then passed through a lock gate and opened out to the long arm of the Dal Lake where the house-boats were.

And suddenly it was beautiful like he remembered, the sun

shimmering off the lake, the mountains rising brown, then grey, and finally snow-white out of the water, the brilliantly-painted houseboats in one long row all down the mile-long stretch towards the Shalimar Garden. The broad-armed boat-men paddled their shikaras between the boats, and near the lock one thin line of ducks with their heads nodding in cadence cut through the floating green weed to leave a slowly closing, water-coloured trail behind the last of them. *The Yellow Rose, Queen of Kashmir, Pride of the Lake, Blue Moon, Bombay Star* and *Kaiser-i-Hind,* with the navs and doongas standing between, stretched far out of sight down the lake. Their lattice verandas, chintz curtains, deck-chairs and sun-shades were augmented by notice boards proclaiming hot water and flush toilets. It seemed to him that nothing had changed in—good God!—seventeen years. A war, an empire dragged off their backs, Partition, another war, and here they were still selling teapots and toothbrushes, hanging chintz curtains in the windows and posting their handwritten tariff cards to colonels in Bournemouth dead of age.

'Houseboat, sahib. Houseboat. Hot water, sahib, sun-lounge, own shikara.'

A thin bearded man ran crazily beside the tonga wheels waving a bunch of papers under Ernie's nose.

'I have testimonials from British officers. Diplomatic per-sonnel, please you read. Lieutenant-Colonel Whitehead, he still writes to me. . . .'

But he urged the driver on for another half-mile, watching the boats on the opposite bank. Then he gave a sudden order, and the tonga slowed down at a ghat where a half-dozen men were sleeping in the shade of the shikaras. They came awake like cats and his tonga was dragged to a sudden stop, lifting him abruptly from his seat.

'Houseboat best, sahib, best on lake—I swear to you, cheapest possible rate.'

He told the tongawallah to wait and walked to the edge of the ghat. Opposite was a large blue-painted boat lying fat in the water with a doonga alongside. The board read : 'Shalimar, prop. A Butt, hotan cold water, flush toilettes, vegetarian kichen.'

'That one looks the best,' he said.

'Sahib, sahib.' He was tugged towards a cushioned shikara with velvet curtains hung on both sides against the sun. The boatman took him in three or four broad-armed strokes gently up against the side of *Shalimar* and steadied him with exaggerated attention as he climbed the steps. There was no one waiting to greet him; he crossed the tiny whiteboard veranda and ducked through the door. Inside on a Victorian settee sat a fat Hindu in a gurrah-cloth dhoti, fleshy feet cushioned in a thick green rug.

He said : 'Mr Butt?'

'Yes, I am Mr Butt.'

Ernie glanced behind and saw he was alone. 'Please show me your security card.'

'First I must contemplate yours.' Mr Butt stared curiously at his visitor; he had not expected an Anglo, it was extraordinary whom they trusted these days. Not even an eight-anna that one though; more like twelve. Mr Butt's teeth moved slowly on betel, and little bits of the leaf were stuck to his lip. Gold flashed expensively every time he moved, from his fingers, his teeth, a bangle on his wrist.

Ernie took out his wallet and held it open. His own dusky face stared up from the dog-eared card, strangely young and unfamiliar.

Mr Butt produced his own card, then put it away under his vest. 'You are welcome. Any help I can offer will be to my delighting service.'

Ernie kept his voice low. 'Is it safe?'

'There is only the boatman and he is speaking no English, you may rest assured,' Mr Butt said, and leaned his head out of the window to squirt a stream of pan juice into the lake.

'I believe I must go to Baramula.'

'Yes, first to Baramula would accord with existing probabilities. But he is always on the move, you understand that. A month ago, let me see, I think it was only a month ago though perhaps it was five weeks. Or ten . . . we had a report that he was specified in Sopur.'

'Have we got anyone in Baramula?'

Mr Butt stroked his stomach; it sat in front of him like a pet animal and stirred with pleasure under his hand.

'Government are too mean to pay another agent. It is as much as I can do to keep up my own position. We have only the soldiers in Baramula.'

'But you think the gunrunner will be somewhere in or near Baramula?'

'No no no, it is not as easy as that. Obviously he keeps as anonymous as possible. He is rarely in the towns, my dear chap. He is training fighters sometimes. And he is bringing in arms several times a year. No, you will not necessarily meet him in Baramula but it is the only place to start looking.'

He pushed his bulbous feet further into the carpet; they were pale and soft as if left too long in the dark. Then he leaned forward and regarded his Anglo visitor with fresh interest.

'You know this man, I believe?'

Ernie frowned and looked out of the window; a child of about three was plying his shikara through the weed. The Minister had promised. . . . But there were no secrets in India.

'You do not have to answer,' the man grumbled. 'But I am only indicating interest. We are on the same side. Are we not?' and arranged his features in an expression of innocent enquiry.

'You're a long way from Calcutta,' Ernie said, and immediately regretted it; he found it too easy to show contempt by insult, to aggravate what were supposed to be his colleagues. But the reference to the Bengali character went unnoticed, and Mr Butt pressed relentlessly on.

'I am thinking you were with him at Oxford University.'

'Listen,' Ernie said, 'I am in a hurry. I told them at the tourist centre I would be wanting horses. Is that right? Where will I get some?'

'Horses?' Mr. Butt's eyes opened wide. 'But we have a jeep for you. Why do you wish for horses?'

'A jeep—I don't understand.' But he did, of course, it was inevitable, and he felt a sudden gust of cold anger at the stupidity of everything, the class jealousies, the property-conscious attitudes and the proudly smiling face of Mr Butt.

'It was not easy, I am telling you. But we Ministry chaps must stick together. I have managed to extricate jeep from police department, I am more important than them. Do not worry, you may rest assured you will not be driving the smelly thing yourself. One of the soldiers—'

'Soldiers!' This was even worse! 'Do you think I am going to take soldiers with me?'

'Oh but you must absolutely take soldiers with you. They are an essential necessity. You cannot attack this man by yourself, and—'

'But Mr Butt, it is not a question of attack. I am to intercept, hold discussion, talk terms. It is my duty to—but never mind, I have my orders and I am handling it in my own way.'

Mr Butt smiled slyly. 'You fellows from Oxford, you are being of loyalty to each other.'

He felt the thin blade touch his nerve and thought Oh God! is this stupid babu going to bring me to it? Against his special sickness even preparedness was no defence. He said, 'I have my orders. There is no need for soldiers and there is no need for jeeps.'

'I am your superior,' shouted Mr Butt.

'And I have orders from the Minister,' Ernie said, but the blade slid forward.

'Oh dear, have it your own way, I am not minding.' Mr

Butt showed no annoyance and smiled pleasantly as he settled back into the cushions and began to pick his teeth. 'Other jaiwans have died,' he admitted. 'If soldiers go into the hills they are shot by some of the tribesmen. And sometimes by infiltrators from Pakistan. Soldiers are no good to you at all,' said Mr Butt, 'so why you ask me for soldiers I cannot comprehend.'

Ernie turned swiftly to the curtained doorway for he could feel the old sickness coming on, the pain of frustrated anger. His hands started to tremble and there was sweat on his neck and temples despite the coolness of the room. For a few seconds his mind swam darkly as he struggled to control it. Then the lake, the sleeping boatman, the strong line of Shankracharya Hill and the clicking sounds of Mr Butt's teeth settled back into one dimension. He had fought the sickness down as he often could these days, and he turned back to Mr Butt and spoke to him quite calmly.

'We are agreed, Inspector-sahib, that I will go to Baramula by myself?'

'Yes, yes, that is correct.'

'And for that I will need horses. Do you know,' and it seemed he had been asking the question for many hours, 'where they can be hired?'

'Yes, but why not go by bus?'

'There is a bus?'

'Twice a week there is a bus. One leaves today but you would not get on it. You can make reservation on Thursday's bus. Until then you may care to stay on my houseboat, my charges are extraordinarily reasonable. You would have the use of my personal kitchen,' said Mr Butt, who had nothing to do with the one mentioned on his notice board.

'It's a long time since I was here. Is that how a tourist would travel to Baramula, by bus?'

'A tourist is not travelling to Baramula.' Mr Butt smiled, and some of the crimson juice trickled down his chin and bloodied his dhoti. 'There are few tourists now, in this season.

You may wish to travel without soldiers but no one is thinking you are only a tourist.'

'Is that the Chenab River?'

The man beside Ernie leaned over and stared out through the bus's cracked window. Every passenger who had heard the question leaned forward, interested.

'No, no,' said the man, after studying it for longer than seemed necessary. 'That is the Jhelum River. You are a stranger here.'

He looked curiously at Ernie's dusky skin, but hesitated at his accent. 'You are Bengali.'

'I am from Delhi.'

The man nodded but his gaze lingered.

'I believe you do not see many strangers now.' Ernie led into it carefully; though how did you find a man in hiding without asking questions?

'Only soldiers,' the man said. 'Sometimes Indian soldiers, sometimes the other ones. One set comes from the south, the other from the west. They are not strangers, really.'

'You sound very bitter.'

The man regarded him. 'You are Government.'

'Yes, but now I am on leave.'

'Look out of that window. Is it not beautiful?'

Ernie looked out at the flat brown fields and the lines of poplars.

'Kashmir is the best place in India. We eat plenty, we are rich. But we are not happy.'

'I am sorry,' Ernie said. The passengers had closed in mentally about him, and this man was their spokesman. He was going to hear a list of grievances.

'We are not happy because India pulls and Pakistan pulls but nobody is asking the Kashmiri what they want.'

Ernie said: 'It is very difficult.' Who the devil were they to be asked what they wanted? India was a democratic republic; so was Pakistan. Did anyone ever ask what others wanted? Had he been asked by—? You didn't get asked what you wanted.

'Congress are jackals.' The familiar, tired, generalized plaints were warming up. 'They do not care about us. We were better off under the British, at least there was money in our pockets. We are Muslims up here but a Hindu government tells us what to do.'

The trouble with democracy, like Christianity, was that simple people thought they understood it. The stock answers were always available; but he couldn't be bothered.

'Once we had many tourists. Now no tourists. We are all starving and still they tax us.'

Robbery of the poor and slaughter of the weak. The road to riches . . . but only a moment ago they'd been saying they had plenty to eat.

'I am asking you then,' Ernie said, 'what do you want? If India and Pakistan both said to you, what do you want, what would you choose?'

There was a silence. 'Independence,' someone said.

'No, that is ridiculous. You have no industry, you cannot support yourselves. You would have no status in the world. You would be defenceless against attack by any country.'

The first man said, thrusting out his beard: 'We want what Sheikh Abdullah wants.'

'Yes, yes, yes.'

'Sheikh Abdullah.'

'He is a true son of Kashmir. He is a great man. He saved us from famine.'

'If Nehru said to Sheikh Abdullah, you decide for your people, we would be happy.'

And if Sheikh Abdullah knew what he wanted we would all be happy. Like Abdullah, you have nothing but national pride, ignorance, and fear of religious domination. But your Sheikh Abdullah has had his day.

He said: 'You all have my sympathy. But you cannot turn

India from a colony into a country in one night. But before long your troubles will be solved, I am sure, with the blessing of Mahomet and your father Abu.'

A Pathan spat. 'There are Shiites here. You would do well to remember that, Government.'

He turned aside and folded his arms; the others went back to their seats and the bus became quiet. The Delhi man was a tourist after all.

The bus took two hours to reach Baramula. The road was straight from village to village and ran across dead flat country between the white-boled poplar trees. The villages were built of wood, and wood-smoke drifted from their chimneys. Out on the wide fields men and boys were scattering fertilizer from the deep-walled carts.

This is not India, he thought before he could stifle it. On the road were some smart tongas with quick, fat little horses trotting briskly. Nothing moved briskly in India. He did not often see a mosque, though there was sometimes a small one with peeling white paint and cracked window frames standing away from the road; and sometimes by the roadside was a Hindu shrine with pictures of Brahma and Vishnu and a cup of yellow flowers.

The road started to rise just before it entered the town of Baramula. They were back beside the Jhelum and the Baramula Gorge lay beyond the town. This had been the site of bitter fighting in 1947 when the Maharajah of Kashmir had opted for accession to India. Pakistan had sent in guerillas to whip up the Muslims to revolt, then sent in their own troops for support. The Maharajah had appealed for Indian troops, and rather to his surprise found his own soldiers fighting on their side. After the first fury it had dragged on for over a year, and now the border was only twelve miles down the road. Half the town had been destroyed and much of it had never been rebuilt. There were gaps in the houses, a broken drainpipe still spilled refuse across the road, and the poster outside the Hindu cinema had been promising the same pro-

gramme for the last ten years. Life was too uncertain to engage
in building. Unlike India, where life like the white cor-
puscle absorbed death, here they dwelt in uneasy juxta-
position.

Beyond the town were high mountains, far away. The river
ran swiftly down and half-circled the town before flowing
away to the south. There was a large mosque with flattened
dome standing above the house roofs. There were several tea-
houses in the courtyard where the bus drew up, and from
the tables many long, dark-eyed faces watched with interest
as the passengers descended.

Ernie looked round at the high encircling walls. It was midday, but cool in the earthen yard. In one corner where the
horses stood the ground was muddy, and steamed gently. An
odour drifted across from a pile of rotting potatoes covered
with sacks; a dog lay on top of them, asleep but moving its
thin brows in nervous enquiry. The bags were thrown down
from the roof, borne away by their owners, and soon he was
the only passenger remaining, already conspicuous. The tea
drinkers leaned a bit closer.

He gave a porter four annas and asked what hotels there
were.

'No hotels,' the man said. 'Only Mahbub Ali.'

'What is he?'

'Teahouse. He has rooms upstairs. Clean, okay for sahib.'

It sounded just right; that was where all the travellers and
farmers would collect, the starting place of all the gossip. But
he should not appear too anxious.

'Is there not a dak bungalow?'

'Not since Partition.'

Good. The porter rode with him on the tonga to Mahbub
Ali's teahouse. The owner sat on a bench against the wall, a
large Persian-looking man in karakul and baggy white
trousers covered with an incongruous patched overcoat, smoking a hubble-bubble. He raised his eyebrows slightly and
turned away boredly in the same movement. Behind the tea-

house, clouds sailed on the dark river's surface, and a few boats lay on the mud beside their rotting mooring posts.

'This way, sahib.' The porter had taken charge for he carried Ernie's bags through the door and began to walk them one at a time like crutches up the dark stairs.

'Is this not the owner? I must talk with him.'

'There is no need. I show you the way. I know the best room.' It seemed as if workers here were interchangeable, they performed any service and collected the tips that were going. Mahbub Ali stared with misty eyes over the river, showing no interest. There was probably something else under the coals, more interesting than tobacco.

A door at the top of the stairs opened and closed again; he recognized his neighbour from the bus, and had a swift, covert glimpse of a woman in a blue sari, a whiff of cooking. The waiter carried the bags down to the end of the passage and from the top of the stairs Ernie could hear the water bubbling in Mahbub Ali's pipe.

The porter stuck his head out impatiently. 'Sahib!'

He walked down the passage and went in. Again that feeling of a foreign land; no water basin, no bars at the window or religious water colours on the wall; but a stove in the room's centre and a crooked pipe going through the ceiling. He looked at the bed.

'The sheets we will change,' the porter said.

The Jhelum River lay almost underneath; when he opened the window he could hear the water birds calling. A few black, bare-armed trees stood at the river's edge, the debris of the last spring flood in their lower branches. There were hills and mountains beyond the river and through some breaks in the mountain range he glimpsed the surprising whiteness of snow.

He had to start his investigations quickly before he was common news, and after lunch he took his papers and went to look for the army post. It was a small town; from any street he could see the river. The centre was paved and other streets were cobbled for they were under flood water in the spring. He walked away from the river for ten minutes towards the army post but then found the river in front of him again, bending away to the south. The army hut was a long wooden building on a concrete foundation, a dirt yard in front and an empty flagpole encircled by the concentric wheel-marks of an army Land Rover. A Muslim corporal came out of the small brick lavatory at one side of the yard, waving his left hand in the air to dry.

'Tourist,' announced Ernie loudly, but once inside the door he took out his papers. 'Get me the lieutenant.'

'In bed,' the corporal announced and started to leaf avariciously through the papers till he had them snatched from his hand.

'You will please awaken the lieutenant. I am here on—' he searched for the right time-saving phrase—'important Government business.'

The corporal immediately collected himself, saluted, and went out through one of the two doors behind the counter.

He was back in India again. The room was strangely like his office in Calcutta: untidy files, rubber stamps with the occasional small mistake (premitted, signiture), trays for In, Out, Filing. Handcuffs hung selfconsciously on a nail, and a tray of dusty tea-cups stood on a shelf as if they had long been part of the furniture. On the counter he twisted his head to read some of the entries in the upside down logbook . . . I was proceeding in a westerly direction on Imperial Avenue when a Muslim fellow who appeared to be in an inebriated condition. . . . The British influence lingered like a weed: you could grub it all up and toss it away, but soon it would be back as strong as ever, covering the new seeds, choking their growth.

The lieutenant entered in his pyjamas, said Excuse me, and walked outside. Ernie could hear the man washing himself under the tap and hawking noisily. When he returned he scrutinized Ernie warily as if searching for evidence.

'Government business?' he ventured.

'Important and very urgent Government business,' Ernie insisted.

The lieutenant stretched out his hand for the papers. Ernie passed them over and settled back; he knew nothing more would happen until they had been scrutinized by the lieutenant and his corporal right down to the small type and the printer's address. The lieutenant was a long, morose-faced man with large squared eyebrows and a nose like a Pathan. He was in his mid-forties and must have missed promotion a few times before accepting the command of a small post that could well spring into the news any day if only the Pakistani fellows would attack. It was all he could hope for; good men were not appreciated.

It was now three o'clock, so apparently yesterday's shave was to see him through the day.

He cleared his throat; it had crept up on him again since the washing at the tap.

'Namaste,' he said from a sitting position. 'I am Lieutenant Hurree Mokerjee, Officer Commanding Baramula Section. From 1935 to 1936 I am attending at the University of Bombay where I came very near to receiving diploma.'

'I am honoured,' Ernie said. A pundit; it was going to be a session.

'It is about the Posts and Telegraph,' Lieutenant Mokerjee suggested.

'That comes under a different ministry,' Ernie said. He knew everything would seize up if he pushed too hard, but he was not designed for this . . . his impatience stirred again with the papers' sharp rustling.

'It is all Government to me,' Mokerjee said. He fanned himself with Ernie's folded travel warrant, creasing it irritatingly in one corner. 'It is very beastly hot in here. But if you are coming from Ambala you will not be thinking so.'

'Delhi,' Ernie said shortly.

Mokerjee hesitated, and turned again to the papers on his

desk. His hand moved through them like a snake through leaves and Ernie jumped up and snatched his papers away.

'Damn it! I will not—I am on urgent business. You have read my Minister's letter. Now you must do as I say and I have no time to waste on nonsense.'

Mokerjee had turned a shade paler; but at the mention of the Minister he could not resist another peep down at the letter between his hands on the table. A sentence impressed itself upon his mind like a rubber-stamped admonition. 'It says here,' he said, 'that you are looking for the gun-runner. . . .'

'Yes.' Yes!

Lieutenant Mokerjee folded his arms . . . the stripes of the pyjamas ran into each other.

'Then you may rest assured, for this man he is not existing.'

'You mean he's not here?'

'I mean,' Mokerjee said with an aggravating yawn, 'that he is figment of Governmental imagination. Up here before the police have come, soldiers have come, but they are not finding him.'

'That is why I am here,' Ernie said. 'I am finding him.' And then felt angry and disappointed at the man who should have been closest to the whole situation but was just another junglie of no help at all.

The lieutenant remained calm. 'It is very regrettable that you have journeyed for nothing. But he is not existing. We have never seen this British fellow in Baramula.'

'You may not have seen him. I am not disputing that he may not have forced himself on your attention. But others have seen him very recently. People have died trying to arrest him. He brings in arms from Pakistan and distributes them to caches in the villages. He has been seen four times in Baramula in two years, and all the evidence shows that he uses this town, or somewhere near it, as a base.'

Mokerjee's face turned from calm to distress that his advice was not heeded.

'It is not true what Government say, Baramula is a small town, perhaps five thousand people. I know every person and from what place they are coming. There are no unofficial persons coming from Pakistan, there is only one road and it is guarded by army.'

'Do you never have people coming from the direction of the border? Or the cease-fire line? Forget the Jhelum Valley Road. What about the town of Shaburah, or Uri? What about the farming villages in between? What about the gujers in the hills, what might they conceal?'

'The villages also are known to me. I know all people. There is not a person unknown to me on this side of the valley and if I do not know them my jaiwans do.'

'And Shaburah? And Punch?'

'Shaburah there is no practicable road. Punch is on the cease-fire line and travellers are inspected coming from there. Also I am driving the road two times per week and by jove I am inspecting all the baggages.' He threw himself morosely back in his chair and started to pick his long nose furiously.

Two jaiwans had just come in and stood blocking the light from the door; they were both Sikhs and looked very smart. One of them had the indented scars of smallpox on his face. Ernie glanced often at them as he argued with Mokerjee.

'You are not denying, Lieutenant, that there has been a dangerous increase in arms and ammunition all over Srinagar and Kashmir North?'

'Certainly these village fellows have guns. They have always had guns, for the shooting of wild pigeon and duck.'

The corporal was leaning on the counter with his elbows, his chin pensively in his hands. Though his face registered a careful impartiality Ernie could see it was only one degree from disaster, like milk about to boil over.

'I am not talking about sporting guns.' He would report this man to the Minister. 'I am talking about automatic rifles and Thompson guns and grenades. American weapons.' He consulted a list from his pocket. 'Browning automatic rifles, M.14 semi-automatics and Garand rifles. Pakistan's army is supplied by America and these tribesmen and infiltrators are armed by Pakistan.'

'Ah, certainly the Pakistanis are villains, I am not denying it. It is in their inherent history. During the Mutiny—'

'For the love of Mike!' His fist banged on the counter and made the corporal jump. 'You are incapable of sensible talk. Will you stick to the point?' You never knew, though, if to lose your temper or keep it was the quickest way. He could see the two Sikhs smiling, and wondered if it was directed against Mokerjee or himself.

'I am asking you,' he said to Mokerjee, who bore a look of injured innocence, 'if there has been an increase of guns among the villagers in the past twelve months. And if yes, where have they come from?'

He turned to glare crossly at the Sikhs, who stared back disarmingly; the pockmarked one grinned and winked, pointing his face at the lieutenant.

'Indeed there has been undue increase in firearms equipment,' Mokerjee said coldly, 'evidence for which is increase of murder crimes in area and thefts from arsenals. We have on numerous occasions apprehended criminals and confiscated their loot. However, this contraband does not enter Kashmir from area of Pakistan.'

'Have you any ideas on the subject?' Ernie enquired. The Sikhs grinned and nudged each other delightedly. The toecaps of their boots shone with effort and their brass buttons sparkled like reminders of promotion.

Mokerjee stood and began to pace between the door and the dusty tea cups, his arms held out from his body like a baby learning to walk, perhaps because the pyjamas were sticking to his flabby outline. 'Well, you see,' he began unpromisingly, 'those Pakistani fellows, they are all occupied upon the cease-fire line established by United Nations in January 1949. This cease-fire line is existing until holding of

plebiscite, arrangements for which unfortunately broke down
in negotiations. So there you are, you see. Much guns and
equipments are engaged on this line and there are none to
spare for engagement on alternative fronts. Nor are arms
coming from Afghanistan because Afghanistan unfriendly to
Pakistan—'

'Get to the point,' Ernie commanded. He wondered how
many people had learned of his presence in Baramula in the
half-hour he'd spent in this room. The Sikhs were watching
Mokerjee like dogs waiting for a thrown ball.

'Obviously arms are not coming from south for customs
would be apprehending. So—' the lieutenant said, and turned
to face the room triumphantly : 'they are coming from east-
wards.'

There was a silence, broken only by a slight giggle from
near the door, and Mokerjee sank slowly back on his heels
with the frustrated look of a man who has just bowled four
byes.

'Well, there you are, you see . . . looking towards where
fellows have aspirations in present area, you are aware that
the arms are coming from no place but China.'

It had been one of those intuitive times when he had
known, one instant beforehand, what Mokerjee would say;
the giggling of the Sikhs, the sinking of the corporal's face
deeper into his cupped hands, had warned him in advance
of his own anger. Here was one of those Indians (there were
many of them) who were carried along by the oral effect of
what they were saying; he knew that if questioned vigorously
now, or even casually in a few days' time, Mokerjee would
certainly deny that his words had meant firearms were being
brought across the Himalayas from China. He felt mainly
relief that the conversation, the meeting, the whole burden
of the afternoon in the army post, could now be brought to
a convenient end.

'Lieutenant Mokerjee, I am afraid I consider you to be a
fool. Now my job is to find the gunrunner and I require your

co-operation without any more reading of papers or expounding of stupid theories.'

Mokerjee had just achieved one climax of self-expression and now he had to dredge up a shadow of it. 'How dare you,' he uttered drearily. 'That is an outrage. To insult me before my subordinates. . . .' and giving up the pale effort he turned and went back into the bedroom.

'He will return,' the corporal said. He spoke automatically, as if he were used to covering up his boss's social gaffes, just a matter of throwing another handful of sawdust on to a dirty floor.

Ernie turned to the Sikhs; they straightened up and saluted together as if worked by the same lever.

'Have you seen any strangers in Baramula?'

They looked at each other.

'Or any visitor at all, anyone who doesn't live in the town?'

They turned back to him and nodded at the same time. The pockmarked one said: 'There are always comings and goings, sahib. All of them we know, but some we see only two or three times a year.'

'That's the type that interest me. Are there any in the town today?'

The same one spoke again; his face looked as if it had been beaten from a copper plate. 'There are a few. Mostly they have come to sell autumn rice on speculation.'

'There are people in the district who are friends of the gunrunner,' Ernie said, watching their faces. They looked intelligent and he trusted them. 'They are men whose occasional absence is not missed, who have justification for travelling about Kashmir.'

They looked swiftly at each other and turned back again. Ernie suddenly remembered the corporal; it was important to have them all on his side, even the lieutenant, if it wasn't too late.

'I hope you will allow me to give the jaiwans their orders,

corporal. I would not usurp your authority, but I have direct instructions from the Minister—'

The Muslim corporal smiled disarmingly, with what was very close to a sneer; he wondered how this cheechee would have addressed him before '47. The lieutenant was the boss, the Sikhs were the smart ones; he just did all the work. He made a permissive gesture of one hand which didn't commit him very deeply.

'You will please keep your eyes open,' Ernie said. He had the Sikhs' confidence and began to feel he was getting somewhere. 'Tonight at Mahbub Ali's teahouse you will bring me a list of all strangers in town today. I want to know where they come from and what they carry in their baggage.'

The Sikhs smiled and nodded eagerly, and the corporal's smile lengthened rather than broadened; anything that went wrong would be his fault in the end.

'Don't alarm anyone,' Ernie said. 'It must appear normal routine. When you come to me pretend you are inspecting my papers too.'

They saluted like two clockwork soldiers. Ernie looked at them approvingly; they were good fellows.

He decided to walk back along the river bank, to learn more of the town. There was a narrow path there between the cherry groves and some children were playing with sticks, carving pictures in the mud. The river was very wide at this bend, the level was low, and there were white banks of sand and pebbles gleaming far out in the water. Women were beating their clothes at the water's edge and kept their heads down as he walked past.

There were a few boats drifting in the stream with the fishing lines out, and there were other small boats moored to posts or beached on the pebbles. This was as far as the boats could come before the Jhelum plunged into the Baramula Gorge. There were canals passing to the backs of the houses on his left hand.

Round the next bend were more women beating clothes

with their long flat clubs. As he drew level he tried to think of a greeting but they covered their mouths and kept their backs to him. From one of the houses he could hear the sounds of a wedding, the first regular thump of a drum and the crying chant of women, that he remembered from days in Delhi before . . . before everything. And then all the things ran together in his mind and he found himself remembering all he could of the time he had been here before, when his life held such opportunity for happiness, before the racial curtain drew across his future and the pit opened behind to cut him off from his past.

He returned to the teahouse and entered through the back way, a feeble token of secrecy. There were still two hours before dinner and he took out his maps and spread them on the table. The oil lamp swayed irritatingly from the ceiling until he unhooked it and set it by his elbow.

There was only one road from Pakistan, alongside the Jhelum River through Muzaffarabad. It had been a popular route for tourists before Partition; they had ridden from serai to serai with their guides and bearers on the beautiful mountain road. There were ninety miles between Srinagar and Muzaffarabad, and Uri stood about halfway between them with the present cease-fire line running through the town. A baggage train could not possibly pass Uri without being searched by Pakistani and Indian soldiers.

At Uri was a trail branching south; it went across mountains as far as Punch, then turned north-west to cross the border at Murree. It was a possibility but a bare one. The trail would be virtually impassable for five months of the year. But surely that could leave only the Muzaffarabad road.

He searched the country on the other side of the road, to the north. There was a reasonable road up beside the Wular River for a while, but stopping short of Shaburah. And the mountains between Shaburah and the border rose to 16,000 feet.

He consulted the list Ram Lal had given him. There had been four suspected consignments in 1955 and five in 1956. Now it was June 1957 and intelligence reports stated there had been two. The third was due about now. Much of this was guesswork but it indicated something.

It was fifty-five miles from Muzaffarabad to Baramula and the road was first class. But there were only four or five trips each year. There were many possible reasons, of course: shortage of supplies, for one. Or the arsenal might be a long way into Pakistan, at Rawalpindi or even Peshawar (though they'd come by train to Rawalpindi of course). And whatever role was adopted for disguise might involve its own delay, the need to act like a surveyor or a farmer travelling between the markets.

Even twelve trips a year would not have brought in enough to make more than a small difference in a war, should the Pakistani army attack. It was not an entirely serious exercise, the effort outweighed the useful result. It indicated something about the personality of the gunrunner which, of course, Ernie already knew.

The oil lamp had been flickering for the last ten minutes, and now smoke poured up to the ceiling. He searched along the passage for another lamp, but there was only one outside his door, too high to reach. There was a noise coming up from the restaurant which reminded him of hunger, so he locked up the maps and went downstairs.

The big room was very crowded now. The acrid smoke from hubble-bubbles drifted to the ceiling with a noise like twenty men snoring. It was too warm for the big stove to be lit, but the tables were grouped close in around it through habit. There was a lot of noise. Mahbub Ali and a boy were busy serving tea and meals of rice and meat.

He took the only table left, facing the door. He could see through the door and across the river into a blue darkness.

Two boats were moving up and down with their fishing lights.
The moon was not up yet.

'Food,' he said to the boy when he came near. 'Rice, mutton,
chai.'

It was a long time coming; there was no competition in
Baramula. A man with a cough shuffled from one of the tables
to ask who he was. Ernie told him he was a tourist and the
man smiled politely; he was getting the same reaction as film
stars assuring the press they were good friends. Did the sahib
have a cigarette? About ten more men came in and sat down
with a great shuffling of chairs close together. The man got
a cigarette from one of them and went back to his table, still
coughing.

The food was good, when it came, and he ate it quickly,
watching the faces coming through the door. A boy came in
with newspapers and Hindi film magazines. He bought a Kasmiri newspaper which he could not read but it was an excuse
to linger without becoming involved in conversation.

The next time he looked up one of the Sikh jaiwans stood
in the doorway. He caught the man's eye, then frowned and
looked down at his newspaper. The Sikh stood for another
moment, then went out.

Ernie turned to Mahbub Ali and called, 'Chai!'

There had been a lull in the noise as the Sikh entered; his
uniform drew silent attention. In the seconds needed to adjust
to his departure the room's noise was muted and Ernie's voice
was injected into an awkward quietness.

'Bring more chai,' he called again to break the spell.

A few men were looking at him curiously. The group behind him at the long table had been talking noisily, but were
now quiet. Damn the Sikh's foolishness; they had realized the
connection, now no one trusted him. Mahbub Ali was staring
curiously from behind the samovar, his face mysterious with
tobacco smoke. The Sikh might have had an urgent message
. . . but now he had sent him away. Perhaps there would be
a note slipped under his door. But he mustn't move yet or

his going would be associated with the Sikh's appearance. Or was that going too far? This wasn't a spy film. Feeling foolish, he was about to rise when he heard Mahbub Ali call out: 'Use the other door. Hey, you, then!'

He looked round and saw the door to the passage pulled swiftly back and a figure silhouetted against the lamp outside; then a cloak swirled and disappeared through the closing door.

'That only leads to the bedrooms,' Mahbub Ali grumbled. 'He'll be going through them like a thief.' But there was a pipe under his hand . . . his face showed only a temporary interest before the pipe was firmly between his teeth.

Ernie sat stiffly for several seconds . . . the silhouetted figure formed again in his mind. He jumped to his feet; then saw, at the table next to him, every eye on his face, and one chair empty. He fumbled for his seat again; his hand brought the chai glass to his lips. He had seen . . . but now he was watched. He could have panicked but he was amazingly calm. He even glanced again at the newspaper, trying to guess a caption from the pictures below it, a bus overturned in Tangmarg, his thoughts flicked confusedly towards irrelevance. . . .

Then still slowly he got up and walked outside. He didn't dare to look to see if they watched.

He walked quickly round the building and entered again at the back door. There was a short passage beside the stairwell; light and noise buffeted the café door but it was quiet in the passage. A draught from somewhere blew a page of newspaper along the wooden floor. He turned and went up the stairs. The passage led away to right and left; opposite was the Indian woman's room, to the left was his own. He hesitated for another minute, then walked quickly along the passage to his room and thrust open the door.

'Rob—' he began, but the room was empty.

He went back downstairs and out to the street. There was the tea-room's noise again, as if it held all the town's life. The moon was up now, making the dark places darker. What was it that had reminded him so fast? He had been standing in

the strong light from outside; Ernie had seen just a karakul
hat, a line of shoulder and arm under the cloak. But the visual
memory had compressed all the time in between. He experienced a jolt of happiness, heavy like a burden. After ten
years. . . .

He wandered through the 'own hoping the miracle would
be repeated, that Robert would stroll out from a doorway, slap
him on the back, and then they'd go somewhere to talk. For
shock dulls the senses . . . for the first time in ten years he
did not hate Robert King.

He came back to the teahouse after half an hour of search.
He had still not given up hope. Perhaps Robert had doubled
back and now waited for Ernie in the room, sitting on the
bed and swinging his long legs. They would talk, about
Oxford . . . everything. He did not think beyond that . . .
things would be taken care of, the search was over. He trod
heavily on the stairs, wanting to be heard. He pushed upon
the door, letting it swing forward, and felt a stab of disappointment. Then as he moved inside in the gloom his toe kicked
something big and soft.

He felt the turban first, then the warm blood behind the
ear. He felt something else, too.

He returned to the swinging door and propped it open,
letting the poor light slant in through the gap. He went back
and this time saw the twine clearly, knotted into two looped
handles, curled about the Sikh jaiwan's neck. It was the one
who had come for him in the teahouse. Blood from a bruise
on his head had trickled down into his hairnet, matting the
beard; his bangle was smashed on the floor. A cold wind blew
into Ernie's face as he took hold of the thin wire. It was not
pulled tight; there was no mark on his windpipe and he was
still breathing; no one had ever been closer to death than
that.

He had seen this sort of thing in Bengal, in the troubles,
but had not expected to see it ever again. The cool draught
was from the open window, someone had gone through it a

short while before, someone who had not had time to finish what he was at.

Like everything else, he thought bitterly, memory had turned sour with time. He had been recalling the happy years, Oxford, schooldays . . . but they were no longer children and innocence had gone.

He thought irrelevantly of his father . . . how shocked Victor would have been; how unBritish to garrott a fellow member of the Empire. But the thought would have been ten years out of date, and Empires can die as fast as anything else.

Plains

There was a new boy at the school, a captain's son; and at the morning break the class made a rush for him.

'To the tree! To the tree!'

The thin, nervous boy struggled in token resistance; his muted cries meant that he was not actually calling the master, but hoping desperately he would hear. But he was borne from the playground like a football game's hero.

'It's the rule. All new boys climb the tree.'

Ernie followed, for he had not seen the ceremony before: 'all' new boys did not include him.

His first weeks at the school were met with restrained hostility. He was ignored rather than disliked. The British boys were still establishing an attitude to their first coloured intruder and they avoided him until he could be labelled and identified. Robert was his only contact, but trusting Robert was tying himself to the roc's claw. Sometimes it was the days of football again; but often there was no greater threat than the blond-headed boy who commanded all paths and retreats, was master of after-school hours, and enjoyed a position even the teachers did not challenge.

It was the season of cricket and the game was strange to him. He and his friends had always played football, for anything served—a tennis ball, a bundle of rags. But cricket needed equipment, and an attitude; he could not manage the overarm action of bowling, or the gentle prod of the bat that won more credit than the wild, boundary-scoring swing. It seemed merciless that a single miss could tumble his stumps and send him off the field for the rest of the game.

Robert was wonderful at cricket; already the teachers were

saying he would play for England. He looked like a Greek athlete at the wicket, striking the ball with easy, rounded strokes. He could bowl clever, twisting balls that paralysed the bat, or fast ones that made the batsman protect his shins instead of the wicket, and accept the crash of the stumps behind him. Sometimes Robert would hand over his bat with a 'Here you are, I mustn't be selfish. Someone else's turn.' And of course he was a terribly good sport: if ever a boy did bowl him out he would run down the pitch to shake hands. Ernie was always placed well down the batting list but if Robert was bowling for the other side he would get his turn all right. Then he would be out after half a dozen strokes, scoring perhaps two fours but then the ball hitting his foot; and the rest of the team would mutter at his letting the side down. But not Robert: 'Never mind old man. Better luck next time. But you must watch that footwork. . . .'

In the gymnasium his supple body could perform feats the British boys had never seriously considered, but he soon found it worked to his disadvantage. There was something 'wrong' to be able to twist about like that, hardly natural. Once he heard the word 'monkey' whispered behind him, and after that he pretended he could no longer climb the ropes, and leap the box with folded arms. This made the teacher angry, but grown-ups' disapproval was easy to bear.

Occasionally the barriers would crumble. The occasional mood of rebellion ('Sir, I've finished already, have you another sum ready?') stirred him to defy convention; he recognized his classroom ability was exceptional, and used this power when he could. He yearned to be as British as any of them, but when Victor added his earnest persuasions to the schoolboys' silent watchfulness it became all too much, and his heart called him back to familiarity, like Mowgli from the hearthstones of men.

Down along the eastern side of the cantonment, on the edge of the servants' compound, stood a banyan tree beside a wide black pond. There the sweepers watered their buffaloes, and their naked children played for hours on the broad rough backs. The banyan tree was stripped of bark and blackened with charcoal at the base, but the branches grew strongly and already were curving to their destination in the ground : for the branches of a banyan take root and put out further branches, which continue their lives after the main trunk has died, like men.

Over the hill the boys came pouring like water into the pond, dragging their victim so that he had to run to keep balance. The compound children abandoned the pond and ran off, then crept back to watch what would come.

Ernie followed until the boys stopped at the tree, then glanced round in uneasy recognition.

'I've been here before.'

He had spoken quickly, before memory became recall. There was a strange familiarity, like a thought working backwards. Then he caught sight of the land beyond the compound, the thin asphalt strip a buffalo cart wide, the equidistant keekar trees painted with consecutive numbers to prevent theft, and his two identities shouldered against each other. Here was one of the villages he had cycled to, which he now saw from the opposite side.

'I didn't realize,' he said to no one but himself, and he felt something tremendous about to happen, that life had been preparing for years.

They threw stones to drive away the buffaloes, then let the new boy go and pointed. One of the branches stretched across a corner of the pond. It reached to just short of the bank, eight feet above the green slime on the surface.

'You have to climb up.'

'Who says?' But the boy had abandoned hope from the beginning; now he only sought an interval before humiliation.

'You've got to. All new boys climb the tree or they're crying babies.'

The branch stopped short of the bank but a boy's weight

would lower it nearly to the water; he would have to swing
forward to get his feet on the bank. It was not difficult, most
boys could have done it; but not this one.

'I can't—I can't climb. . . .'

'Coward.'

'Mummy's baby.'

'Diddums. He's going to wet himself.'

The boy said: 'I can't climb. I'll do something else. . . .' But
the rules did not admit variation; imagination needs experience. They pushed him to the banyan's trunk and placed
his hands in position, embarrassed as he. The boy stood like
a dummy fixed in position, refusing to move. There was a
moment of hateful silence and Ernie stepped forward.

'It's not fair. Not everyone does this thing. I was not com-
pelled to.'

There was a hush. 'You don't count,' someone said.

And he gave a grim smile; it was what he had hoped for,
and now they could not stop him riding to triumph at their
own expense. It was not sympathy for the boy which made
him act; how unjust that this little baby be offered the opportunity he was denied.

'I'll show you.' And he leaped for the tree. He went straight
up the shortest way, ignoring the time-carved footholds,
scrambling like a cat. He reached the branch, found it wide
and unslippery, and raced along it crouching to the tip. He
knew without looking that every face was bent up towards
him; turning, he grasped the slender branch and hung with
his sandals a yard above the water. He swung twice more for
momentum, then dropped safely on all fours and let the
motion carry him over backwards to land, finally, on his feet,
smiling in triumph.

His slightly dizzy glance picked out Robert's face, watching
him with a mysterious smile of pleasure and possession. But a
few seconds later the thought began to pick at the edge of his
triumph that his very expertise had somehow detracted from
the performance.

There was the laughter of relief when a boy called: 'It's all right for a monkey.' He turned, prepared to fight; another step towards acceptance.

'We've all done that, Maher, except Grizzleguts here. If you really want to show off do it from the next branch up.'

'Certainly,' he raged; then looked up and knew he had over-reached himself. But already he had started towards the tree again; reserves of strength are contained in the elements that make up fear.

The next branch up was the top one of the tree. It grew out exactly above the lower one but several feet higher, and overlapped the bank. It needed a straight drop to the ground. The top would bend under his weight; but how much? It was too late to think of now.

He climbed steadily, conserving his strength. He still panted from the previous effort; it was less than a minute since he had landed with a backward somersault in the dust.

It seemed a long time after he passed the first branch when he reached the second. The boys' upturned faces seemed merged into one expression. But they did not realize: it is from the tree's top you judge the height, from under the harrow-blade you feel the prick. Observers have the double delusion, thinking they understand.

From where Ernie crouched the upturned sheet of faces, the black pond and the lower branch, all seemed on the same dimension, and he was up high on his own.

So far he had been acting ahead of fear, but halfway along the branch it moved up and took him by the elbow. The bough was not going to bend . . . he couldn't drop twenty feet. He pushed further along, moving with slow reluctance. Now the branch did begin to bend but already he had only eight feet to go . . . he slipped a little, and the strain was thrown forward on to his hands, he felt a little crack in his wrist. . . .

Any further and the time for retreat would be past. He hesitated at the final point of safety, conscious of the communal demand from below. The branch might bend another five or six feet: it was not certain. By hanging from the extreme tip his feet would be . . . no! he shuddered; he would be left swinging like a spider.

He moved back and peered down at the distant sea of faces.

'I can do it if somebody weighs down the branch.'

He expected jeers, but they were so quiet he was not certain they understood.

'If one of you fellows will come up. . . .'

Then he saw someone had already begun to climb. It was Robert King. Good old Robert! The blond head moved steadily up the trunk until it appeared above the branch, and scrambled towards him.

'Are you going to do it?'

'Of course. If you'll just—'

'It's a long way. Sure you're not scared?'

He wished Robert hadn't said that, it was difficult enough to keep his nerve. He had hoped to get used to the height but with each head-flicking glance the ground did not look any closer. He wished now he had done it right away.

'You don't have to do it, you know. None of the chaps would blame you.'

'I want to. Those rotters down there. . . .'

They moved up together. Once past the fork the branch began to bend dangerously and he felt the strain again in his wrists. He eased one arm beneath and, holding his breath, slipped round so that now he hung from all limbs like a sloth, his ankles crossed over the branch. He moved along another couple of feet, until he was past the black water and directly above the bank.

The branch now bent nearly vertical; there was no grip left for the ankles and he had to let go. All his weight hung from his thin arms. . . . The crowd beneath gave a concerted gasp, it had sensed danger even before Ernie, for only now did he tighten his legs in a sudden shameful fear.

'You can do it.'

Robert was craning down towards him, the thin branch

wobbling. 'Go on!' But his voice did not carry the same conviction, and suddenly the thought occurred to Ernie that he
could die.

'I can't. Robert, help me, I can't move—'

Visions of his mother's face moved like shadowy ghosts into
the front of his memory and back. A sudden warm dampness
in his trousers warned him he had lost control of his fear.

'Ernie, come back then.'

But it was too late now. Swinging high above the pond's
bank he cried, but soundlessly, as if even in this moment loss
of pride were a greater fear than maiming.

'Ernie!' Robert was shouting. 'Look at me. Move your hands
back. . . .'

'I can't.' It was the only phrase left; he was past thinking.

'You can! Move your bloody hands back—'

'Stop—stop shouting so much . . . Robert I'm going to fall,
my arms are breaking. . . .'

He grabbed with one hand inches up the branch, then had
to follow swiftly with the other as the fingers slid on the
smooth bark.

'Do that again.' Robert shouted; then, louder: 'Come on,
you can do it. Courage, Ernie.'

Again he performed the double grasp. Now he was back
over the water: pain prised open his fingers and dragged on
his arm sockets. But he moved another hand back and felt
Robert's reassuring grip on his wrist.

'Come on, Ernie. A last effort!'

'Quietly,' he sobbed, one fear surmounting the other.
Robert's hands were under his armpits and he was pulled back
into the safety of the fork.

'I'm—I'm sorry Robert.'

He was terribly ashamed for King to see him crying, but
he had no more control over that than the other thing. He
wished Robert hadn't been so rotten and shouted . . . but he'd
been wonderful, he'd saved him; he was overwhelmingly angry
and grateful.

'All right now?'

He nodded, blinking. Robert had saved his life all right. His gratitude was too much for expression.

'Right, move over will you?'

'What?'

'Mind yourself. I want to get past.'

'What are you going to do?' The fear closed in again.

'I'm going to have a shot at it myself.'

He hung on to Robert's arm. 'Don't—'

'I want to.'

'No, you mustn't!'

'Why not?' Robert knocked the restraining hand off his arm.

'You will fall. It is too far—'

'That's not why you don't want me to do it.'

'I don't know what you mean.'

Beneath, the sheet of upturned faces watched the new development. How much he tried to like Robert and how much he wished he could. But always the cruel pressure of the handshake, the grin behind the smile.

'You're trying to stop me. I'm not a coward.'

'Robert, I beg you—'

'Shut up or I'll punch you in the face.'

Robert pulled his arm free and moved quickly hand over hand along the branch until it began to bend above him. He glanced back with a controlled steadiness of voice.

'Just sit out as far as you like, will you?'

Ernie nodded. Dumbly he moved down the branch and took a grip.

'Well, I'm going, then,' Robert said.

He moved on until his hands gripped the very end of the branch. It stretched down tightly with his weight; he was directly beneath so that Ernie could see only the white-knuckled hands and the hateful sheen of blond hair. Then he fell away and hit the ground a second later.

Slowly Ernie turned and climbed down. None of the boys

were looking at him as he reached the ground and walked away; he hated everybody.

But Robert overtook him and placed a friendly arm round his shoulders.

'Ernie—'

'I don't want you. You didn't have to do that. . . .'

Robert smiled. 'No one's blaming you. The fellows are all being awfully decent. I just didn't want to let the side down.'

He felt tears of exasperation pricking the back of his eyes.

'Come on, Ern. Please stop sulking.'

And next morning Robert met him at the gates with a friendly smile. 'I've told my ma about you.'

'What have you told?'

'That we're friends and everything. I've got to invite you to tea.'

'I don't want your rotten tea.'

'All right,' Robert said instantly; and Ernie began wondering what it would be like to go to Robert's house and have tea there. They lived in the cantonment and there was a sign on the gate saying *Maj. R. King, Adj.* He had cycled past it once, carrying a message for his father, and he had stopped outside the Kings' gate pretending rest, fearing and hoping Robert would come out and say hullo. But Robert hadn't come, and he had never yet been into a cantonment house.

Robert linked arms and said: 'Do you like it at this school?'

'No, it's rotten.' But that sounded like an admission of defeat and he added: 'Some of it's all right. The lessons, of course, are very easy.'

'I'm going to school in England. I shall wear a uniform and a cap. They play other schools at football and cricket.'

Ernie was kicking at a stone, dribbling it through the confusion of legs in the playground. His imagination conjured tackles and a cheering crowd and he shot brilliantly to score against the doorpost; he had heard what Robert said.

'Didn't you hear? They live in lots of little rooms of their own and get pocket money and play football every day.'

One temptation overcame the other. 'I don't care,' he said.

'I'm going to the best school in the world. It's the best in England so it must be the best in the world. Then I'll go to university.'

And Robert had struck true at last. For Ernie a university was almost equitable with paradise. Or perhaps it was the Styx; what lay beyond was not imaginable from the common world he knew. To have gone to Oxford or Cambridge (he knew of no others), to be England-returned, was to command respect and future success unquestioned. Robert would go, of course, because he was British; he wouldn't need to be clever.

'You could go to university, Ern.' But he tried not to listen, as in a dream of proffered wealth one tries to sustain disbelief.

'You're jolly clever at lessons and everything. You're marvellous at maths. It's not impossible, Ernie.'

The school bell began to ring, and his answer was stifled by the realization of how far they had strolled from the gate. They raced back up the road and into the playground.

'When am I going to come to tea?' Ernie gasped. 'Look, hurry, we're going to be last in.'

'My ma says Thursday,' Robert puffed, and they trotted into the classroom. The teacher did not reprimand them, for they were his two best pupils and he liked to see them such good friends; it was also good for British-Indian relations.

When Robert stepped towards him off the Thursday bus Ernie expected he would confirm the tea that afternoon. He got ready to say something like: 'Oh yes, I'd forgotten; but I'll be able to come.'

But Robert wanted only to compare homework. He went off without mentioning tea and left Ernie puzzled and apprehensive. Had Robert forgotten? He'd been looking forward to it all week. Victor had bought him a new shirt for the occasion from the store at a discount price. Could he remind him? . . . No, there was a convention he dare not break.

School over, he waited tensely at the front door. But Robert went by with his hand on someone's shoulder, talking solemnly of cricket. 'He keeps a straight bat,' Ernie heard him saying, and just for a moment thought Robert noticed him but without remembrance showing in his face.

He hesitated; should he speak? Robert had forgotten or changed his mind. It didn't matter, anyway, he didn't care.

But it would be silly if—

He hurried to the gate. Robert had been talking to Dingwall the vice-captain; they would be drawing up the team to play Mathura, or collecting equipment from the store. Forty or fifty children walked and cycled through the gate, diminishing Ernie's hopes. Then at last Robert appeared, still talking to Dingwall, looking very important. They walked through the gate together, and at last parted as Dingwall went for the bus and Robert turned towards the cantonment.

Ernie fell uncertainly into step beside him.

'Come on, then,' Robert said.

Before they reached the lines he tucked in his shirt and tried to scuff his sandles against his socks as he walked, wiping off dust. As he caught himself in the act a ball of temper moved in his chest; the British houses were nothing to him; did they have the Jama Masjid, the Red Fort? He was proud to be Indian. He said 'Sat sri akal' to an old Punjabi mali as they walked past and refused to respond to Robert's silence by looking at him.

But as they walked sullenly in the centre of the road a thin flat shape moved out of the storm ditch in front of them.

'A snake,' Robert cried. 'A poisonous one. Get some stones.'

There were a few small stones lying on the road and he flung them all at the snake's head, missing each time.

'Get some large ones from the ditch. It's a Russell's viper. Hurry up.' Then he turned to see Ernie still standing quietly with a grey face, hands to his throat like a startled girl.

'Here, what's the matter. . . ?'

Robert's command seemed to release a trigger. Ernie took six or seven jerky steps backward as if someone had pushed him and he was trying to keep balance.

'Come on, Ern . . . find some rocks.'

Now a dog had run from a nearby garden and stood barking excitedly at the curving menace, its hindquarters arched for instant flight. Robert came staggering from the ditch with a heavy stone in his two hands. He ran as close as he dared and lobbed it at the snake's head. The heavy thud on the tarmac awakened the snake to danger. In a few seconds it had disappeared in the long grass at the roadside and the dog was barking at a memory.

Robert turned. 'What's the matter with you?'

Ernie stood ten yards down the road, staring into the grass where the snake had disappeared.

'You're scared,' Robert ventured.

Ernie said nothing.

'You're scared of snakes.' Robert's face was bright with interest and hope.

'I just don't like them,' Ernie muttered. His face was the colour of porridge and he shivered in spite of the heat.

'You're scared. You're scared of snakes. It wasn't even near you. . . .'

'I can't help it.' He looked at Robert appealingly. 'Are we near your house yet? Are we late?'

Robert made a schoolboy jeering noise. 'Don't try to get out of it. Admit you were scared.'

'I'm not worried about anything else . . . jackals, or spiders . . . I just can't help it with snakes. Lots of people—'

'Don't lie. You were scared like a girl. My sisters have got more guts than you.'

But he had taken it precisely far enough; now he stored the knowledge against a future need and they walked on down the leafy road of the cantonment. A few bearers were cycling with invitations to teas and cocktails. Dogs dozed under the keekar trees. On the verandas ladies fanned themselves with the airmail edition of *The Times* and wrote letters to aunts in Dorking. A white-trousered mali was watering the path as the boys turned in through the gate. Under a thatched roof a big Austin car was parked out of the sun and Ernie's eye lingered as they passed into the house.

'First we must wash,' Robert commanded.

A bearer was setting out clean towels in the bathroom beside the front door; the towels he took away looked no less white than their successors. The Mahers had a bearer at home; and a gardener too whom they shared with three other families. And their house had a veranda and lawn, but it was nothing like this, the bearer's uniform, the woodblocked floor, the elegance of everything and having to wash before tea. He moved in the bathroom as if his presence were an intrusion.

'I must put on a clean shirt,' Robert said. 'You wait here.'

Robert ran upstairs, shoes scraping the banisters, and Ernie felt as uncomfortable as if Robert were misbehaving in church. He washed his hands and face, trying not to dirty the bowl . . . the enamel was swan-white and showed stains like wounds.

He dried his face in front of the mirror and when he lowered the towel he saw a girl standing before and behind him.

She was about ten years old, dressed in a green frock and white plimsolls; she sat two seats in front of him at school.

'What are you doing here?' Surprise startled him from his careful manners.

The girl said: 'I'm Susan.'

He knew that.

'Susan King,' the girl said.

Robert's sister! 'But he never told me he had a sister.' At the same moment he recalled Robert's words out on the road, comparing him with his sisters, and hesitated in confusion.

'He's got two,' she said. 'The other one's Rowena and she's

very serious-minded,' the overheard phrase coming awkwardly off her tongue.

Her hair was not so fair as Robert's; it was darker and golden. It had about two more years to decide whether she was going to be blonde or turn darker with puberty. With one ankle-socked foot poised against the other, twisting a skein of hair round her finger, she seemed like a timid animal wanting to flee but held by a cord around her heart.

'How did you get here?' he asked with a child's need for logic.

'On my bike. Robert left his behind,' she said, 'because you were coming. He said you'd be too poor to have one. Are you poor?' she asked.

'No.'

'Mummy's outside,' she answered and went away, as if this confession limited to the grown-up world his potential of interest.

'We're rather late,' Robert called from the stairs as if the blame were to be shared between them.

He had changed his shirt and shorts and put on polished black shoes instead of the open sandals. Ernie wished for time to comb his hair but Robert hurried him out of the front door and round the side of the house, past two large chestnut trees and the mali sprinkling the same square yard of grass and on to a lawn with acacia bushes in flower at the far end. An overweight labrador got to its feet and waited to greet them.

Mrs King was tall and beautifully dressed. She rose to greet Ernie, fluttering and anxious like a large white moth. The tea-table was set like a careful chessboard between elegant walnut chairs from the dining room, and the two girls were already seated but politely waiting, Susan still curling her hair round one finger, and Rowena, whom he also recognized from class. She was dark like her father, and quiet like him, and looked rather unfriendly. He hoped he wouldn't sit next to her; and as if Mrs King had seen the thought written on his forehead

she placed him between herself and Susan, patting the chair
before he sat as if giving it one last, anxious attention.

Perhaps he had forgotten something tremendous, for Robert
was regarding him critically. He said the words thank you in
a small, general way as if to cover every possibility . . . but
Mrs King was speaking. He noticed she was never still: her
hands arranged spoons and plucked at cake and rose to attend
her hair, and her glance darted about the tea-table as if any
slackening of vigilance would allow its component parts to fly
away on their own.

'Help yourself to lots of tea, Ernest. We've plenty of food
for growing boys. Don't let that fly sit on your plate. There's
jam and there's honey and there's black treacle. Would you
like nimbopani or would you prefer a nice cup of tea?'

'Nimbo—' he began, then saw with dismay the white-coated
bearer turn with the empty jug towards the house. 'It's all
right—tea . . .' he began and saw the bearer's glance brush
his face as Mrs King said: 'Certainly not. . . .'

He looked secretly at Susan who was eating with concentration, not looking up. He tried to think of something to say to
her.

'Robert tells me you are very clever at school,' Mrs King
accused him.

'Oh no—no, it's not so. Robert is heaps better than me—
than I—than me. . . .'

'And football. You play football together?'

And now he could see that Robert's mother was as nervous
as himself. It was very strange; he was frightened of them and
yet they were all uneasy themselves in his presence. Mrs
King was chatty, Susan shy, Rowena quiet. Only Robert
was at ease, knowing both camps, able to attack in either
direction.

The bearer moved silently about between them, a presence
without substance, stepping carefully round the labrador
which moved its head and frowned at him. A deferential
second after Mrs King had put down her empty cup he took

it and, seeing Ernie had nearly finished his nimbopani, hovered
at his elbow.

Ernie swallowed two hasty mouthfuls and handed the glass
up over his shoulder.

'There's no need for that, dear. Radu will look after you,
won't you Radu?'

'Ernie is like that,' Robert said suddenly. It was his first
word since sitting down. 'He speaks to malis in Hindi, don't
you Ernie?'

Well, he had been expecting it . . . he didn't know why
he ever bothered with Robert King. He had wanted desperately
for the others to like him, but Robert was going to spoil it
all if he could.

'Do you speak Hindi?' Mrs King was bending towards him
with delight; she spoke as if it were something magical like
sword-swallowing.

'You're very clever to speak Hindi. The Major has been trying to learn it for years.'

Ernie looked directly at Robert and added another triumph
to the first.

'It wasn't Hindi, it was Punjabi Robert heard me speak.
But I *can* speak Hindi, and Urdu a little. And I shall learn
Sanskrit when I'm bigger.'

'That's *very* clever. But then you boys often know lots of
languages.'

He looked at Robert who was staring into his glass. 'Do you
speak any languages except English, Robert?'

He would pay for it, he knew; his quicker brain was no
defence against Robert's omnipotence. But now he felt happier;
Mrs King was very nice, and the girls too, especially Susan.
She looked like a little doll he could have held on his palm.
She tucked one foot under her on the chair and for a second
until Mrs King spoke he had a disturbing view of her white
knickers. He had never been really close to a girl before. It
was nice; Robert was lucky to have a sister.

And Mrs King was bending towards him again as if they

were two conspirators. 'Tell me why you wish to learn Sanskrit, Ernest? Is it not a dead language?'

'It has nice poetry. All the old poetry was in Sanskrit. I'm
going to read all the Sanskrit books.' He quoted the futile
claim with apprehension, trusting her niceness not to challenge it.

'Like Latin in Europe,' she said. 'You're a very clever little
boy.'

'Bearer!' Robert gestured imperiously. 'Bring me another
nimbopani.'

'Please,' his mother added in a murmur, but neither the
bearer nor her son took any notice.

'Wouldn't you like another one, Ernest dear?'

'Oh yes—it doesn't matter,' he stammered as the stiff figure
disappeared behind the chestnut trees.

'He'll be back in a moment.'

Ernie looked again at Susan, who had exhausted the possibilities of the table and was now searching the sky for another thing to engage her attention. She had not revealed
shyness in the house, but her mother's presence acted like a
catalyst.

'Do you like school, Susan?'

'Susan, our guest is talking to you,' her mother said immediately.

The girl had been about to reply but now swallowed air.
She smiled and looked back into the sky.

'Susan!'

She looked down, and up again. 'Yes,' she shouted, and
reached for a cake she didn't want. She took one small bite
and for the rest of the meal broke off little pieces in her fingers
and fed them to the panting dog who demolished them as if
he were paid for it, conscientiously.

The impassive bearer returned and Robert sent him back
for another nimbopani. The sun now peered from below the
shade of the acacias but it was cool enough, with the approach
of winter, for them to remain where they were. Two big

mynah birds were hopping on the lawn in search of crumbs
but the labrador had done a thorough job.

'I have a great admiration for your father,' Mrs King was
saying.

'Yes, ma'am.'

'A most loyal and trustworthy man. I think it is very nice
you and Robert are friends'—the boys glanced at each other
—'it's very broadening. The Major has always said that we
should be more—I mean that we should accept. . . .'

Only her mind and Ernie's were quick enough to be ahead
of the words, the implied condescension hovering unspoken
behind them. Further disconcerted by the child's knowledge
she made a clumsy recovery.

'And how long has he been with the regiment, then?'

And he saw in her face the immediate recognition of her
mistake. You never enquire into an Anglo's past. You certainly never touch the sensitive nerve in every Anglo-Indian's
breast which reminds him of his military antecedents. And
only one type of Indian woman could give her body to
such an irreligious act. . . .

He had learned this even before the business of offering a
lady a seat, saying thank you for gifts; and his young mind,
full of the wrong kind of experience, saw her rally her forces,
overestimating the danger, and continue to shoot long after
the last sniper was flushed out of the trees.

'. . . But of course one never knows about one's own father,
does one? Do you know, I was nearly fifteen before I realized
that my father ever had been a boy. It had just never occurred
to me. I've never told you two girls about that, have I, or you
Robert? But it's true, you know, and I'm sure you must think
me very silly, but I've often thought how nice it would be if
we knew more about our own families. Now the Major's
family, oh dear. I wanted to trace it back to William the Conqueror—you know who he was, I hope, dear—but I'm afraid
the bend sinister . . . not that you'd know what that is, and
nor should you, a little boy like you. . . .'

He rode home that night in the big Austin car. She had asked the Major to take him, for it would have been a long walk. Robert and Susan went with him for the ride, which was a relief, for he would have feared conversation or silence with the forbidding Major King. Rowena did not accompany them; she had picked up a book immediately after tea and had not even heard them say goodbye. She read with the absorption of one who finds more safety and truth in story books than in the unreality of the world around them. And he could share that feeling; for however different their lives were from his, it was with them that he identified himself as he grew towards age.

One day Susan fell into step beside him as he left school and walked through the barracks. She was often hanging around now, to his fearful embarrassment; she must have looked very fair beside him with her straw-coloured hair and white school clothes.

'Are you going to see your father?'

She moved in a peculiar, hopping walk, and after speaking would sometimes jerk her head up and back as if listening with her mouth.

'Yes, that is correct,' and he hoped the obvious dullness of the errand would dissuade her. But she clung to his arm as she tried to hop, one white-painted stone at a time, along the border of the gravelled path.

You're doing awfully well at school aren't you?'

'Yes.'

But she was quiet for so long that it made him feel nervous.

'I like composition best,' he said. 'And maths and everything.'

'I don't like anything much. I like history.'

This surprised him: she had been bottom of the class in the last test. But nothing this girl said could be taken very seriously.

'Old Bates was cross with you, wasn't he?'

It wasn't her fault that she renewed his humiliation; thoughts in her became words, like clouds produced rain. The teacher Bates was new from England and had a habit of taking off his spectacles to rub his eyes, fingers in one eye and thumb in the other, as if trying to push them deep into his head.

'Which of you is Maher?'

Ernie stood up.

'Oh!' It implied an uncertain change of direction. 'Nevertheless—'

He picked up an exercise book which Ernie recognized; he had often watched its open cover expectantly while the previous teacher had read from it to the class, as an example of good work.

'I asked you all over the weekend to write about your favourite work of literature. Was it unreasonable of me to expect it would be from among those you have read here at school.'

His sentences often seemed to be a few words too long. For some seconds after his meaning was made clear, words continued to drop like stones.

'Answer me, boy.'

Already it was a familiar trick, demanding an answer which made the boy ridiculous either way.

'Yes sir . . . no sir. . . .'

'But what is this you have written about in your exercise book here? The Bar—the Baa—'

'*Bhagavad Gita*, sir.'

'Who wrote this mighty work of literary merit? No don't tell me . . . Shakespeare? Milton?'

'No one knows, sir.'

'I should think no one wants to know.' The tired phrase slipped across the desk to gain a token response. Any kind of humour did in the classroom; it was not necessary to be funny.

'Of course, I cannot expect to understand the Eastern philosophical attitudes like you do.'

There was another shameful reluctant titter from the class.

'I naturally expected you to write about Macbeth as most of the others have done here. Did you think this Bar thing a superior work of literature to Macbeth?'

'Sir?'

'Do you think it's better than Macbeth?'

'I don't know sir. I liked it better.'

He knew by the silence the whole class was against him : Maher showing off again. Robert two rows in front was staring straight ahead, stiff-necked.

'Yes I do think it's better,' he said.

It provoked a stunned silence, alarm at his courage. . . . But reaction followed : Maher, of course, could get away with being peculiar.

Mr Bates took off his glasses and wiped them thoroughly with his handkerchief. Then he rubbed his eyes with finger and thumb and when he took his hand away his eyes were red at the outside corners. But the moment for anger had passed : he contented himself with saying, 'In that case, young man, I don't know what you are doing in an English school.'

And afterwards Robert had said : 'Ern, you're a bloody fool, you are.'

'What's the matter with you. . . ?'

'Putting in that Indian thing for your homework. Ungrateful little twerp. Do you want to be a wog all your life?'

'Shut up calling me a wog.'

'Well, don't act like one. It's not the first time either. Been on any more bike-rides lately. . . ? Oh yes, I've seen you. My father says you'll get in trouble, doing that.'

'It has nothing to do with you.' But he was frightened; it had been his secret.

'You want to go to university, don't you. You're always saying you do.'

He kept silent. Like the name of God, it was something you didn't speak of lightly.

'Then why don't you act more like us?' Robert was used to

running his own conversations, handling both arguments.
'You're just as good as some of these English lads but you
start going all woggy.'

'The *Bhagavad Gita*,' Ernie said, 'was written before Shakespeare and Milton were even heard of.'

'All right, all right. But you're with English people. This
is a British school.'

'And I am half Indian. There's nothing wrong—'

Robert seemed suddenly to lose his anger. He gripped Ernie's
arm in a rough, friendly way. 'If you ever went to England
. . . it wouldn't matter. Some people wouldn't even know—'

'You seem to think I'm ashamed of it.'

'It's just bad luck, that's all. We can't all be born British.
You could have been Chinese.'

'So could you.'

'Oh, go and do what you like. Put on a dhoti and go and
shit in the gutter. Go on a pilgrimage to Benares. Or be someone's bearer, or shovel nightsoil. It's your choice.'

There were plenty of choices but they all connected with
each other, overlapping like a fortune-teller's hand of cards.

'I was on your side, Ernie. I didn't laugh like the others.'

Susan looked up at him appealingly but he did not answer.
What was she doing walking with him anyway? They would
be at the store soon and people were looking at them.

'I don't like Shakespeare either.'

He suddenly felt amazingly grown-up in front of her. He
knew so much more than she did. Adulthood, then, didn't
come suddenly like initiation; parts of life developed as others
faded behind, and thus came the progression, as with the
amoeba they had been drawing in their books at school.

When they reached the store he made her wait outside. He
gave his father the message he had carried from school, handed
to him by a sergeant's son with a demand for urgency.

'Why couldn't Sergeant Martin have come himself,' Victor

grumbled. 'He knows me very well. I got a very good carpet for him last month at a special price.'

'It's your half-day, Father. Will you take me home on your crossbar?'

Victor frowned with reluctance and Ernie said, 'All right, it doesn't matter.'

'Go and wait by the main gates,' Victor said. 'I'll be up there in ten minutes.' He did not want to be seen in the compound two on a bike, like the Indians.

Ernie came out of the store and found Susan sitting like a lonely kitten on the grass.

'Anyway, Robert was against me,' he said. 'And I bet you were on Robert's side.'

'No I wasn't. I was on your side. No one can make me laugh when I don't want to.'

She followed him as he walked up to the main gate and some passing wives stared at them curiously. He shook off her arm.

'Where are you going, anyway?'

'I'm just walking with you.'

'Why?'

But she was immune to innuendo, like a deaf man to curses. 'I like being with you,' she stated, and gave the characteristic jerk of her head. Then her gaze went past, over his shoulder, and a look of fear seemed to shrink her thin body.

Looking towards Jangpura, they could see a large ragged-winged vulture drifting slowly down towards a column of dirty black smoke. Ernie had not noticed the smoke because it was always there, a permanent smudge on the near horizon of the ridge where the villagers had a burning ground. The vulture came slowly in and settled heavily in the branches of a tree with the smoke blowing through it. Two other birds were already sitting hunched in the dead branches.

'What's the matter?' He tried clumsily to comfort her. 'It's not you they're after. It's all right.'

Two more birds were flapping their ugly way over the Jaipur Road, and to his horror she started to cry. He glanced uneasily up the road; it was temporarily deserted but someone could appear at any time.

'It's so horrible,' she sobbed.

He wondered if she knew in fact what the birds were after.

'They're only vultures. They don't attack you. They just look horrible.'

'Robert told me,' she cried. 'I begged him not to tell me, but he did.'

'But then, how did you know—?' But he realized logical argument would not help him. She lifted her dress to wipe at her eyes; she was always showing her knickers. Perhaps he should just walk away from her. Girls were so peculiar, she hadn't cried at all when they heard about the Bengal earthquakes.

'It's only if there's not enough wood,' he said. 'It's a very rich compound over there, they've got tons of wood.'

'You're telling lies,' she said, but she was interested; she had dropped her dress now and was wiping her face with her bare arms, high up near the elbows.

'No, honest, the brother of one of them owns a forest. They can keep fires burning all day.'

One of her sobs sounded very like a giggle. She knew it was nonsense, but his falsehoods were comforting.

'I just hate to think of it happening,' she said.

He did too. 'We'll send them after old Bates. They'll sit on his shoulders and pull out his hair.'

She started to smile.

'Then they'll peck all his clothes off in the square,' he went on with his nonsense.

Her face was almost dry already, as if the tears were dew and the sun of her smile was drying them.

'And then—no listen—you be one of them and I'll be the other one and we'll lift him up and fly off and drop him in the Jamuna with a splash.'

She giggled and waited for him to continue; more tears were in reserve. But his feeble imagination was exhausted.

'Robert, your brother you know,' he said, thinking fast, 'he's marvellous, isn't he?'

'No, he's a pig.'

'Oh!' he said with interest; he'd caught a quick, guilty glimpse into another secret world, of Robert King through the eyes of another. 'Oh no he's jolly well not,' he said, keeping it moving.

'He's a pig! He's a fat old pig!'

'What—' he said anxiously; it could easily get away.

'He thinks he's a hundred years old. He thinks he's my boss.'

'Yes—?'

'He leaves me out of everything.' She could manage only the vaguest grumblings; it was not with her brother she was angry this afternoon. 'But I still like him,' she conceded at last. She made pronouncements one at a time, and the last took priority like her father's military commands.

'How can you like him if he's all those other things?'

'He's nice,' she said, and her argument turned and retraced its steps, striving for expression. 'He's terribly strong. He likes me best, I'm going to marry him when we're grown up. I like it when the other girls know he's my brother. I don't mind if he's . . . if he doesn't talk to me sometimes at school.'

'He can be rotten sometimes.'

'I don't care. He can't. Anyway I'm glad—I don't want anyone else to like him. He's terribly strong, he can lift me up.'

During the past minutes Ernie had forgotten to keep a look-out and now Victor suddenly stood there astride his bicycle, jingling the bell.

He looked as if he wanted to make the English girl's acquaintance, but children don't make introductions; you have to know or guess.

'Goodbye,' Ernie said, and wriggled up on to Victor's cross-bar.

Victor stood on the pedals and turned left, on to the Jaipur Road, to branch off soon on a footpath through the bush leading to the Ring Road.

'Who was that English girl?' Victor asked; and Ernie, who had been waiting for the question, said, 'Robert King's sister.'

'She is a very pretty little girl.'

He stared out over Victor's shirt-sleeved arm. They passed the burning ghat which was still smoking. A villager was throwing stones at the last, most patient vulture, and as they cycled past it rose from the branch uncomplainingly and Ernie watched it flap heavily away towards the railway tracks. He was thinking of Susan's remarks about her brother which had brought on such a sudden, acute loneliness, a fear only aggravated by the Kings' closeness to his life.

Mountains

Ernie sat and watched the body of Prithi Singh ascending back into life. The closer the hunter draws, the nearer to becoming the quarry. There is needed such a small adjustment of time and circumstance to change love into apathy, draw strength from fear, or be standing at the wrong end of the rifle. Chance has only its own laws, and the man who pulls the trapdoor could also be the one to drop.

Mokerjee came in and asked, 'Is he awake yet?'

Ernie didn't answer, but let the lieutenant make his own deduction. The jaiwan's breathing was regular and his groans almost theatrical. The wound in his head had started to bleed again in the tossing jeep and soaked through the bandage. Mokerjee said, 'He nearly bought it, eh?' and giggled as he went out.

Break a limb and the pain doesn't start till later. He busied himself with Prithi Singh to prolong his own respite, avoiding the realities of blood and the looped handles of wire. He shifted the man's head to a different position and thought about making tea.

Mokerjee came back again like an irritating habit.

'We are searching the town. We are making arrests before dawn.'

'Who are you looking for?' Ernie asked, 'the Chinese?' Immediately he regretted it; he would need Mokerjee yet, so he said: 'Have you heard from Sopur yet, Lieutenant?'

They had telegraphed to the main police station twelve miles down the Srinagar road. At least ten men would be needed to cover all the roads and paths out of Baramula. 'No dramatic arrests,' the Minister had said, but the events of an hour could invalidate a month of planning.

'I am still waiting,' Mokerjee said. 'The lieutenant was not there.'

Ernie made tea for them both in the cracked pot and the dirty cups. The cups had never been clean for more than two minutes in their lives: they were used, then left till they were washed and used again. Before he had finished Prithi Singh was moving and Ernie stirred six spoonfuls of sugar into one of the cups and held it to his mouth.

Prithi Singh needed only five minutes to recover, then started to talk in formal sentences as if for an official entry in the log, a report on a case of petty larceny.

'During the afternoon I was making enquiries, sahib, accompanied by Jaiwan Attar Singh. I discovered four men who visit Baramula sometimes but do not reside here. At 1930 hours I reported to Mahbub Ali's teahouse to warn you, sah, that they were seated at table behind you. When told to disperse, sah, I waited in your room, taking the liberty, sah.'

'Did you see an Englishman?'

'I saw nothing, sah, but stars in my head. Now I have almighty pain instead.'

Back it came into his mind, however hard he resisted . . . the coiled wire like a snake, the handles looped for a firm grip. The man mistook Ernie's stare.

'It was nothing, sah. It is like a hangover that will be gone tomorrow. If I may be permitted sick leave of absence—'

'Of course—'

'Just until midday, sah, and then I can resume my duties.' He was sitting upright now at a sort of attention; unconsciously his left hand was caressing the scuffed buttons of his jacket.

'Sahib. . . .' He looked puzzled; memory was not returning logically, but as with glimpses of a photo album pasted down in the wrong order. 'I think I did not go immediately to your room. There was a man, a big man who went out the back way.'

'Go on.'

'I followed him, sah. He was one of the strangers. But I lost him. He went towards the river.'

'Most careless of you,' interrupted Lieutenant Mokerjee. 'Very damn careless.'

'Do you remember if the light was on behind you? Or was there light also in the room? Did your attacker have a torch?'

The Sikh pondered for a moment; the log book should not have erasures.

'Only behind me, sahib. There are oil lamps in the passage. I had just opened the door when he hit me . . . I think.'

'Then your attacker would not have seen you properly. It was probably me they were after and I am sorry you have suffered.'

'It was my duty, sah.'

It was almost irritating, this man's aggressive loyalty. Surely there were duties that took precedence over getting killed for someone else. Ten seconds more and the jaiwan would have had a thin line of blood across his windpipe; the same day would have seen him dressed for death, spaded under, and the small pension sent back to the family in the Punjab. Another entry in the log. A small gap in the establishment. One of the cups would not have been cleaned again.

During the night a suspect was brought in, dressed in an old army uniform and smelling of resin. They had found him burying a Browning automatic under a pile of sawdust in a lumbermill. His shoes had been made in Pakistan but this didn't prove very much; there was nothing else to identify him. When Ernie tried to question the man he maintained a bored-looking silence, occasionally spitting accurately between Ernie's toes. They put him in a cell.

He went outside and found the other jaiwan, Attar Singh,

walking up the path with a torch, his pocked face reflecting the beam curiously.

'Where is the jeep?'

'The corporal has taken it. He is searching the Uri road.'

'Then find another vehicle. I want you to go to Sopur. I want at least a dozen men with rifles back here before dawn. We have telegraphed ahead so they should be ready.'

Attar Singh looked doubtful. 'I am only a jaiwan, sah. If there should be some difficulty—'

'I tell you we have already telegraphed. You are just to hurry them.'

He watched Attar running with his swinging torch beam back into the town. He would find a vehicle all right. There were several lighted windows down there, at an hour past midnight. There were few people who would still think him a casual tourist but the time for pretence was past.

The fear and the rage were beginning to get him. He hadn't known it would be like this, suspicion and fear and garrotting in the dark. Taking all in all, he had not hated Robert King after all this time; he had been ready to come to terms with the events of ten years ago. But he now recognized that it would have been dependent on capturing Robert and having him in his power, triumph repaying defeat. What had happened tonight only increased the debt.

Mokerjee was inside with his prisoner, and the rest were searching the roads. For something to do he walked back to the teahouse. Mahbub Ali was not in bed; he sat wrapped in his patched overcoat in front of the samovar, reading a newspaper by the dim light of a dirty bulb ten feet away. He held the paper at an angle for the light to slant on it.

He looked up at Ernie without lowering the paper.

'You are having a restless night.'

'I nearly slept a long time . . . in your room up there.'

Mahbub Ali shook his head, denying responsibility. 'That is serious. A most regrettable incident, very bad for trade. I wish to offer the apologies of the house.'

'Did you know any of those men?'

'I told the lieutenant. They went out after you left. I never saw them before.' He moved the newspaper back towards his eyes an inch or two.

'You will find my bag upstairs, still unpacked. In the morning you will please have it sent to the police post.'

'Where are you sleeping tonight?'

'Anywhere but here,' Ernie said.

He helped himself to tea from the samovar and took out his purse.

'For you nothing,' the man said, studying his newspaper. 'The room is with the compliments of the management.' But Ernie put ten rupee notes down on the counter and said: 'Would you prefer Kashmir to be joined to Pakistan?'

'I like Kashmir as it is. Let people leave us alone.'

'But if you had to choose?'

'I don't know. What difference? Pakistan I suppose, I am a Muslim. But neither preferably, and no more fighting. I have my business to run.'

The answer was simple and honest, and easy to believe. War was the Government's affair, and only rarely did it loom more important than a wedding or a funeral, a comfortable fire, the samovar and the pipe.

When he walked back up the slope he could see the first glow of a false dawn above the mountains, and he heard the jeep returning from Uri as he reached the gate. Its headlamps lit the pale trees and swung in a wide arc that took in the whole compound before coming to rest on the petrol tanks.

The corporal stepped out. 'I discovered no persons on the road, your honour.'

Ernie was not surprised. Anybody wanting to avoid being seen would have had about ten minutes' warning from those headlamps.

Mokerjee came out to the veranda, staggering slightly from tiredness.

'The suspect has talked,' he announced proudly. 'His name is Sultan and he is coming from Lahore City.'

'Well done,' Ernie said. He hurried through the office to the cell at the back. At the cell door he stood for a long while . . . then walked slowly back to the lieutenant.

'We beat him,' explained Mokerjee unnecessarily.

'You are a fool. I shall report you. That is against the law. You might have killed him, you might have killed an innocent man.'

'Oh nonsense, man. You have to beat these fellows.'

'Now he is unconscious.'

'Oh yes,' Mokerjee said as if insensibility were the object of the action, the position gained from a planned advance.

'So tell me what you have learned.'

'His name is Sultan. He is coming from Lahore City.'

'Yes, what else? Did he come with the gunrunner? Where are the others now? Where are their headquarters? By what route did he enter Kashmir? Quickly, just the main points.'

'Well. . . .' Mokerjee sensed that his answer was going to be insufficient. 'His name is Sultan, as I said. He is coming from . . . well, we have beaten him and now when he wakes up he will certainly talk. I am telling you.'

'Were you born so stupid? Or did you learn it from the University of Bombay? You are a damned idiot and I shall report you for this if it's the last concrete thing I achieve here.'

Mokerjee shrugged. They stared at each other in dislike. Their mutual antagonism was so well established that it had become necessary, a point of understanding between them.

They both heard the jeep at the same time and Ernie went to the door and stared off to the right, up the road to Srinagar where the sky was paling. The sound of the Sikh's erratic driving came in blocks of sound from the narrow streets, and then in a noisy progress up the hill. There were no other vehicles with it.

The jeep turned a dusty circle round the flagpole and stopped with its back to him. The flap was flung back on to the canvas roof and a fat sergeant climbed heavily out.

He dusted himself down carefully, staring at Ernie. Another man, a jaiwan, stepped backwards down from the jeep and dragged out two rifles. They stood looking curiously at Ernie as Mokerjee came down the steps behind him.

'You're alone?' Ernie cried. 'Where are the others?'

Attar Singh jumped down from the driver's seat.

"Sahib, I am most amazingly apologetic. I could not make them believe. The C.O. thought it a matter of no importance.'

Sudden blankness, and the insertion of pain into a level of his head like a card into a slot, told Ernie he had the old fight before him again. The sickness sprang at him, the cold sweat stung his forehead like a wet towel. He struggled for breath but fell to his knees with Attar Singh holding him.

'Sahib, you are ill—'

'Get away!'

He stood up, knees shaking. 'Bastards!' He addressed them all. 'What are you here? Is this a posting for imbeciles?'

He tottered several steps forward. Mokerjee backed away in alarm.

'Bloody choors! Robert King is in this town or a few miles from it and the soldiers of Kashmir don't care a pig's penis. No wonder you have gunrunners, no wonder you will lose Kashmir to Pakistan—'

He stopped. It was a sign of danger when he swore in Hindi and the danger of the sickness wasn't past; it never passed.

Mokerjee said, 'Kashmir is an integral part of India.'

Ernie slammed into the hut while he still had control; he left them looking like actors on stage who have missed a cue.

He knew very well now it could not have been Robert; garrotting was a peculiarly Indian custom. Robert was too confident, he did not have fear enough to kill.

He heard the jeep leaving again, and his ear watched it turn towards Uri, and after waiting another five minutes he went out to see the dawn really coming at last, over the Ladakh Hills. He was tired now, at the wrong end of the night. Everyone had gone, the compound was cleared like a stage, and he could hear Prithi Singh on Mokerjee's bed, snoring into his bloodied beard.

The sun rose higher; the near hills assumed their daytime colour. He could see the first soft outline of mountains right back to the snowline, the mist drawing up like a curtain. Already, as he watched, the gullies were turning brown and cultivated patches bloomed on their slopes.

He had heard the river murmuring all night but now it gave way to other sounds. A truck was revving down in the town. A donkey, twice its size with kindling wood, trotted despondently in front of a small girl with a stick. He heard ducks calling down on the river, and a dull thumping that would be the day's first dhobi-woman breaking rocks with her master's shirts. He heard Prithi Singh end his snoring; and, across the compound, Attar approaching him accompanied by a second pair of feet in faltering cadence.

'Sahib!'

The man was still a soldier, his uniform arranged with stern discipline. Since returning from Sopur he had found time to polish his boots.

'The man from Sopur has something to tell you. He saw something on the road.'

'Well, let him talk.'

'He speaks no English, sah.'

'I speak Hindi.'

'He has not command of Hindi either. He is from Assam but knows some rough Kasmiri.'

Attar Singh spoke swiftly, establishing concise information from the uneasy replies. The man seemed to be regretting a chance remark that had now dragged him into the unwelcome light.

'As he sat in my jeep he saw three horsemen about a half-mile from the road on the far side of the river. There was a full moon, sahib. They were going towards Sopur.'

Ernie shook his head. 'That is no good. They would be going the other way, westwards. They are not our men.'

'There was something else—' He broke off and exchanged a swift sentence with the jaiwan. 'There were donkeys, heavily loaded. He thinks about three or four. It was too far to see what the loads were.'

'But does he think they could have been guns?'

That was the sort of sentence which invited the Indian yes: he had spoken unthinkingly. But Attar Singh was reliable.

'I wondered why the men should not be using the road. They were on a path which connects some farms and eventually leads down to Sopur. But it is a longer way. And why did they choose to ride at night?'

Ernie stood mentally disputing all these facts, unwilling to admit his instant belief in a hope. . . .

'The path leads only to farms, sahib,' Attar said softly. 'You don't travel on horses at night.'

It was getting warm already. The curtain had lifted from the long hills of snow and Ernie wiped a handkerchief across his forehead and said, 'Where is the lieutenant?'

'At breakfast in the bazar.'

'And the Sopur sergeant?'

'Searching the Uri road, sahib. It would not take very long to find them.' Attar spoke seductively, and stroked the shoulder which was allowed to carry a rifle in a declared emergency.

'How would we—?'

'There is a pontoon three miles down river. Some of us could cross there and the others could go on down to Sopur and cross at the bridge. That would trap the dacoits between us. Perhaps reinforcements could be picked up at Sopur.'

'Did you say trapped? Could they not get off the path if they saw us coming?'

'They could, sahib. But they couldn't take loaded donkeys

into the bush. Shall I go and look for the sergeant, sah?' and he shifted his right shoulder at the uncomfortable lack of weight.

Attar Singh went out in the jeep and brought the fat sergeant back. The corporal arrived at the same time, and as they were preparing to go Prithi Singh came to the door of the building and waved the jeep down.

'You are not well,' Ernie commanded.

The man had already got one leg over the tailboard and now, avoiding Ernie's stare, watched the other leg move up as if against his will. 'I am quite recovered, sahib,' he muttered; and added on inspiration, 'You will need me to identify the criminals.' And the corporal moved into gear and Ernie said no more.

They bounced down the slope towards the town and Attar said: 'Shall we fetch Lieutenant Mokerjee?'

Ernie stared ahead. 'I don't think that will be necessary.'

'It is against regulations,' Attar murmured, to cover himself for the future, and Ernie said: 'It would be wrong to disturb his breakfast, a hungry man is not a happy man,' adding the absurd words as if they constituted a recognized maxim of great appositeness, and they all chuckled now that Government had declared himself.

They reached Sopur in a half-hour, slowed briefly for the corporal to jump out at the police post, then scattering a herd of goats they crossed the narrow bridge and went up into the hills above the river. They had left the sergeant and his man at the pontoon and already they would be coming along the path towards Sopur, driving the men with the donkeys like an unwitting herd.

The path went up steeply for a mile. They drove through a walnut plantation and past a whitewashed Hindu shrine with a grey concrete dome. A hundred yards further on the path became too narrow for the jeep, so they reversed towards

the shrine to park in the open space by its doorway. A fat
Vishnu stared at the car with bored arrogance from deep in
the temple's shadow.

'There must be no shooting unless absolutely in self-defence.
That must be clearly understood. In particular no one is to
shoot at the Englishman. If he shoots at you then you must
withdraw. I am very strict about that.'

They both nodded with eager haste.

'I mean it,' Ernie said; the obese statue sneered down and he
inspected the Sikhs doubtfully, like sporting dogs recently
tamed. But he hadn't much choice. 'The Englishman is tall
and wears a karakul,' he said as they moved off, and watched
the new blood flowing brightly through the long curly hair
at the base of Prithi's turban.

The path wound right and left across the face of the hill.
There was low brush and the occasional rice field on both
sides, the gentle slope on their right, the steeper one on their
left down to the river a mile away. Attar walked twenty yards
ahead, carrying his rifle as if there was a bayonet on the end
of it. He peered carefully around each corner before advancing.

They walked for an hour and then Ernie had to beg a rest.
Office work had not fitted him for this and he was exhausted.
Cessation of movement brought out the sweat on his face,
and his legs trembled at the completed effort. They had
already climbed five hundred feet since leaving the jeep. The
Sikhs were not sweating; it was something which marked his
difference. Indians complain of the heat as much as anyone
but they don't sweat. As a boy he had played football in
summer, but now he sweated; it was the one quality he had
brought back with him from England, that and a hatred which
even the destruction of its cause could never cure, like snake-
bite.

Attar Singh said, 'Sahib!'

A horseman was galloping round the next bend, the echo
of hoofs bumping from the hill behind. It was a moment before
they recognized the Sopur jaiwan riding very clumsily with

one hand clutching the horse's mane. He disappeared for a moment in an angle of the path, then came galloping out towards them, not seeing the party till he was nearly level.

He reined in twenty yards down the path, looking uncertain how it was done.

'We have discovered, sahib! Dozens of rifles. The four donkeys are loaded with them.'

'Where?'

'In an orchard—a mile away—'

'And the Eng—?'

'The men are not to be seen, sahib. They must have observed our approach and made hasty escape. The donkeys are not even tethered—'

'Where is the sergeant?'

'Staying near the donkeys.'

'Good fellow.' He trembled at a sudden fear. 'We will come as fast as we can. Go back and help, but there is to be no shooting.'

He started running with the Sikhs at his heels. The jaiwan took over a minute to turn his horse, as if fumbling with the gears, then went by leaving them running in his dust.

They walked and ran, making their own time. As they reached the orchard the sergeant stepped out of the trees.

'We have kept close observation. The bandits are hiding, they are not in the farmhouse.'

'Who is?'

'The farmer. And his wife.'

'Arrest them! No—afterwards. And don't bother with the donkeys. We must all spread out and search.' He tried to think of a sensible dispersal of his forces but the sergeant was already in command and suddenly he was alone. 'No shooting,' he was going to say, but it was too late, and he thought nervously of the Sikhs beyond his influence, caressing their rifles like loved objects.

He moved through the orchard, over the thin grass. It sloped

downwards, and he came into the open with a ditch in front
and a steep field of corn rising on the other side. It fell away
on the left to bare earth and stones, with another hill rising
behind it, heavily wooded after the first hundred yards. A
breeze rustled the long grass in the ditch. As he ran forward
to jump he remembered one second too late he should have
looked along it first. There was a crack in his ears; he screamed
and fell, clutching his groin . . . and then there was quietness
and he had not been hit and the memory of the sound placed
it ahead of him, to the left, near the wooded hillside.

He started running. The shot had not been for him; there
was another shot from the orchard and Ernie saw a quick
movement as a man raced across the hill, head down. He fell
a yard from the trees and lay there, turning.

Out of the orchard ran Attar Singh, down towards the
ditch. His turban was knocked aside and the hair streamed
down his back. Ernie could hear the click as he drew back the
bolt.

'Attar Singh! Stop shooting, you bastard. Stop it!'

At the edge of the wood the fallen man stirred and raised
an uncertain arm . . . but the arm dropped and the rifle bang
echoed from the hill, and a swarm of birds flew up from the
trees.

He ran to the Sikh and kicked him twice in a fury. 'You
crazy Sikh! He was already hit. If it was the Englishman—'

The fire in Attar's eyes died slowly. 'He was escaping. . . .'
He held the rifle to his chest like a wounded animal and his
dark eyes peered nervously through the spilled hair from the
turban. 'He fired first, by the beard of the Guru—'

But Ernie turned to the hill, for he had just remembered
something seen as he ran beside the ditch, a small irrelevant
movement which could have been some animal, in the crevice
between the hills. . . .

But the sergeant ran lightly out of the orchard, carrying
his bulk like a dancing master.

'We have another one. He was hiding up a tree.' He giggled.

'I left Prithi Singh to guard him, you know how Sikhs love Muslims.'

The jaiwan joined them, limping, for he had hurt his ankle. Attar stood at Ernie's heels like a dispirited dog, crying tears of excitement or remorse.

'Now,' the sergeant said, 'there is only the Englishman.'

He pointed with his rifle towards the field of corn and swung it to cover the woods. He held the rifle one-handed at the butt and must have been tremendously strong.

'That is where he would go—'

'No!'

'There is no cover down in the orchard. It's small and noisy—'

'The Englishman is not up there, sergeant. I was watching.'

The man didn't believe him. His eyes were saying But you've only just arrived. He shaded his eyes up at the hill again and Ernie said: 'I saw him go that way, round the orchard.'

Was he being foolish? This man stood a better chance than him. He struggled with this thought while trying to identify his motive.

But the sergeant took Attar with him round one side of the orchard and sent the jaiwan limping off the other way. Ernie watched them moving off through the long grass and waited another full minute before turning to stare up the dip between the hills, where he knew Robert had gone.

On the left-hand hill was the fir plantation with the man lying dead below the trees. At its foot was a crevice with a trickle of water, a line of saltbush, and a worn path going up both sides.

He kept his eyes fastened on the spot. A rabbit bounded away across the slope but he didn't even see it go.

When he reached the place there were, of course, no incriminating footprints, no Craven A cigarette paper chucked down or strand of English worsted caught on a bush. The ground was bare and dusty and he moved on up the hill. He climbed for twenty exhausting minutes, using the rifle like a crutch.

He reached the top. The bare hill on his right continued up and away. On his left the line of firs had retreated and now lay a mile back. In front of him was a thousand yards of flat ground before the next hill, littered with broken white rocks and a man stumbling over them. . . .

Robert! He walked forward into the stones but gave up after twenty yards. That was how things happened, then. He watched the tall figure making its painful progress over the rocks and thin grass. He could not follow: this after no dramatic chase or exchange of bullets. . . . Drama is only the ordinary enlivened by passion. He was exhausted, it was hot, and he didn't want to cross the scree.

He stood in the sun and watched for ten minutes more the long figure moving towards the hill. The karakul was off and the blond hair shone, even at that distance. He started once as Robert fell. . . . It would have been too hot to follow and too difficult to know what to do when. . . .

He could have used the rifle but . . . he was too far off now, anyway. He watched until Robert reached the slope and scaled it . . . and then a sudden long stillness told him that Robert was standing, looking back, and he had been seen.

He made an awkward gesture, the rifle bumping his shoulder. A cloud sailed across the sun and he watched the shadow travelling away across the scree. . . . Now he regretted he had waved, for it somehow suggested an offer he was unable to make.

There was a dak bungalow in Sopur; Ernie was given a bed and slept through until ten o'clock. He had eaten rice and chapatti before falling off, but when he woke he was hungry again. He lay in the dark room and heard, without listening, the noises of the town. Even in a darkened room, eyes closed, you could tell this was Pak—this was Kashmir. There was not the slow, tedious creak of the bullock carts straining by, the bells jangling in Hindu temples, and the odour of heat. They were different smells of food that came drifting through the evening window. From his sleep he remembered the song of the muezzin at sunset.

He reached down for the blanket and drew it up to his chest. Then he heard what had woken him, a gentle tapping on the door. Attar Singh came in with a tray.

'Chai?' Ernie sat up.

Attar smiled proudly. 'Coppee. It is nescoppee, I obtained it from the bearer of the local magistrate.'

'Is the local magistrate aware of his generosity?'

'He will acquire merit,' Attar said, 'by giving without self-gratification.' But he was nervous, watching sadly as Ernie drank and ate the greasy omelette that looked as if it had been dropped at least once on its journey from the kitchen.

'Now sahib, there is some news. King sahib was in Sopur this afternoon.'

Ernie stared.

'Yes, sahib. After the encounter in the orchard he came straight back here. He arrived before us.'

'That is impossible.'

'No sahib. By the beard of the Guru, he was here.' His voice trembled with the desire to regain confidence. 'He was on horseback, sahib. I have asked many reliable persons of the town. One of the horses was missing afterwards and he must have taken it.'

'But the reinforcements would have met him on the road.'

'No. The corporal says he saw no one. But he could have observed the party and hidden off the road until they passed.'

He should have been ready for something like that; Robert always played to his own rules.

'He came to buy horses, two horses, and traded in the other. Then he rode away.'

'In which direction?' The frying smell of kebab came sliding between the bars of a window from a nearby compound.

Attar's pockmarks dilated as he frowned in sad perplexity. 'It makes no sense, sahib.'

'Which direction?'

'He rode away to Khadzil.'

'No, you have made a mistake. Go and check with the man who sold him the horses.'

'Sahib, I too am not understanding. There is nothing in Khadzil and there are only mountains beyond. Please believe me, sahib.'

'All right,' Ernie said. 'Let me think about it.'

Khadzil was at the far north end of the Vale, on the River Sharif which flowed into the Jhelum at Sopur. He couldn't remember much about it. It nestled up against the Pangi foothills, but there was no way up into them.

'It doesn't make sense,' he muttered. 'He is going nowhere.'

'Maybe he is frightened, sahib.'

Ernie looked at him. 'Of what?'

'He is frightened of you, because you are from Government. He runs north because you would not think of it.'

No, not Robert! Let the Sikh think so, it was a tempting idea. But Robert would not leave a game if he was losing, and going north would be like going offside.

'He has not used his brains, sahib, because he is trapped in Khadzil. The road ends there.'

But he had not concealed his destination from the horse-trader. He had sometimes played cricket lefthanded, to give the bowler a chance, and if there were enough people watching.

'Khadzil cannot be far from the ceasefire lines?' Ernie suggested.

'Thirty miles, sahib. But only if he goes north-west, and he would have to be a bird.'

'Perhaps he knows a way across the mountains. There are plenty of people in Kashmir who would help him.'

'It is impossible, sahib. Anyway, there were plenty mules available but he bought horses.'

'And are horses not good? I once rode a horse over the Banihal Pass from Jammu.'

Attar faltered; he had served with the British on the northwest frontier and liked his officers infallible.

'The Banihal Pass is an anthill, begging your liberty, sahib. You would not take horses into real mountains. They might die in the snow. Also they do not like heavy loads and they cannot carry loads downhill. And they break their legs too easily and they get winded.'

'Any other reasons?'

'Sah?'

'Never mind,' Ernie said. 'You're doing very well. Now, just tell me why Robert King, fugitive from justice, is going towards mountains that can't be crossed.'

'You shall know when you capture him, sahib. Shall I be making arrangements for you to follow? If we start at five—'

'Wait a minute.' He pointed to the tray. 'Attar Singh, will you go and rob that magistrate again?'

'Instantly, sahib!' He ran delightedly from the room and Ernie could hear his shouted orders to the chowkedar, a door banging, and later the cracking of a thorn fire near his window.

In his haste Attar had thoughtlessly taken the lamp and night had slammed back into the room. He felt in the dark for his map, then moved along the wall with his hand, searching for the light switch. It was stuck up with paint, had probably never worked since the place was built. He took an oil lamp from the passage and brought it back to the table.

Khadzil was a town of about two thousand people, thirty miles from Sopur. The road went alongside the Wular River until the fork to Shaburah, then turned left. There was not much more he could tell from the map except that the mountains to the west were marked as uncrossable.

Robert was on his own now, armed of course but not defended by hillmen with garottes. By merely following he would have him. But why this hesitation? He didn't want it to end. After years of chasing figures he was now hunting a man; and what a man! The best possible revenge! But the chase was everything; the kill meant only grubby disillusion and a return to the files in Calcutta.

Well, for a few more days perhaps, the relationship would be sustained.

He turned again to the map. Behind Khadzil the Muzaffarabad Range rose to thirteen thousand feet before dropping to the Kishen Ganga River, then rose again to sixteen thousand feet on the other side in Pakistan. The Kishen Ganga lay just inside the cease-fire line. There was no way of crossing the Muzaffarabad mountains, there was no town or village west of Khadzil, there were no roads or paths, but Robert was there and the game was still waiting to be played.

Prithi came for him at six o'clock. 'Everything is ready. There are horses waiting at the bridge. We were stern with the man and there will be little to pay.'

It was still cool and the town lay in the shadow of the hills. Behind him, as he walked on the cobbled road, he could see the sunlight moving down the hillside; it had dropped another twenty yards each time he turned. Below, the earth still slept in a haze of blue shadow, but just as he reached the bridge the sun dropped on his shoulders and warmed him under his jacket.

A small group of men waited by the tongas at the far end of the bridge. Attar was there, and the Sopur sergeant. The horse dealer was arguing vehemently; Prithi could not have been quite stern enough.

Prithi stepped forward. 'All is ready, sahib. Give me your things.' He began to unpack Ernie's suitcase into the saddle-bags on the packhorse.

Attar led forward a bay mare and made a step with his hands. Ernie settled in the saddle and immediately felt good, bouncing once or twice to get the feel of it, staring between

the mare's ears up the Khadzil road. He glanced round and
saw Prithi in the saddle of a grey pony; he stared, and Prithi
grinned and patted his mount's neck and looked up at the
mountains. He turned the other way and saw Attar also in
the saddle, leaning down to place rupee notes one by one into
the dealer's hands.

'We are ready, sahib.'

'Attar Singh . . . Prithi . . . there has been a mistake.'

'Sahib?'

How could he possibly explain to them, in any way that
made sense? His memory peeled back the years; the journey
they had done before, the blue kingfisher and the hat on the
water. There was no way of explaining even to himself. He
said: 'You are not coming with me. Nobody is,' and stared
between the mare's ears, along the barrel of a rifle, into a past
without hope.

'There has been a misunderstanding, that's all. I am going
to travel alone.' His bay took a few unbidden steps forward
and for an instant the whole scene slipped behind him and
the two men cried out in disbelief.

'Sahib, you must take us. It is not safe alone!'

'I am very sorry. I appreciate your loyalty and sense of duty,
but my orders. . . .' He got down to hitch the pack pony to his
own saddle while he was still ahead of them in resolution and
doubt.

He shook Prithi's hand and said: 'How is your head now?'

Prithi blinked with big eyes. 'It is clear, sahib. But I think
yours is not, to go after a bandit alone.' He touched the wound
at his ear. 'If it should happen to you—'

He turned to the other man. 'Attar Singh, you have done
splendidly. You shall both be rewarded, I shall put in a report.'
But a tear trickled down Attar's broken face.

'You are remembering yesterday in the orchard. I will leave
my rifle behind, I beg you!'

'No, Attar Singh, that is forgotten.'

He went back to the mare which the big sergeant was holding still with one large hand against its chest. His face was disapproving.

'If you should fail,' the sergeant muttered; Ernie could see him visibly weighing his loyalties and he said sharply, 'The responsibility is mine, sergeant,' and got back into the saddle. It was important to keep moving.

'Sahib, there is food in the bags. Your map is in the pocket of the left-hand one. You must keep your rifle dry with the oilskin.'

'Namaste,' Ernie said. 'Sat sri akal,' and clattered over the bridge with the odd repetition of the pack-pony's hoofs behind. He turned right and trotted up beside the river, waving to the small paddling children who took no notice. Indian children do not smile or wave back; strangers are not welcomed. At the edge of the town he faced along a dusty road that led irrevocably on and up into the hills which were now green and brown in the sun.

Plains

'Robert, are you really going to England?'

'Yes, of course.'

'In the summer?'

'Before then,' Robert said, studying his long tanned body with satisfaction. 'I'm going from Bombay on May 26th on the *Orion*. My folks are seeing me off.'

It was March. Already the air was warmer in the mornings, so that people were rising early to sit on their verandas around the green and take lungfuls of air while it was still some pleasure to breathe. The roses in the trim beds beside the cantonment swimming pool were enjoying their month of bloom before April shrivelled them brown.

'I didn't know it was so soon,' Ernie said. They were lying at the edge of the pool. Robert had been diving all morning, conscious of the attention he attracted. He was a beautiful boy, scaling the ladder with easy grace, falling from diving board to water like a hungry seal; his perfect pubescent body trembled on the edge of manhood. The wives watched him from their deck-chairs, and middle-aged officers sucked in their stomachs and swum steady, conscientious lengths of their own.

'I suppose you won't bother with me any more.'

'Don't be daft. Ma's already told you to come up whenever you like. And your girl-friend's pining without you.'

He ignored (but for an angry blush) the reference to Susan. He refused to admit his tenderness for her; only in a crowd did he feel safe.

'Yes, but I mean you. Your ma's terribly nice, but. . . .'

'I'll write to you Ern, honest. I shall, well, miss you.' It is difficult for children, who live only in the present, to think beyond a parting.

'I'll write and tell you about England. And you can tell me what's going on here—all the things my ma wouldn't tell me.'

They both paused and tried to think of subjects in that category, conjuring a world beyond their experience.

'You'll be going to the Lady Fowler School in five months.'

The British School catered only for boys who left for their boarding schools at the age of twelve or thirteen. The Lady Fowler School was for the children who stayed. It kept abreast of the School Certificate syllabus and the examination was taken at the end of the third year.

'Robert, will we stay friends?'

''Course. Why not?'

'I don't know. I wonder if friendships last when you go to different schools. Different countries too. And you're English.'

The reference did not often arise between them: it was a cloud in the future which they could ignore for a while, like a difference in religion between an engaged couple. But two months only remained, and if their friendship was over then, it was over now.

'I shall be coming back every summer holiday,' Robert said.

'You'll be too posh to take any notice of me. You'll have all your English friends. They play cricket and everything.' He spoke like the devil's advocate, raising objections to himself. 'We won't have anything to talk about after a whole year.'

'But you're British too,' Robert said. 'In a way, you are.'

Ernie stared at the flush of goose-pimples on his arms and felt utterly miserable.

'You're an old misery guts,' Robert said.

After ten minutes of silence they picked up their towels and went in to dress. They drank a nimbopani, and walked down the corridors of jacarandas in the cantonment, flicking at each other half-heartedly with their damp towels. The heat bounced up from the roads, their shoes stuck slightly as they walked and a passing bearer on a bicycle left a perceptible trail behind him in the tar.

Mrs King waved from the veranda, but her arm dropped as though it held a heavy object. The veranda deck-chair was an unhappy compromise between the discomforts of heat and the stuffiness indoors.

'Hello dears, have you had a nice swim? Your towels are all dirty.' Her hand hesitated over a perspiring nimbopani, then retreated to turn another damp page of *The Times*. All the nervous energy which found a release in movement during winter months was now trapped in her chairbound flesh and she had adopted what Robert called her summer grumbles, a vague but sustained comment on her immediate surroundings.

'I can't think how you get your towels so grubby. Don't tread the dust into the hall, now.' It always seemed to be hotter in March, just after the winter, than in August at twenty degrees higher.

They went upstairs. Robert had two cases already packed for the journey to England, his initials on the side in black letters.

'There'll be a third one,' he said, 'for all my clothes. But I shan't need any of these cotton things, it's too cold in England for bush shirts.' He spoke of England with authority though he had last seen it at three years old, and his frequent references owed more to imagination than memory.

'Are you taking your football?'

'Shan't need that thing. They play rugby at my school.'

'It's not your school yet. You needn't show off.'

'I've had my name down for it for eight years,' Robert asserted. 'My father went there.'

'What's rugby anyway?'

'Oh . . . it's difficult to understand if you're not—unless you've seen it.' In fact, he had no knowledge of it except for the odd-shaped ball and a long passage in *Tom Brown's School-*

days which didn't seem to make much sense. 'You hold the ball in your hands, you see. And you have dozens of players on each side. You have to be very brave to play it.'

'Aren't you scared?'

'Of course not; British boys don't funk it.'

'Do you wear top hats?'

'Don't be stupid. We wear straw boaters in the summer and caps in the winter.'

'You'll be terribly cold when you get there.'

'No, I don't remember it as too cold in July,' Robert said gravely.

Downstairs, Mrs King said : 'Are you stopping for lunch, Ernest?'

'Ooh yes.' Susan answered for him. Ernie saw Robert turn to watch his reaction, and he blushed angrily. 'I can't—my father doesn't know.'

'We shall telephone him.'

'We do not have a telephone at home.'

'Then we'll send Radu on his bicycle. The Major bought Radu a bicycle six months ago, you know, and Radu is paying it back at five rupees a month, not that he seems to be very grateful for it.' She craned her head to each side of the veranda, trying to peer round the corners, but sank back. 'Robert dear, I can't imagine what you're grinning at. Please just run along and find Radu. It's so hot.'

Rowena was reading a book at the other end of the veranda, crouched in her wicker chair as if it was a dark cave. He recognized the title from a Christmas present and said, '*The Twins at Drear Castle*. I've read that. It's good.'

The girl moved the book very slightly out of his shadow but did not look up or speak.

'You won't get any change out of her, dear. She doesn't hear you when she's reading. At least she pretends she doesn't but she can hear when she wants to all right.'

Rowena looked up from the page. 'Did you speak to me, Mummy?'

'There you are,' Mrs King offered, but for the first time the experience of doubt caused her words to falter. She loved her children, but was a little frightened of things around her she could not control. After all, she read her *Times* every week without shutting off the world as if it had no existence. Rowena had always been too serious-minded for a young girl.

They had been waiting at the table for ten minutes before the Major returned from his office and sat down with the usual abstracted air. Ernie always felt that for the Major his every visit to the house was a first experience. The man never remembered his name, and rarely spoke. But his son and daughters worshipped him.

Afterwards they separated, the Major back to his office, Mrs King to a cold bath, Rowena to Drear Castle. Susan had abandoned the attempt to capture the boys' attention and now enticed her overfed dog into clumsy play on the lawn. Upstairs the boys refought the battles of the Boer War with toy soldiers and guns, Robert taking the British side of course, and having sole access to the clockwork train and the books by Roberts and Baden-Powell. Radu brought them cold drinks at three-thirty, and an hour later served tea on the veranda as the sun went behind the trees.

Ernie was driven home in the Austin. The Major did not speak to him. He had plenty of time to think about his afternoon with the family and nurse the fear that, however uneasy his friendship, Robert was the tiestone that held it all together, and Robert's departure might leave him stranded in his own unfamiliar home.

There was a dust storm on the day of Robert's departure. Mrs King and the girls had their hair tied up with scarves. The boys used handkerchiefs to cover their mouths and secretly shot each other with their extended fingers, then fell suddenly quiet and took to shaking hands very formally.

'Cheerio then. Goodbye old man.' He was already testing his new school language.

Luggage and people moved past, separating and rejoining them like corks on a sea. A smell of curry and heat wafted from the third-class end of the train and porters stumbled with sacks of ice into the buffet car. It seemed to Ernie a long time before the whistle blew and all the family stepped into their compartment and leaned out of the window.

Suddenly Mrs King opened the door and jumped down, glancing nervously at the guard with his flag.

'Ernest dear, you look so unhappy, poor little man. When we come back we'll tell you all about Bombay.'

He looked doubtfully up at her, concealing grief. The train began to move in the long slow acceleration timed to accommodate goodbyes and completion of pan vendors' sales.

'Ernest dear, please come.' She had to turn his face back with her hand. 'I shall miss Robert so much and you must help to fill the place. . . .'

But now she had to leap back into the carriage. Her foot slipped on the moving step and one shoe nearly fell off on to the track. He stumbled after her as she leaned dangerously down with her mouth against his ear.

'I'm Indian,' he muttered fiercely. 'You don't want me.'

'You're a little boy,' she had wanted to whisper, but the noise of the train made her shout. 'To me you're just as English as my Robert.'

'But—' he tried to say.

'Yes, yes, yes! Come in a turban if you like. But come please. . . .'

Incongruously he was having to trot to keep their faces close, avoiding luggage and babies. His shoulder brushed a chapatti-wallah and he heard an angry yell as his foot trod into something soft and he felt the wet dough clinging to his shoe. With the train's acceleration it had become a thing important in itself to match his speed with it, to sustain communication as long as possible with the anxious face bearing slowly away from him. But the platform's end ran forward

to meet him and he stopped against the final rail and waved to
her in agreement.

On his bicycle Ernie crossed Connaught Circus and pedalled
down the Qtub Road beside the railway track. Between the
track and the road was a sweeper village burdened by the smell
of dryness, and beside the road was a ditch with steep banks
holding rats' nests and a black pool, stiff with ordure. Children
squatted to defecate on the bank and he kept his eyes averted
as he hurried past. Sometimes when he came this way the
villagers would jeer and throw rocks under his wheels. He
kept as far to his own side as possible, until he was past the
last wood and corrugated-iron hut and was crossing the Sadar
Bazar. But then he eased off and let the slope carry him; his
legs were tired and there were still more than two miles to the
university.

Victor had said to him, on the day he returned from lunch
with Robert's family, 'So now you have bearers to deliver your
messages.' He couldn't keep the envy slipping off his tongue,
but in fact he saw it as the end of the first battle in a long
campaign. For Victor had never been invited to lunch in the
cantonment. He had occasionally drunk in the club bar and
been invited to noisy parties in the sergeants' mess, but lunch
at an officer's house had not been achieved. But his son was a
scholar at the British School and now he was going to Lady
Fowler School. The regiment was paying half the fees, his
good friend the Adjutant had helped him there.

'You're more British than me,' Victor said, with a sad envy
that time and circumstance could achieve so much. And with
the exaggerated nonchalance of a man about to commit a
robbery, he said, 'Do you perhaps have other British friends.
Now that Robert is in England?'

Ernie said, 'I have friends, but most of the British boys are
stupid.' But the words lacked force; in the face of token rejection Victor felt himself nearing the end of a long journey.

'If you do well at Lady Fowler you could go to British university. You do realize that, I am hoping.'

'I—I don't know—'

'You could go to Oxford or to Cambridge. It is possible.' They had had this conversation before; every few weeks they renewed their faith like the Sat Bhai.

'You will have to work harder than a slave but I am telling you, you can do it.'

'It would cost much money—'

'I will pay. We will sell things . . .' and thoughts of university lay before them like a vision.

Three months after Robert went away, Ernie started at the Lady Fowler School in Lodi Road. The school opened at seven o'clock and closed after lunch; for those six hours he chafed under the restriction of timetable and syllabus, sighing through the empty minutes accummulated by finishing essays ahead of time, fretting at the slowness of group reading. He took to inventing work for himself, and every morning presented his teacher with an essay written the night before, begging him to mark it. If Victor took him to a film he would write the story down to the extent of his ability to recall. He joined the British and American libraries and read books by torch-light into forbidden hours of the night. He was growing fast during this year, the thin body shooting up, and the growth outstripped his energy; he stayed thin, his eyes stared from pale depressions over his cheekbones, he fell suddenly tired in the afternoons and twice went to bed for a week to rest his body and his brain.

He discovered the game of hockey and worked hard at that too, and his Indian pride took him again like an old fever. India was the world's hockey champion and with every goal he scored he drew closer to his Indian identity. Ernie was never below the top five in the monthly exams.

It had to be this way, for the biggest difference between himself and the English boys was that they were insured against failure. The result of poor work for them was a matter of degree only, while he would be finished. He had the advantage of the hare, running for its life, over the dog which chased only its dinner.

And his visits to the university were all part of the great endeavour.

'Hallo Vijay. Mr Lal. Naresh Tandan.'

The students passing out of the university gates saw Ernie's familiar figure bicycling anxiously up the road.

'Hallo, it's the little pundit.'

'What books are you reading today? Tell me please.' He jumped from his bicycle and pushed it along the kerb, looking up expectantly into their faces. He had learned they liked to tease him a little first, dangling their knowledge agonizingly just out of reach. Vijay and Naresh elbowed each other and dropped their books over the road.

'Please tell me. I want to be clever like you.'

'Today we have done no reading. We have been changing rupees into gold.' They giggled together, showing their teeth. But Ernie kept his face stern; he had no time for humour.

'Then tell me please, what are you reading yesterday?'

'An English grammar, you nutcut. One that informs us of the relationship between tenses.' The two bent over with exaggerated mirth and dropped their books a second time. Ram Lal did not join them; he had a pale, lizard face and rarely smiled.

'Why, what is wrong with my sentence? Explain to me please.' He waited in frowning patience.

'Hey you little shaitan, would you have our lessons gratis? Well then, today we have been studying the works of the poet Browning.'

'Browning? I have not heard of him. What poems has he written. Tell me please.'

Ram Lal said goodbye abstractedly and strolled away to the bus stop. At Imperial Avenue the other two would go different ways and Ernie fidgeted uneasily. But they had never actually said goodbye without, breathlessly, at the last moment, telling him: it was like giving conspicuously to charity.

'Please tell me.'

Vijay said: 'It was the poem entitled *Porphyria's Lover*. That is a very good poem.

'Who was Porphyria?'

The two students looked at each other uncertainly.

'It is about a man who loved his sweetheart so much that he strangled her.'

'But that is an apparent contradiction, is it not?'

'No, that is not so. When you are as clever as us, little pundit, you will understand such things. It is a very good poem.'

'How do you spell it?'

He searched for a pencil, but found he had nothing on which to write. Vijay read it to him haltingly from a book and Ernie was turning his bicycle about before he had finished, lips working in memory. He cycled back past the sweeper village, across the wide space of Connaught Circus, and past Parliament Street on to Willingdon Crescent. The library at Willingdon Crescent closed at five o'clock and he stood anxiously on the pedals, to avoid the waste of an evening.

He took out a copy of Browning's poems, checked that the volume contained *Porphyria's Lover*, and read it with snatched glances on the long ride home. But his attention was disturbed; he had to keep glancing up from the page at a thickening traffic. There seemed to be twice as many people as usual, and when he reached the racecourse he had to dismount as another dense crowd came slowly up Club Road. Where were they going . . . was there a riot? A funeral? The faces were grave and quiet, there was a startling hush over the whole marching crowd. He felt himself and his bicycle pulled along with the relentless movement, and ahead of him, on a high wooden platform, was a thin dhoti-wrapped man with a bare arm and shoulder. He was tiny and bald but he held the surging crowd like the unmoving centre of a wheel.

He heard a sudden cheering and all the people behind him pressed forward. He was pushed up against the people in front, fearful but fascinated. A microphone blared suddenly from a tree, starting in mid-sentence, but before his brain adjusted to the Hindi words it cut off again and he heard a roar of cheering beyond the platform. He strove for another glimpse of the man in the spectacles . . . then felt a firm hand on his shoulder.

'Mr Lal!'

The student beckoned. 'Come with me.'

'Why—I want to watch. What is happening—?'

'Come away,' the young man said in a voice calm with authority. He pressed backwards, making a path for Ernie to push his bicycle. When they were clear of the crowd he put a hand under the boy's elbow and pulled him along.

'There is going to be trouble.'

'What? How. . . ?' He twisted round to catch a last glimpse of the little man in the dhoti and suddenly all the memories ran together and brought out on his lips the word 'Gandhi!'

'This is no place for you. Don't be impatient, little one, there will be plenty opportunities. But today there is going to be trouble.' The microphones were blaring again and he heard a few isolated words (republic, swaraj, congress) before another bend in the road reduced the voice to a murmur.

'How can you tell something will happen?' He trotted along, pushing his bicycle, to keep up with Ram Lal's determined strides. Lal looked down at him with an expression of complicity and hope.

'We are always prepared for it. We know that today it is coming. Those men on the platform are martyrs.'

Then Ernie heard the lorries coming; in his heightened awareness he was instantly receptive to the changing scenes as they performed for him one by one. He heard Ram Lal saying, 'We have already said goodbye to them . . .' before he too became aware of the approaching noise. They stood against the hedge and watched them go past, a dozen large black lorries with native policemen and dogs, and then a line of motorcars with British officers. Ram Lal watched them go by, and pulled with his fingers at that part of his face which would never grow a moustache.

'If they want us to show violence . . .' but he let the sentence drift by. Another swift picture of the thin, bespectacled Gandhi flicked past Ernie's eyes and Lal said: 'He is their saviour as well as ours. He is a saint.'

He gripped Ernie's arm again. 'Come on, you're still too near. What's that you've got in your shirt?' There was a square bulge on Ernie's chest.

He blushed, but with hesitant pleasure he pulled out the thin copy of Browning.

Ram Lal's pale gloomy face softened. 'You are a determined little one. You will be a great pundit.' He stopped again suddenly in the middle of the road. 'But where do you stand, hey?'

'Where do I—?'

'You look as Indian as me. But I have seen your father.'

'I don't—I am not like him—'

'We are not racial, understand that.' He had meant to speak stirringly but his face couldn't support it; the eyelids drooped, and he pulled again at the moustache that was not there. 'We hate nobody. When India is free there will be a good life for everyone—Muslim, Hindu and British. We only want'—his hands gestured despairingly—'dignity.'

But Ernie thought of the thin-shanked man on the platform with his impotent microphones, and the lines of policemen coming to take him away. Dignity was a big word: it meant the British Army, Government House, the photo of the King Emperor on the wall of his father's dining room. Could there really be anything else?

'Where do you live?' Ram Lal demanded.

Ernie told him, and Lal said, 'I will come and see you sometimes. Do not worry about your father. I am at university, next month I am working in Indian Civil Service. I have great respectability.'

Ernie felt an excited glow in his chest. This was what India meant to him: history and culture, political expression, intellectual involvement and university graduates. The sweeper villages were but dust on an ancient parchment.

'You wish to call on me?'

'You are young at the moment. But in five years' time you will not be too young. We will need people like you for the new India. Go home now. I must return and see what has happened. There has been trouble, certainly,' he said with gloomy satisfaction and walked swiftly away down the road, his pale lizard face glowing with the late afternoon sunlight.

At home a letter was waiting with a British stamp. It stood propped on the mantelshelf like a certificate of influence. Victor said with heavy casualness, 'You have a letter from Robert King.'

But it began: 'Dear Ernie. . . .' Robert did not use salutations.

He had not returned that summer after all. Major King had used an accumulation of leave to take his family back to the home they had not seen for nine years. Robert had written twice during that year, letters full of school and rugby and the O.T.C. camps. They were friendly letters but Ernie felt increasingly that he was missing shades of meaning, as if they were from a foreigner who could not write colloquially.

The King family was still in England and this letter was from Susan. He read it with surprise and pleasure. He had not had a letter from her before and it seemed to offer a different picture of her, in clearer focus by being further away. She described their large stone house in Wiltshire, the green hedges and nettle-strewn lanes, the English-looking cows leaning over the fence on wet mornings. Her immature phrases evoked a vicarious sort of nostalgia, as if the grey house and the lanes belonged to him from a distant childhood. 'There's a funny old greenhouse down by the river. It is always empty. It is made of glass. I go there heaps of times and it's fun. Nobody can sneak up and I pretend I'm grown-up and having women to tea. Robert is most posh. He wears his school clothes all the time, even his cap as well. Mummy says he wears them in bed, but he doesn't. Mummy is very proud of him.'

The radio broke into his train of thought. Victor had switched it on in time to be arrested by an item of news, and now stood as if on guard with an angry stare in his dark eyes. Each repetition of the word 'Gandhi' left another bruise on his dignity.

There had been trouble at a political meeting. The police had tried to disperse it with dogs and the crowd had panicked, aided by paid agitators. Shots had been fired; someone had been killed. Gandhi and four others had been taken into custody. 'It's disgraceful,' Victor shouted. 'He should be executed, we are far too tolerant. He is a menace to the community.'

The announcer turned to the sports news, it had been a fine day and Gloucestershire were still batting. . . . Ernie folded his letter and put it between the leaves of Browning. He thought of Ram Lal pacing awkwardly down the afternoon street, his face too sad to look angry, begging for dignity. His sudden dislike for his father rose swiftly to something less containable, a feeling of superiority.

He glanced at the clock, arranging his schedule. He had an hour of maths homework. He would write a voluntary essay describing the political meeting. That would still leave an hour for Browning before bed; *Porphyria's Lover* did not look a very long poem. . . .

Susan returned from England to a list of demanding questions: Robert's school, his uniform, the game of rugby; had they seen the King and was Wiltshire near Oxford or Cambridge? He was met with insubstantiality: England was pretty, London was big, the greenhouse was very nice. The vision was blurred again with closeness. But next year Robert did come back.

He looked years older as he stepped down from the train. His mother and sisters rushed forward, Major King following, but Ernie stayed back in the shadow of a pile of mailbags. He shouldn't have come, he was out of place . . . and next week they'd all be off to Kashmir for the summer and he'd be alone.

He could see Robert's broad grin from thirty yards. Gosh, he was bigger! He was hugging his mother and shaking the Major's hand over her shoulder. He threw a grin and a wave at Ernie and then they were all moving down the platform towards him.

'Hullo, Ern old man.'

The voice had broken; it belonged to someone else. He hesitated at the unexpected sound and Robert said, 'Tongue-tied, eh?'

Damn him! He'd been about to speak but now the accusing words cut back his reply. Now he felt himself blushing . . . but Robert put an arm round his shoulder and said, 'Here, I've got you something.'

He had to unwrap it right there on the platform. The string knotted; he tugged at it angrily. Inside the box lay a handsome knife in a leather sheath.

'I say . . . thank you!'

They moved down the wide steps to the Austin and the pile of suitcases. It had all been too familiar; first the authority established, then the act of generosity putting him in a grudging sort of debt.

'Sit with me, Ern.'

He squeezed past Robert's mother and sisters and took his seat with pride. He had been longing for this day for two years. Now, although he was somehow unsatisfied, he felt consoled by the thought that for complete happiness he would have had to pay too high a price.

Susan was prattling happily, unaware of strangeness; and by the following day it was she who had drawn the boys together, an alliance against the awkward female presence. They spent so much of the day together that Mrs King sent Victor a note suggesting that Ernie stay at the cantonment for the next week of the holidays; it would spare the boy the cycle ride to his home in the evening and the long return the next morning. Victor spent two hours writing a delighted note of acceptance in the florid style of the printed invitation cards he sold in his store, and Ernie moved in.

A week after Robert's return he came across the family in the living room, sitting in an atmosphere of intrigue as if they were preparing a secret joke. Every time he caught their gaze they smiled quietly and turned away.

'Ernest dear. . . .'

He had done something silly or wrong. They were going to be decent about it.

'Ernest, what are you going to do for the rest of the holiday, whilst we are away?'

'I suppose . . .' he began, then said determinedly: 'It will give me the chance to study, I have not been working hard enough.'

Susan giggled and he turned on her fiercely. He hated jokes he couldn't understand. 'I am working very hard indeed. I am top of my class.'

'Ernest, isn't there something you would rather do?' She looked rather like her daughter at that moment of archness. 'Think of the thing you'd like to do more than anything.'

A flame of hope brushed his soul. But to turn dream to reality is to chase it all away. He waited with his mind concentrated and empty.

'Come on, Ernest—'

'I don't know.'

'Have you ever seen Kashmir?'

Oh God, how he wanted it! But he trembled at the emotional demand on him. The bright faces awaited his gratitude. Only Rowena, surprisingly a calm spot in the turbulence, seemed to understand his fear.

'Why don't you tell him?' she demanded in her voice which could often sound severe. 'It's horrid to be teased.'

They had rented a houseboat on the Dal Lake in Srinagar, the capital town of Kashmir. The Major could not go, but he was sending his family up for two months. Mrs King and the girls were going by rail to Rawalpindi, then driving along the Jhelum Valley Road to Srinagar.

But Robert and Ernie were to ride. First by train to Jammu, where they would hire a guide and ponies; then a ride to the Vale from the south. They would go from serai to serai, crossing the Chenab River, climbing the twelve-thousand-foot peak at Kulgam, and Robert would shoot pigeons and wild duck and take photographs with the box camera he had bought in Bombay; and at Srinagar they would all swim and go boating on the lake in a shikara. From the lake they would be able to see mountains of permanent snow.

'Will you be my friend up there?' Susan asked him the evening before they left.

He felt very grown-up before her these days. 'We are friends already,' he told her.

'But I know you two. You'll go off every day and leave me stuck with Rowena and Mummy.'

'Well, of course. . . .'

'I want to be with you.'

'I expect you will be,' he said, blushing, 'some of the time.'

'You're very brave, riding through the mountains, just the two of you.'

He did not remind her they would have a guide. He saw himself on horseback carving a path in the wilderness, repulsing the attack of enemies. He peered ahead to imaginary hills and his dark eyes glowed.

'Aren't you handsome?' she said.

He hated her when she said things like that. She was a girl, and English; there was no way of really knowing her mind. It was like being friends with a timid wolf.

An hour before they would reach Srinagar and the lake Robert slowed his pace and, when Ernie still did not draw level, reined in entirely. When Ernie reached him he moved forward again, trying to engage Ernie's eyes, which were staring straight ahead.

'I'll never tell them,' Robert said.

The ponies were sweaty beneath the saddles and against the boys' trousered legs. The ground was still rising gently from the Jhelum River valley.

'Honest, Ern, if you don't say anything they won't ever hear it from me. It's our secret. It's nothing to worry about.'

The guide Ali Hoseyn turned round to give them a friendly grin. There had been sulks for the last three days, but now it was the end of the journey and the time for tipping was near. He pointed to a tiny blue bird hovering over a stream with hard-whirring wings and imparted information worth paying for.

'Bird, sahibs. It eating fish very much. It going down, splash, it going up. Eat plenty fish, sahibs.'

He punctuated with a toothy grin and turned his back again. The bird made a right-angled turn, then spun off downstream taking Ernie's thoughts with it, for he would never again see a kingfisher without remembering Islamabad.

If only Robert had not been there. . . . They had gone up by train overnight to Jammu, catching the connection from Sialkot while it was still early enough to be cool. A lieutenant from Major King's company met them off the train and took them to his quarters for breakfast. Ernie's dusky face was a shock to him; they had watched him thinking about it on the walk to his house, and then he had produced rice and kichree from his bearer's kitchen. Robert sent it back and shared his egg and bacon with Ernie, and thereafter the officer's treatment of them was cool. He took them to the stables and argued terms with a hard-faced hajji in Urdu, the hajji throwing in the occasional Kasmiri expletive which the officer fortunately did not understand. They hired two horses, a guide and a pack pony, and next morning were on the trail.

The road cut through bamboo, deodar and pine forests, straddling the rushing streams of cold blue water. On the third day they crossed the Chenab River, and on the fifth day went through the Maroul Pass and began the descent to the Jhelum. The road was lined with the slender poplars planted by the Mogul kings to mark the way to their summer palaces. It was a land so much like Ernie's dreams of it that a day or two passed before it had any substance for him.

It was difficult for Ernie at the serais; he looked more Indian than ever up here where the Kashmiris were famous for their fair skins. Many of them were lighter than he, and the serai wardens would regard him closely, then bend their heads to reread the letter of identity from Major King. 'He is English, of Indian ancestry,' Robert had learned to say in his defence, and Ernie felt grateful for the description which would have angered him so much from anyone else.

At Islamabad they stayed two nights with the District Commissioner, a friend of the Major's. They needed the rest after six days' riding. He was a disconcerting companion—for that is what he insisted on being. He liked boys, he had none of his own, and he thought the way to their affection was to behave like a boy himself. He welcomed Ernie with self-conscious *bonhomie*; he even offered a room to the guide, but Ali Hoseyn had his own ideas on accommodation and drifted down to the small wooden houses in the unlit streets near the mosque.

On the third morning they set out again and two hours out from Islamabad Ernie's horse brushed a hanging bush with its knees and a greenish-yellow, six-foot snake dropped from the branch and landed with an audible thud on the path.

The cry Ernie heard he thought was his own, but it was drowned by the scream of the horse. They had sounded as one; and when the mare's hoofs touched the earth again she gathered herself and shot away down the road. The road bent to the left, a narrow trail led straight on, and the bushes were lashing Ernie's face. In the first few seconds he had heard Robert's cries—'the trees! the trees!' it had sounded like—

but now he could do nothing but crouch low to avoid the whipping branches, trembling at the rush of wind and the memory of the long green body before his eyes. He knelt low on the horse's neck, feeling the dampness of its spittle and his own tears on the back of his hands. Then he was galloping beside a sheet of water and immediately turned the mare into it. . . . Seconds later a blow along his back knocked the air from his body. He could hear it coming out in a long consistent moan from, it seemed, yards away. Then Robert's strong arms lifted him from the water before he could drown.

Dumbly he watched Robert drag his inert body through the water and across the mud into the long grass of the bank. Small children had gathered instantly, and he watched them peering down at him, silhouetted against the sky.

Suddenly he could breathe again. It was as if a plug had been pulled from somewhere and he was all right after all, without injury. His helplessness disappeared so spontaneously that for a moment he continued the pretence, feeling dully foolish; what a fuss, Robert must be thinking, about getting wet.

The guide gave a shout and he turned his head. The man was cantering up the narrow path holding the wriggling snake in his hand, a wide grin on his face.

'Sahib, see! No death. Bites no death. See!' He held the back of his hand against the thin smooth head, then nuzzled it against his cheek, grinning. 'It eat mouse, rat, little thing. But no venom. No eat sahibs.' Then he flung the snake at the watching children, who screamed and fled.

'Shut up you fool. Get away.' Robert bent down and whispered in Ernie's ear. 'Take no notice of the jungly fool. Your horse bolted, rotten business. . . . When you can stand up. . . .'

The man was standing outraged like a stage comedian whose best joke had failed.

'It eat mouse,' he protested. He turned to find it again but there were only some shallow scraped depressions in the soft mud.

'I understand,' Robert said. 'I know how you feel about snakes. It's not your fault.'

Ernie turned his face away and saw a tiny blue kingfisher hovering over a shape on the water. It was his sunhat, still floating. The bird hesitated, turning this way and that over the spot. Then it darted away for several yards and bounced on the water with a splash of whiteness.

'Go and get it,' Robert told the guide.

The man looked mutinous, but waded in up to his knees and brought the hat back. He flung it down on the bank still half full of water, and wandered off to look for the mare. Some children pointed the way along the bank and he scattered them again with a raised fist.

The mare had a slight limp when the guide brought it back and Robert decided they would return to the D.C.'s house at Islamabad. The guide was furious. His home was in Srinagar; he wanted to keep to the schedule. Probably there was a wedding or a birthday he would miss. He rode far ahead of them back down the road.

Ernie was nearly recovered now. The immediate concern of remounting and riding had gathered his composure.

'Didn't you hear me calling?' Robert asked.

'What?' He arranged his thoughts like positions of defence.

'I shouted at you to turn the horse into the trees. No horse will gallop with a tree in front of him.'

'It was out of control.'

But Robert wouldn't have let a horse out of control, he knew that. He was hating Robert's quiet air of understanding—he would have preferred his mocking laughter. He would have laughed at one of his English friends; why was he so different from them? He didn't want Robert's rotten kindness. The thought of the banyan tree, the drop from the branch, came strangely into his mind, and he pondered over the connection between the two events on the long ride back to Islamabad.

That night he went through it all again. He felt the wind in his hair, the tears on the back of his hands. The mare's mane whipped his face and the green and yellow shape rose towards him. He was flung through the air but before his body could break he awoke sobbing, the sheets damp with his perspiration.

He heard Robert get out of his bed and come towards him in the dark. If he tried to stop crying he only choked. The mosquito net was drawn back and the bed creaked beneath Robert's weight. He gripped the strong arm as if the reality of physical contact could draw him up from dreams into the daylight.

'Robert—I'm sorry—I can't help it.' And he moved away because even though Robert knew he was crying he didn't want his tears to splash on the bare arm. He went slowly back to sleep holding Robert's hand, but as he was about to take the last breath into rest he jerked awake again, and the thin greenness uncoiled before his eyes.

'Oh hell, Ern.' Robert turned the pillow over and pushed Ernie's head gently down on to it. 'Come on, now.'

He didn't resist any more; he let the tears come uncontrollably. What did it matter? He couldn't help himself. Tomorrow the shame would come; now all he wanted was comfort and sleep and what Robert was doing to him. The bed sank as Robert moved slightly. He started drifting again, and his last conscious thought was for the delicate blue kingfisher, picking a delicate path on its tiny wings, moving precisely above the calm surface of the water.

'Hope you make it this time,' the D.C. said jovially. He caught Ernie's reluctant eye and gave him a broad wink, belching loudly from a recent breakfast.

'Where's that feller of yours?' He had carroty hair and a flushed, freckled face; drops of perspiration had already started their day-long progress down his hot skin.

'Whoring in some harpy's den, the rogue. He'll catch more than he wants.' He winked, and waited disappointedly for the boys' reaction; knowing that boys like to be thought men, he yet mistook the scope of their ambition.

Ali Hoseyn slouched up to meet them ten minutes later, pulling his horse behind as if too lazy to climb into the saddle. He moved past without a word and on up the road towards Srinagar.

'Insolent bugger,' the D.C. muttered loudly; but when at last he turned to see the effect of his words he was saddened at their look of blankness. It is demoralizing to have your gifts refused; he waved the boys away, then turned back into his office to bully the staff.

Once across the Jhelum River the old atmosphere was almost restored. They were in the Vale of Kashmir now, the hills behind at last, and they moved out on to the great brown plain with the tips of mountains far away like house-roofs on the horizon. They passed between the corn, rice and barley fields surrounding the tall, three-storeyed wooden houses of the fair-skinned Kashmiri farmers, along the true, straight, white avenues marked for miles ahead across the plain with the slender poplars. In the towns they were offered walnuts, apples, peaches and cherries from stalls coated with the road's white dust.

At last, under the watchful circlings of the broad-winged hawks, they came to the town of Srinagar. Among the wooden houses were the solid brick ones, the D.C.'s house, Brown's Hotel, the Club, a dak bungalow, and momentarily Ernie felt himself back in India, but when they had moved through the untidy town sprawled over rock knolls and sluggish canals and came at last to the Dal Lake he was startled at the beauty of it. There was the dark blueness of the water, the snow-peaks reflected in the surface like clouds, the shikaras plying between the shore and the mile-long line of houseboats along the bund, and the sound of water everywhere, water enough to waste, to use for ornamentation in gardens. It seemed a long way from India.

They rode out along the bund to where the houseboat

floated, Mrs King waving from the deck, Susan running towards them to be first with all the news.

A year after his trip to Kashmir, a week after his fifteenth
birthday, Ernie started at Warren Hastings College. At the
end of the first month he was called to the headmaster's study.
'You are Maher?'
'Yes, Mr Archer.'
'You're a brilliant young man.'
Ernie said: 'Yes sir, I think so. . . .'
'What do you want to do?'
'I want to go to Oxford.'
'And afterwards?'
'Well. . . .' Ram Lal's pale face rose before him like a warn-
ing signal, and he said: 'I think perhaps Oxford will help me
to make up my mind, sir.'
The man nodded approvingly. 'With your retentive memory
and gift for expression I would recommend a course in the
Classics. But I'll be frank with you, you're most unusual. The
field is wide open. If you put yourself in my care and carry
on as you have done, then I think you can be reasonably sure
of a place. You play hockey, don't you?'
'Yes sir. . . .'
Of course he played hockey; after only two years he was
playing for one of the big teams in Delhi.
'Keep that up too,' Mr Archer said. 'I shall be writing about
you to the Warden of my old College and they're rather keen
on sport. It can be important, you know.'
'Sir . . . can you really—promise—?'
'All other things being equal. Nothing can be promised in
these disturbed times. If that little nuisance Gandhi is allowed
to carry on for much longer, then it'll put an end to all sorts of
opportunities awaiting this country. But I'm sure you don't
need to be told that.'
'No sir.'

Plains 137

'Let us just say that if anyone can organize a grant for you
to go to Oxford, that person is me, and I shall do my very
best for you.'

A week later Ram Lal paid him a visit.

'How are you managing? You must not be discouraged if
it is a little strange. . . .'

'Oh,' Ernie said, and smiled. 'You need not worry. It is all
the other boys who are worried.'

Lal pulled at his upper lip and said : 'Socrates was the wisest
man in Greece because he knew how ignorant he was. Do not
be too cocky, little pundit, it will work against you.'

Victor had overheard; he took his ear from the door and
walked stiffly into the room.

'I hear what you say, Mr Lal. With other boys it would be
boasting but with my boy it is true. He is a genius.'

Ram Lal almost managed to look angry.

'Mr Maher, at the moment your boy is a very big little fish.
But he is swimming in a very tiny pond.'

Victor had never quite overcome his suspicion of the smooth-
talking Indian youth; he suspected the Congress activities.
But he recognized his influence and treated him with respect-
ful care.

'Oxford or Cambridge Universities are very big little pools.
He will be nothing special and he must not be encouraged
into idleness now.'

'Well, Mr Lal, so long as you can get him into an English
university. . . .'

But Lal waited till Victor had left the room before he said
to Ernie: 'You must soon be thinking what you will read at
Oxford.'

'English literature,' Ernie said.

Lal shook his head. 'You would be starting a race with a
handicap. English boys have a natural advantage with their
own classics. And you would need Latin, it is a waste . . . and
you must remember what your future will be.'

For Ernie to think of a future beyond university was like

an agnostic contemplating paradise. Lal moved from his sad and classical pose by the mantelpiece and sat down close where he could not be overheard from the other side of the door.

'A new India is coming.' He tried to whisper, but every fourth word boomed like a rusty gong. 'It may be ten years yet but it is coming. And it will not be an India which greatly values English literature. You must study economics or law. I have brought you some books,' he said, and looked round for them but he had left them behind.

'You must read newspapers, the liberal English ones like *Manchester Guardian* and *New Statesman*. You must understand the economic background to independence. I have brought,' and he looked first into his pocket to make sure, 'the text of a talk by our Gandhi, concerning support for the cause in England. You can investigate these things while you are at university. When Gandhi is our prime minister,' and he smiled tenderly at the hope, 'you will be able to serve our country in the way it needs. And no one would know,' he said, studying Ernie's face closely, 'that you are not an Indian.'

Hastings College lay in the shadow of Hardinge Bridge, with the great trains rumbling overhead from Agra and the south. All during the summer the traffic increased and Ernie could watch the military trains with special understanding: for he read *The Times, Manchester Guardian, New Statesman* and *Picture Post*, weeks late sometimes, the covers faded and pages missing, but he rarely failed to track each issue down. When on one of his visits to the Kings he was told Robert would not be coming that year he understood more of the reason than Mrs King did.

'It's Germany, dear. They're being rather bullies to the little countries and we have to be a sort of school prefect to them. I wonder if the Major will be back early tonight for the Colonel's golfing picnic.'

'Which particular European countries are involved at the moment, Mrs King?' He had reached the age of sarcasm.

'Oh I don't know, dear. Most of them I think. France is the

one we may have to protect. But it won't affect us very much over here. . . .'

'But India will be fighting as well. I read it in *The Times*.'

'Yes, but . . . it's all a long way away. We're not the British Army after all. Ah, here comes the Major now. Why don't you run along? Susan, go and show Ernest the dress you'll be wearing at the tennis club party.'

Up in Susan's room Ernie said: 'You know, your mother is not quite right. It's Poland, not France, that will make England declare war. Though it's all much more complicated than that,' he said with the confidence of one who appropriates what will not be missed.

'This is the dress,' Susan said. She held it up against her body and did a little twirl; her big eyes sparkled at him over the silk. The thought that she was pretty occurred to him like the answer to a problem, a truth long guessed at but unsubstantiated until the final gathering of evidence. He was aware of her beauty in the sort of second-hand way he knew Gandhi was clever and Hitler was bad, supplementary to his understanding. How long had he been staring at her, at her startled blue eyes? He felt his heart leap at, strangely, a memory of Susan hopping on the stones in her white plimsolls, and the vultures sitting in the smoke.

Susan coloured, and spent a long time examining the collar of the dress. When she looked up Ernie was still staring at her.

'Did you like it?' Already she had developed the feminine need for words to confirm the obvious.

With a sudden anger he said: 'You're not listening. I'm talking about the war in Europe. It's going to be another world war. Your father's a soldier, you should be interested—'

He saw that tears were going to come, and hating her ignorance at that moment he stumbled on: 'All the countries in Europe are going to fight. It's about National Socialism in Germany. But none of you people seem to be worried by it.'

He had frightened her now, adding a second reason for the

tears pricking her eyes. He put a comforting arm round her
shoulders . . . then turned his face towards hers and their young
mouths bumped awkwardly together. The green dress slid to
the floor and he felt her tears on his own cheek. She is a very
pretty little girl, Victor had often insisted, and he tore sharply
away and said: 'There's going to be a war, that's all I'm
saying. You people. . . .'

She seemed to be utterly unaware of the large drops still
trickling on her face.

'Daddy says there's nothing to worry about. It'll be all right
when England joins in. It's only the stupid Germans.' She
looked regretfully down at the silk dress on the floor as if the
war constituted a threat to the tennis club party.

'You kissed me,' she claimed.

Through the open window they heard the mali open the
squeaking gate before Major King's approaching car. From
her table on the lawn Mrs King called for the teapot to be
refilled.

'Yes,' he admitted.

They looked at each other shyly over the fallen silk. 'Can
I do it again sometimes?'

'But you must promise not to say any more frightening
things,' Susan said. 'If you talk about bad things they can
really happen.'

Europe continued to talk of bad things, and six months
later he saw the only people he loved borne away on the train
to Bombay, there to take ship for the alien land of England.
The Major had been seconded to Singapore; a year later they
were to hear of his death, but they would never feel more
uncertain of their future than they did now, leaving their
world behind them, waiting for the flag to wave them away.

The same bewilderment was reflected in faces all down the
train as service families prepared for repatriation, still not
comprehending the changes that had come upon them. An

unnatural silence hung over the station, cleared of civilians
and pan-sellers; guards patrolled the platforms against Congress demonstrations. He had planned to kiss Susan right there
on the platform, not caring who saw, but sudden orders were
barked over a tannoy and a sergeant with a file of papers
pushed him roughly back. Mrs King and the girls were handed
up meekly into the train, smiling apologetically over their
shoulders. He stood back against the wall and waved to the
vague shadows behind the dusty window. At the last minute
he decided he could not bear to wait for the train's departure.
He turned miserably away back to his own home, to college
and study, and the twilight world of swaraj, to wait for the
war to be over and his own real life to begin.

Mountains

He rode hard all the first day with the hope of catching Robert on the road. Because of course his quarry might be going somewhere else; the road went only to Khadzil but Robert could be turning off anywhere. Perhaps there was a rendezvous somewhere, or an arms cache in the hills; he could even be doubling back to Sopur. It could be acting foolishly to follow Robert blindly in this way but it was what he had chosen. The hunter has all the other advantages, he could not expect to dictate the route.

He pressed on longer than he should have done; the sun sets early in mountains and before he found a convenient spot it was already too dark to prepare food. He pulled a blanket from one of the panniers and rolled up in it on the dusty ground. Remembering Prithi's instructions, he wrapped his rifle in the oilskin and wedged it in a bush, off the ground. He remembered things for a while; Robert, the Sikhs, games of football and the banyan tree, things all in the irrevocable past, a photograph with one half cut away and now the other half was in the past too, and he woke in the cool dawn with his heart empty.

Most men live near their birthplace, marry their sweethearts and can identify their lives with surroundings and events. But for him life was the long unwinding of a film, flashing images which promptly clicked away into the past, leaving him isolated. Nothing was ever sustained and Robert was the only thing that had ever returned. He moved slowly, folding the blanket, checking the map as if the track could lead anywhere but to Khadzil. He didn't stop to make breakfast, but munched an apple as he rode.

It was only ten miles to Khadzil. He had been following the Rula River since leaving the Shaburah fork, and after he had ridden five miles he saw the grey shapes of Khadzil across the plain and the long brown foothills of the Muzaffarabad range. If Robert had not left the road he would now be in the town. The wide river moved slowly, the plain was flat on all sides and the heat began to settle on his shoulders with a physical weight. The horse was warm beneath him, the pack-horse trod monotonously behind, and his thoughts were beginning to drift when he saw a figure on the path ahead.

He had thought it was a rock or tree, the man had stood so still. The fixed pose had a quality of silent menace, but he had been seen and there was nothing to do but keep riding forward until they faced each other.

It was a Pathan. His long hard face looked like a hawk's; so did his eyes, which did not blink so much as close and open again with a steady stare. He held a rifle by the butt, its muzzle resting on his toe, and over his shoulder was a string of four pairs of rabbits. He was so tall that Ernie could nearly meet his eyes at the level without dismounting.

'Why do you come to Khadzil?' When the Pathan did move he was light-footed and slow like an overweight cat.

'Government business.'

'Which government?'

But he would not fall into the trap. He said: 'The State Government of Jammu and Kashmir.'

The man smiled evilly. 'I expect you are surveying for a metalled road.'

It was astonishing, because it was what he had planned to say if challenged. Immediately he was suspicious; he had been vaguely fearing bandits, but now he wondered if the man was connected with Robert—he would have passed the spot within the last twenty hours at most, guessing he would be followed. Could he have set these men as sentries. . . ?

'What are you thinking?'

He didn't like this man; he feared him. His rifle was in the pannier wrapped in oilskin, but he would not have been quick enough to use it even if it were in his hand. The Pathan's rifle was inlaid with brass on the stock and a filigree decorated the barrel; it was his own manufacture and he handled it like a loved child.

He said some words Ernie didn't understand.

'I was asking if you were Kashmiri.'

Ernie told him what he was, and the expression that crossed the swarthy face chilled him. It was true, then; this was a friend of Robert's. A length of thin wire twisted in his mind's grasp, and he thought of kicking the horse forward to trample the man down. But only horses trained to it will do that . . . and over the man's shoulder he saw two others moving up out of the flat land and thought: to have come so far, and now it is over. . . .

'Here are my friends.'

They moved up to the road, Pathans with turbans and patched European jackets. One of them had shot a fox which hung from his shoulder with the blood soaking into his coat.

'I must leave you,' Ernie said desperately.

'No, we will walk with you.' The Pathan said something to the others, who turned to grin at him as if at a joke they all shared.

'I—would prefer to travel alone.'

'Do you think we will steal from you?' the man asked fiercely. He caught at the horse's bridle.

'No—'

'Or do you usually scorn a Muslim's hospitality?'

'I am in a hurry—'

'So are we.' They were bullying him and he was frightened, but somehow it reassured him too; if they were going to kill him they would not be acting like this.

They set off at a fast walk along the path, the big one holding Ernie's snaffle rein with a hand like a bunch of grenades. They talked and laughed together. Once he caught the word 'cheechee'—it was used in many languages. The houses of Khadzil drew nearer with aching slowness, but when they passed the first farm and exchanged salutations with a woman working in a barley field Ernie knew it was going to be all right. The man had dropped his grip on the rein, and they moved into the town attracting little notice. But as they passed the first row of houses the man with the fox exchanged some muttered words and ran up between the houses out of sight.

The town was much poorer than those at the other end of the Vale. The lack of a road from Srinagar showed in the quality of the wattled buildings, the absence of concrete and corrugated iron, or vehicles in the muddy spaces between the houses.

The river bent right in against the town, with an earth wall supporting the bank against the spring flooding. On the other bank sheep and goats were grazing among the spiky bushes, and a muddy area indicated a ford.

'We have brought you here safely, yes?'

'It is very kind of you.'

They laughed, and he wondered if they had been leading him away from a danger spot. Robert could have been back there on the plain watching the encounter. There was so much he had not considered.

'Salaam,' they said, and stood in the road to watch him go. He rode in the direction of an Indian flag flapping idly beyond the town roofs and turned a corner to find a neat wooden building and a yard bordered with white-painted bricks. A rope dipped from one short post to the other to surround flowerbeds and a handkerchief of lawn. A man in beautifully creased khaki appeared at the door and paused on the middle step, the final point in the pattern.

'I say, good heavens.'

A pipe was waved in greeting, then put back between the man's teeth so that the following words were indistinct.

'First stranger for a month. Welcome, dear boy.'

At Oxford, jokes about upper crust Englishmen were told in this sort of accent. The man was frightfully pukka, very fair-skinned, probably a native Kashmiri.

'What Department?'

Instead of answering Ernie said: 'You have a lot of time on your hands.' He pointed to the beds of flowers, the diagonal lines of bricks.

'Nothing ever happens here, old boy.'

'You'd be surprised.' He dismounted painfully, and said: 'I don't recognize your uniform.'

The man looked a little embarrassed. He took the pipe from his mouth and began to knock out the dottle on the polished instep of his boot.

'I'm not the police or army,' he said. 'This town hasn't got either. Actually I'm in the Min of Ag.'

He noticed a white mark on his khaki sleeve caused by brushing against one of the fenceposts, and paused to wipe it completely off. 'Being the only Government man in the area,' he said, and bent further to rub off a particularly obstinate stain. 'I find this khaki gives me a sort of, well . . . authority. You'd be surprised how it helps. . . .'

'Can I come in for a while,' Ernie said. 'I'm rather tired—'

'My dear chap, you're jolly welcome. By the way, my name's Pachai.'

'Maher,' Ernie said as he preceded him up the steps. 'M-A-H-E-R,' for he was used to having to spell it out, and the man raised his eyebrows but said no more as he followed him into the room.

In the coolness Ernie felt suddenly weak . . . he sat in a chair and listened to the thumping under his ribs.

'I say, are you ill?'

'I'm all right. Tired, I think. And hungry.' He remembered he had not eaten for nearly a day.

'I'll dish you up some eggs and bacon. Do you like eggs and bacon?'

'Give me some tea first. I've had a hard time,' he said, and gave a long glance through the window, but there was no sign of the Pathan.

'Tell me about the people here. What do they feel about accession to Pakistan?'

'I don't suppose they ever give it a thought. Why do you ask? Where are you from, by the way?' Ernie started to explain but Pachai said, 'One minute, I'll just go and organize tiffin,' and went to the kitchen.

Ernie was beginning to doze before Pachai returned; a haze of blue smoke hung in the open doorway of the kitchen.

'You were asking me about political feelings. There's none of that in Khadzil, they're more interested in their fields and their wives. We have a very thriving little sericulture outfit here.'

'Sericulture?'

'Silkworms to you and me. That's my line, actually, sort of general adviser and agent. Last year we turned out some very jolly stuff indeed and this year's production is already sold to the sharks down in Srinagar, so if that's what you're after I'm afraid you've rather missed the boat.'

'No.'

'I've got my own outfit in the back room here, through that door. I must show you before you go. Sometimes you can hear them at night all chewing like mad,' and a look of fond emotion entered his soft eyes.

'What is your business?' he asked after another pause. 'You know everything about me and I don't even know where you're from.'

Ernie showed him his identity card. 'I imagine you have heard of Robert King.'

'Robert King? No—'

'The gunrunner. The Englishman who—'

'Ah yes, indeed. He is very infamous, even up here.'

'That's not surprising,' Ernie said, 'because he's here now.'

'Here in Kashmir?'

'Here in Khadzil, or somewhere very near.'

'Oh no!'

'I assure you he is.'

'But he cannot be here.' The pipe had been in his hand for several moments so now he put it back between his teeth and started searching for matches. 'There's nothing for the fellow up here, no guns or anything. Why would a man like that come to Khadzil?'

'I was hoping you could answer that.'

Pachai shook his head, and the bearer came in with tea and put the tray down between them. 'One lump or two?' Pachai asked, and the sugar tongs tinkled against the bowl.

'There's no stranger arrived here in the past twenty-four hours?'

'No. Here, I've given you two lumps.'

The bearer returned with eggs and bacon and cinnamon toast.

'Here we are. This will fill the hollow places and later we'll have some luncheon. I must say it's jolly nice to have a visitor. One doesn't get much chance up here for civilized conversation.

'But I say,' and his knife rattled against the plate. 'Did you say the gunrunner chappie is here now?'

'Yes I did, about five minutes ago.'

'But—how do you actually know? I mean perhaps you just heard from someone—'

'I followed him in.'

'But if you followed—'

'I mean I have been following him from Sopur. He might have arrived yesterday or this morning. Look, I know he's here so this is just wasting time, I want to go—'

'No, wait a moment,' and Pachai carved his knife in the air as if following the circumlocution of his thought. 'This could—I'm not saying it is—but this could be important. . . . Here, will you have some more cinnamon toast—?'

'No, dammit! Say what you're saying.'

'It's probably nothing, I don't want to raise your hopes old chap. But just describe to me what he—'

'He's very tall, over six feet, with blond hair, but he keeps

it hidden under a karakul. He's probably riding one horse and
leading another—'

'Has he got a slightly twisted arm?'

There followed a silence so long and profound that to the
ears of both came the tiny rustling of thousands of teeth on
the mulberry leaves in the back room. Then an expression
mounted on Ernie's face that made Pachai look round
embarrassedly for his pipe; he had left it on the window-sill
and as he reached round he heard a strange sound of grief.

'I could have killed him. . . .'

'What did you say?'

His visitor was staring into space and the look in his eyes
was unnerving.

'I said what did you say?'

'Let me ask you a question,' Ernie said slowly. 'Where did
you see a tall blond man with a twisted arm?'

'Is it him? But surely—'

'Where?'

'In the bazar. Buying mules—'

'Mules!'

Pachai fiddled irritably with his pipe; he was beginning to
feel as if he was on trial. Why shouldn't the beggar buy
mules?

'Mules are for mountains, aren't they?'

'Yes—'

'But there is no way into the mountains from here.'

'But this is hilly country, my dear chap. In winter, in the
snow, hills become mountains—'

'It's not winter now—'

'And,' said Pachai firmly, 'there are farms in the foothills.'

'Wait a minute!' He could see a tension building up but he
had no time to waste; he detested this kind of pompous babu.
'When did you see this man?'

'Yesterday—'

'Then for God's sake! I've been asking if you've seen
strangers. Why didn't you think of it sooner?'

'Because,' Pachai said with angry defiance, 'he is not a stranger.'

'He lives here?'

'No, but he visits often. He comes every few months.' He looked at the new expression on Ernie's face and said: 'Look, don't third-degree me, man. I'm a person of authority in this town.'

'Are you telling me you have seen an Englishman every few months in Khadzil and you never thought of finding out his business? As the person of authority in this town.'

'I didn't know he was an Englishman.'

'But he was a frequent anonymous visitor to a town thirty miles from our enemy's border, buying mules for trips into the mountains.'

'It didn't look suspicious, we don't think about gunrunners up here.'

'That's probably why he chose the place, where you're all too busy with silkworms to think about a war on your doorstep.'

'There's no need to be offensive. It's a difference of view. There's other things than war and politics. We're simple people up here, farmers and—and sericulturalists—gentle people. . . .'

'No Indian is gentle, Mr Pachai. We have violence bred deep in us. None of us escape it.'

'That is your point of view. But I know my own character. There's no violence in me—'

'Perhaps you've never been roused.' He was tempted to add: Perhaps you've never had that pipe knocked out of your mouth. 'There has to be the spark,' he said, remembering his own.

'You couldn't rouse these people. If soldiers came here they'd just accept it as fate. I tell you they are gentle people, timid even.'

'And it is precisely that mixture of timidity and violence that bred the Bengal riots.'

'I wish,' said Pachai, 'you would have the goodness to allow me to finish one single sentence.'

'All right,' Ernie said. 'Now . . . you say you saw this man yesterday?'

'It is enough,' Pachai said defensively, 'to say I saw this man yesterday—not I *say* I saw him yesterday.'

'All right, where is he now?'

'I don't know. He is usually here only a day or two.'

'Mr. Pachai, listen. Why would a gunrunner come to Khadzil?'

'I have no clue. No clue at all.'

'But something has brought him. Is there a path, the smallest possible route, to any part of Pakistan? Is there a strong Pathan element here, or supporters of Abdullah? What about infiltrators from the tribal areas?'

'None of those things. It is a complete mystery. Before you came barging in here today and eating my eggs and bacon—'

'Thank you for the eggs and bacon,' Ernie said drily, 'and also for the cinnamon toast, which is the best I have tasted for many months. I am very grateful and now I want to know why Robert King has come here. You're the person in authority and a criminal visits your town. Not for your cinnamon toast, I imagine.'

'I have no idea.'

'But he is here, Mr Pachai. There is a reason. Think.'

'I don't know it.'

'But surely—'

'Why don't you find him first? Then you'll have all the answers you want.'

There was a pause, and then Ernie stood up, dusting the toastcrumbs from his fingers. He straightened his legs against the stiffness from the morning's ride.

'That's the first intelligent thing you've said this morning.'

'What about the gunrunner?' Pachai said. 'If we do find

him here . . . I mean supposing he has friends, it's not as if I'm actually responsible.'

Ernie spoke from the bathroom, where he was having his first wash for days. They kept up a shouted conversation through the open door.

'Where did you say the army post was?'

'Near Shaburah. It's twenty miles and no road but they could be here in the morning. Shall I send a message?'

'No, that suits me fine.'

'But my dear chap . . . I hope you are not considering tackling this fellow on your own.'

'I am,' Ernie said, emerging from the bathroom, 'because those are my orders. Look, I will tell you, in complete confidence, that I know this man King. We were at school together. That's why I've been chosen for this job; I can approach him as a friend, and—arrest him by stealth. My minister is insisting there be no publicity. That would make him a hero.'

'But if it is just you and him—?'

'Yes?'

'He may get away. He has done it before, has he not? Wouldn't your minister prefer him publicly dead than anonymously alive?'

'He is not to be harmed,' Ernie said, and his fingers trembled slightly as he buttoned on his shirt.

'But if he is armed—the soldiers—'·

'No.'

'But it's ridic—'

'No!'

After a two-second silence the door opened and Pachai's bearer stood there uncertainly.

'No Rajuri, we did not call you.'

'Luncheon is served,' the old man said, if that's what the sahibs wanted.

Pachai said, 'What about it, old chap? You're tired and overwrought and hungry. We'll eat now and then you can have a nice rest. And afterwards—'

But Ernie cut him off; he had to be careful where his loss of temper led.

'I'm going to the bazar. If you would accompany me I'd consider it helpful, but you don't have to. You speak Kasmiri, I imagine?'

'I am Kashmiri.'

'Well, then. . . .'

'I had better come with you. If anything happens it'll fall back on me, that's the trouble with being the only responsible Government man in the place.'

Half the shops in the bazar sold fruit: apples, apricots, guavas, walnuts. All the others revealed the self-supporting nature of the town: copper and brass cooking pots, saddle harness, building tools, rope and buckets and guns. There were some workshops dealing in silver and papier mâché goods but it was not a showpiece for the tourist seeking the primitive. Amongst the copper and leatherwork was a packet of Persil, a plastic cruet set or an old paperback of *The Perfumed Garden*.

At the end of the bazar was a muddy courtyard crowded with tongas and mules. In one corner a sick mule was tethered to a veranda post, its head drooping under a cloud of flies. A sign advertised horses, mules and donkeys for sale and hire, and on the veranda steps the passing of the sun's rays caused a man to sit up from sleep and crawl over to keep up with the warmth.

'That is the mule trader. I think it would be best if you waited here, you have the look of Government about you.'

'Ask him if he knows where—'

'Don't worry.'

Pachai strode across to the mule trader like a number three man going in to bat. His khaki shorts were so rigid with starch that they had a stiff, clockwork action.

Ernie moved back into the cave-like shop behind him, trying to be inconspicuous. He knocked his elbow against a tray of sweetmeats and nearly stepped on to a pile of honeycakes on the floor. A cockroach scampered in shiny brown haste from his boot and the Hindu proprietor watched him carefully, his fingers kneading a yellow dough.

He could see the stockinged legs of Pachai and the patched old trousers of the mule trader; the body of the sick mule obscured the rest of them. He moved a few feet sideways to get a better view, but after a moment the wall he was leaning on felt damp and he withdrew again.

Now two boys were staring at him in the blank-faced Indian manner and he glared, wanting them to retreat. It did not succeed, as he had known it would not, and when a man came peering between their heads into the gloom he abandoned the Hindu's cavern and strolled like a shopper through the bazar.

When Pachai and the mule trader descended the steps he followed them at a careful distance. At the corner of the bazar he saw the man pointing, with Pachai nodding and either taking the pipe from his mouth or putting it back in. But they continued to stand there talking, so after a moment he turned and began another slow walk up the bazar. A great hammering in cadence drew him to a metal workshop where seven men with sledgehammers were beating in orchestral rhythm on a glowing bar. In the next hut a man was shoeing a donkey; the animal stood resignedly with a forehoof tucked backwards, blinking in the smoke.

He returned again to the end of the bazar and at last saw Pachai looking for him. The man just failed to get the pipe into his mouth before Ernie descended on him.

'It is interesting,' Pachai said. 'It is also mysterious.'

'Hurry,' Ernie said. 'And leave your damned pipe alone.'

Pachai bent as much as the starch would allow and tucked the pipe into the garter of his stocking, where for the next few minutes the smoke continued to curl lazily up his leg.

'You are right about the Englishman. The mule trader has dealt with him before. Not directly with him, but through friends—'

'Who?'

'Strangers. Let me finish, there's a good chap. He has not actually dealt with the Englishman, but he's seen him in the background and he'd always understood the mules were for him. He speaks fluent Urdu apparently.'

'He would.'

'Well, anyway . . . the Englishman buys two mules, two only. Then two months later he is back with ten or even twelve mules and sells the lot. It is obvious they have travelled a long way, their shoes are completely worn down. Here—' he took Ernie's elbow and turned him about to point back at the mule trader's veranda.

'You see the sick one?'

He nodded.

'That was brought in with the last lot. It is still suffering from influenza.'

He had the same feeling then as he'd had at Mahbub Ali's tea-house. He had gone back afterwards to gaze at the chair where Robert had been sitting as if the object itself were significant; it had stood back from the others, turned sideways, and the mule drooped under its burden of flies and sickness and travel.

'He says he has not seen the Englishman's friends this time, the ones who do the hiring.'

'No. Two of them are in jail. The other one is dead.'

'The mule trader says he noticed something unusual about his voice but he certainly didn't think he was English. Well, then he rode away. That was only this morning, at ten.'

'Where?'

'Look, let's be walking back while we talk.' Pachai reached down for his pipe and then changed his mind; they moved down the bazar and turned out by the Hindu's sweetshop.

'Our friend the mule trader decided to be curious today and followed your Englishman. Which is very fortunate. At least it would be . . . if it made any sense.'

They crossed the main street and waved away three tongas moving up hopefully behind them.

'Where did he go?'

'He followed the man to the ford and watched him for twenty minutes, so there can't be any mistake. King made a beeline for the mountains south of here, or south-east . . . those mountains,' and he pointed over the roof of his house as they turned the corner and had it in view.

Ernie stared into the distant hills with long banks of cloud lying above; it was difficult to discern any boundary between hills and mist.

'He must have been going to some farm. . . .'

'There are no farms across the river, dear boy. There is nothing. The ground is rocks, you know? It has never grown anything. Your Englishman is riding off into a wilderness.'

'It's a wilderness he rides out of with twelve mules laden with guns.'

'You don't know that yet.'

'I suppose it doesn't—it can't lead to Pakistan?'

'It leads nowhere,' Pachai said firmly. His voice held a note of something like pleasure that Ernie should now be in the defensive role. 'In this country, you know, things don't often go smoothly.'

'A twisted arm, you say?' Ernie asked, as if in response to Pachai's last words. His eyes were tired and he stumbled as he climbed the wooden steps.

'You're washed out,' Pachai said solicitously. 'Have a rest now. Afterwards we'll get the map out. I have a jolly excellent map of the area, perhaps it will give us a clue. Then it will be our turn to start batting.'

'No,' Ernie insisted; 'get the map out now.'

The old servant had kept the food hot and Pachai worked through it in brimming mouthfuls, handling the rice and kichree with his fingers, using the spoon only when the bearer was in the room. 'Just a snack,' he mumbled through a spray of rice, as if to say that of course meals were different, an occasion for manners and cutlery.

They sat side by side with the map spread among the plates before them.

'Khadzil is here,' said Pachai in his new tone of authority, 'and the cease-fire line is here. Here are the mountains, look, the ones you can see through the window. On the other side of them is the Kishen Ganga river.' He paused to push in a lump of kichree, elbow held high and chin out to protect his bush shirt from gravy drops.

'The mountains are quite uncrossable without proper equipment and anyway he'd only come to the cease-fire lines, which are patrolled. And your Englishman is not going in that direction.'

He turned the map among the plates until it was set to the compass. With a curry-stained forefinger he indicated a line slightly south by west.

'Your Englishman seems to be heading for this range of hills. He could cross those, but then he would come to the real hills. And there's nothing there anyway.'

'The cease-fire line bends right in here—'

'Yes, it crosses the peak. But that line was merely drawn on a map. For all practicable purposes the boundary is right back here. That peak has never been climbed.'

'Are you sure about that?'

'Positively so, I am telling you.'

'But, perhaps—?'

'Please! He is one man with two mules. He cannot climb snow peaks.'

'You don't know this man,' Ernie muttered, and Pachai looked at him curiously for several moments, but at last only said: 'I know the mountains,' and moved his chair in a series of irritating scrapes round the table until he was at the south side of the map.

'Now you see, in all this region, there is nothing. No villages or farms, no route to anywhere. I am inclined to think your Englishman does not know what he is doing.'

'There's a village or something here. . . .'

'A mine. A survey team thought they discovered copper and sunk a few shafts. That was a year ago, there's nothing there now.'

'Well, what's this thing up here, at twelve thousand feet?'

Pachai grinned. 'He is not a religious man, your Englishman?'

'Keep to the point,' Ernie said. 'He rode off hours ago, we're wasting time.'

'That is the Shrine of the Sacred Hair.'

Ernie frowned.

'From the Prophet's Beard,' Pachai explained, and a little shower of rice grains splashed down into the Jhelum river. 'It was a temple built to house a hair of Mahomet's beard.'

'Was?'

'The Hair was moved, oh, thirty years ago. . . .'

'I'm beginning to remember. It's in Srinagar now.'

'No, no, that is another one. He was a hirsute fellow, that Mahomet. Or perhaps the Moguls got jealous and decided to discover their own.'

'But the temple itself is still there?'

'Oh yes . . . well, I suppose so. . . .'

He stared at the little spot on the twelve-thousand-foot contour, the summit of a subsidiary peak. The main peak was five thousand feet higher. It was on the edge of the snow line forty miles south-west of Khadzil.

He looked north and south of the peak for fifty miles but it never dropped below fourteen thousand feet. Just what the hell could Robert be doing? Even if he did know a pass not on the map, which was very unlikely, it would still be too high to bring a mule train through. His eyes wandered over the map's empty spaces searching for a clue and eventually returned for lack of direction to the cross marking the Sacred Hair temple.

'How did pilgrims reach it?' he asked.

'Reach what? Oh, the temple. From the south, there was a path.'

'That's no help.'

'I have told you,' Pachai said. 'You are looking for something which does not exist.' He took out a smelly tobacco pouch and began thumbing the contents into his pipe bowl as if tamping down a new grave.

'From the south, you said?' Ernie kept struggling with a thought.

'From the Jhelum Valley road.'

'From Baramula, then?'

'No, from Uri I think. There was a track. But what are you wasting your time for? The temple was abandoned at least thirty years ago. There would hardly be anything left of it.'

'But the track will still be there,' Ernie said quietly.

'After thirty years? Unlikely, old boy. No one is going to keep up an unused road.'

'What about the nomads who live in the mountains?'

'Gujers? Gujers do not build roads.'

'But they might keep up those already in existence,' Ernie said, and stood up to move closer to the temple. 'It would be to their advantage, wouldn't it?'

'Perhaps . . . I suppose . . . I don't know. Really, the questions you ask! I don't know what you're driving at. . . .' The pipe had gone out for lack of attention and he resumed his more or less constant search for matches, like a mole for food.

'The track!' Ernie said. 'There will still be the track, that's what I'm talking about. And Robert King is heading straight for it.'

'It's impossible to say that.'

'It's right on his route. You said yourself he is heading along this line . . . well, here is the temple and from the temple there is a road to Uri. By God, you did say Uri, didn't you—?'

'But my dear fellow . . . there is virgin forest and a twelve-thousand-foot peak between us and the bally temple.'

'What's the matter with you? It's staring you in the face. Robert is making for the temple. He knows it's there all right.

He's going to the temple and that's where the track starts. The track to Uri—'

'Twelve thousand feet,' Pachai hissed.

'So what. Twelve thousand feet is nothing to Robert King. Keep your damned food off the map,' and Pachai jerked his hand away and another drop of gravy splashed down from the kichree in his fist.

'The track leads down to Uri,' Ernie said; he leaned both hands on the table and glared at Pachai. 'Uri is on the cease-fire line, correct? Once beyond Uri he is in Pakistan. Why the hell has no one thought of it before, it's brilliant—'

'The hills cannot be climbed—'

'Oh no? How do you know what this man can or cannot do? He is not a breeder of silkworms, he is an English soldier and an athlete.'

'The hills cannot—'

'They can because he has done it. He returns the mules with worn-down shoes and influenza.' His hand jerked excitedly and knocked Pachai's cup of tea to the floor; the smoke curled sadly up from his pipe. 'Oh Robert, you clever bastard! The Shrine of the Hair. . . .'

He stumbled to the window and gazed out towards the mountains. 'That would appeal to you, wouldn't it?'

'What are you muttering about now?'

Ernie turned back to the room. 'Send your bearer to buy some mules. I am going after King immediately. He has got to be caught before he reaches Uri.'

'Please listen,' Pachai said. 'Even if your crazy bally theory is correct you cannot be charging off into the mountains. You don't know them; you would die. Go back to Sopur, and round to Uri by road.'

'It would take too long.'

'Now you are just deceiving yourself, it would be much quicker and you know it.'

'No! I must follow him.'

'Why?'

'Why? Because it wouldn't be the same. . . .

'Well then,' said Pachai, 'now I am sure you are mad.'

'Yes, I think you're right,' said Ernie, starting to laugh, and for the first time he felt hungry and began to stuff the rice into his mouth in dripping spoonfuls. 'What you don't understand,' he said, waving the spoon under Pachai's nose, 'is that Robert King is not just the state's enemy, he is my personal enemy. And if I retreat to Uri now, I'll never quite convince myself I did it entirely out of duty.'

'He didn't sound like an enemy just now, when you were telling me how admirable he is.'

'It is quite possible to admire your enemies.'

'Nevertheless, with a duty to yourself and a duty to the state you should obviously act in the state's interests . . . though perhaps an eight-anna can't see it like that.'

For the first time in several weeks he was in high spirits, with self-confidence brimming over.

'How beautifully uncluttered your mind is. You're like one of those illustrations with dotted lines and a cross-section through your brainbox to show where everything is.'

'All right, you half-breed pardesi of a Government clerk. Do you think you are better than me, you damn rotter? Go on then, and be killed.' He flung orders at his bearer, then dragged a whisky bottle from his desk drawer and drank off two glasses quickly without offering any.

'I would like to borrow your map,' Ernie said.

'Request refused. You will not be returning, you will be dying in the snow. The map is necessary to the performance of my duties.'

'Then I shall take a copy,' Ernie said happily. He traced the section between Khadzil and Uri, marking the temple with, he noticed afterwards, a capital R. The bearer returned as he finished.

'Where are the mules?'

'He says there are no mules.'

A familiar helplessness, the Indian frustration, stole through him like a chill. 'There must be mules. We saw them in the bazar. . . .'

'He says they were all hired shortly afterwards, by a Pathan. It's never happened before.'

He could turn back now; nobody would blame him, least of all Pachai. It was only stupidity to carry on against the odds and he did not want to encounter the Pathan on any more lonely paths.

It had not seemed like this, back in Delhi. Then he had been overwhelmed by thoughts of the past. Ram Lal and the Minister had regarded it as a diplomatic mission, a negotiable agreement by two Oxonians to do the decent thing. Fear and death, the gun and the garrotte, had probably never entered the mild-mannered Sikh's thoughts; violence for him was the refusal of cigarette privileges in the British jail. Even the physical problems of sleep and hunger would be tabulated as neatly in his mind as the grammar books on his shelves.

From the table he could see through the window, across the river and the wide plain, into the grey-brown hills. A sporting gun hung on a nail by the window; he thought idly that it was careless, for a hand could reach in and take it. And then it brought the memories floating in like the flotsam of his soul. The gunshot in Wiltshire still echoed in the Kashmir hills. It had been a debt he preferred to ignore, but since the meeting with the Minister that had been impossible. There had been the attempted murder in the teahouse, the encounter on the Khadzil road, and now the appropriation of the mules, and so long as he kept on Robert's trail the debt was going to pile up ahead of him.

He caught Pachai looking at him curiously, and brushed away the thoughts that his face might reveal. 'Perhaps,' he said, 'we can obtain mules from elsewhere.'

Pachai said, 'It's curious. There was another place, but it seems that the same man—'

'All right,' Ernie said. 'It doesn't matter anyway. Robert has trapped himself.'

'How?'

'Horses travel faster than mules.' Now he had made up his mind.

Pachai stared. 'You intend to go into the mountains. You must be crazy if you think anyone will give you horses.'

'Then I'll use my own. There would be no time to find others anyway. They're tired, but no more than me.'

He could see the different arguments replacing each other behind the man's eyes; there were plenty to choose from, but at last Pachai simply said: 'Please. Go round by road, stay alive and do the job.'

'No.'

'Because if you go into the hills, knowing as little as you do, you will die. If I could stop you by force, I would.'

'You don't understand,' Ernie said. He went to the window and stared out across the river. His hand played lightly over the shotgun on the wall, and he said: 'I have got to go. Robert is somewhere out there. If I go fast on my horses I will catch him before he gets far. . . . It's been inevitable,' he said tiredly, 'for many years. I don't have a choice any more than your silkworms can stop chewing those leaves.'

'No one can say I didn't try to stop you,' Pachai said, and scraped the contents of his pipe bowl on to the steps. 'My conscience is clear.' He stepped aside for the bearer to sweep up the dottle at his feet.

Ernie didn't answer. He tugged down hard on the packstrap till the buckle reached its grommet and then went under the horse's head to attend to the other side. The horse wrinkled its nose at the smell of the river, and the other one lifted its tail and nearly splashed Pachai's brown leather shoes.

'Those stores will only last you three days.'

'I must go now,' Ernie said. 'Thank you for your assistance. And especially for the sleeping bag.'

Pachai brought out a pistol and its holster from under his

jacket. 'Here, you better take this. You can't always have a rifle ready to hand. You may be caught away from your horse. I am sorry I was rude to you. After loading it, you have to cock it before it will fire.'

He poured a double handful of bullets into Ernie's pocket and held out his hand. 'You are a bloody infuriating fellow but I hope you win through.'

Ernie moved down to the river, feeling the little tugs on his saddle as the packhorse adjusted to the rhythm. He could see in his mind's eye a picture of Pachai standing forlornly on the steps for a few moments, and perhaps bending to flick a spot of dust off his trousers before turning back into the room to his matches, pipe, and the moth larvae spinning out their existence in the back room.

The ford was wide and strong; it took over a minute to cross. He kept his feet tucked up high for dryness. A single line of trees grew on the far bank with a green tidemark round their waists, and his horse slipped twice in climbing the muddy bank.

The path showed as a faint discoloration on the stony ground. A quarter-mile from the river he passed between the upright black stones of a Muslim burial ground; the igneous black slabs glistened as if wet, and a crow lifted heavily from the path and dropped down again among the dead.

To the first line of hills the plain of stones lay level, smoothed by wind and frost to resemble mosaic. The hills ahead reared suddenly from the plain like a boundary wall, and long shelves of cloud obscured the farther hills where lay the Temple of the Sacred Hair. He travelled all afternoon thinking of the Pathans. They had not despatched him on the Khadzil road as so many others had been despatched without hesitation; they had gone through the performance of obstructing him but without hurting him because he still lived under the patronage of the man he sought. A further humiliation....

The hills before him looked bare of trees against the darkening sky; the gullies were filled with deep blue shadow. But the dropping sun behind him at last revealed a gap in the mountain wall; as he hurried forward, it seemed to close against him in darkness. But he could see it now, the mouth of a gully leading back into the hills.

His greatest difficulty, he realized, would be to capture Robert alive and he was probably the worst man the Minister could have chosen. It needed someone decisive and uninvolved. Too many tricks waited on the flick of one card : he wanted to capture Robert; but he didn't want to kill him; but he did want to humiliate him; but. . . . And he didn't trust his skill; it is more difficult to shoot to hurt than to shoot to kill, and memory could turn the bullet as it left the gun. It had once before.

He must remember that if he shot Robert he could not travel back to England and carry the bleeding body through the grey-walled courts of Oxford or expose it on the steps of the Wiltshire house. And to the Minister and Ram Lal his mission was just a piece of obvious duty. But triumph had to be observed, and there was only one spectator who would understand; so Robert must stay alive, ride back to Srinagar in front of his rifle, sit opposite him on the Delhi train with his manacled wrists and listen to the evidence in the court of the Indian Republic.

And be forgiven.

The sun had dropped below the plain and the hawks were floating silently into their nests on the dark mass of the hill. He was getting used to camping out. There was just light enough to find water in the bed of the gully, to scrub down the horses and cover them against the night. He made a meal of the cold baked beans, bread, onions and peppers from the panniers. He had to preserve his strength, the speed of eye and hand. If it came to a shooting match his slightest error could kill Robert, and that would be the end of it all.

He woke two hours before dawn. The moon had only just risen; the black rocks were edged with silver and the standing horses loomed large in the moonlight. Shivering with cold and excitement, he rolled up his sleeping bag and strapped on the pistol under his jacket. He walked the protesting horses beside the stream and as soon as they would do it he made them trot. He should gain three or four hours' advantage from this because Robert would not be in a hurry and, he remembered, he liked his breakfast . . . they might even meet today and the thought made him smile and shiver and increase the pressure of his heels.

There was no path, but there was only one way to go, along the inclined gully beside the stream. He made the horses trot, although the ground was rising; his whole advantage lay in forcing the pace.

But he could not keep the horses trotting and as the sun came up he slowed to a walk. Both horses were sweating hard; the packstraps were twice their width in dark wet patches on the horses' flanks and his own trouser legs were damp. A half-hour later he dismounted and led them up the increasing slope at a fast walk.

He was no longer in the bottom of the gorge. One bank of the stream had become sheer, and later on the other did also and he was forced up on to a ledge which rose steeper than the stream. The ledge bent around the curves of the hill until suddenly the sunlight broke out on to his head while the bottom of the gully was still in gloom. The trail turned and again he was in shadow, a cool air on his face and moisture on the rocks. The horses left their prints in the dew. Again the trail turned; dust blew across the gorge and a screw of paper came bouncing and rolling down the path.

It was almost past him before its presence registered and he leaped down to grab it as it went between the horse's legs.

He could read Urdu. It was the front and back pages of a newspaper printed in Rawalpindi, three months old and smelling faintly of oil. He let it drift from his hand and blow on down the path. A wind caught the paper and carried it out into the gorge where it fluttered down into the gloom like a wounded bird.

Now Robert could be around every next bend. Still moving fast, he reached the top of the gorge an hour later and had a clear view in front for the first time that morning.

He had been climbing a scarp slope; now he looked down the dip. It fell away steeply for two miles of scrubby bushes. There was a level area of ground at the bottom, green with vegetation, and then a narrow river between banks of trees.

Beyond the river the ground sloped up again, to a hilltop as high as the one where he stood. He let his gaze carry on upward and beyond and felt a bump in his chest: there it was at last, the horrible whiteness of snow.

It gave him an extraordinary feeling of smallness and dread. More than anything in nature, snow marked an alien land. It seemed to hang above the clouds like an island on the sea.

A clutch of hawks were circling a half-mile above him on unmoving wings. He felt free air in his face, but down below the air was shimmering off the hot rocks. He thought: they have seen Robert pass down this slope, making a path between the bushes, as now they see me. He searched the shadows and folds of the hill, but it was so difficult to adjust his vision against all the space that he found himself squinting, as when looking for an aeroplane in the sky.

Soon after he started down the slope, the top of the opposite hill had moved up and cut off his sight of the snow. Almost at once the breeze dropped and the warmer air enveloped him like another layer of clothes.

Suddenly there was a flash of grey and red; a fox had started up almost from under his heels. His horse backed up in fear, cannoned into the packhorse behind, then tried to run across the hill until Ernie hauled firmly on one rein and pulled its head round till it was touching his knee. The fox went on across the slope carrying its silver brush like a banner. And as Ernie watched it go he saw, a mile beyond it, entering the shadow of the trees by the river, what he had come to find.

Beside the river was a small clump of firs, the bottle-green shadow of them a contrast to the bright earth. In the time it took his vision to adjust to the distance, two mules passed from light to shade into the trees.

Had he seen it? A mile was a great distance in which to identify a moving target, but his eye had not needed to grope. He had been expecting it for so long that he now recognized it like an old photograph.

Strangely, a sort of pity was the dominant emotion as he hurried down the hill, like the sadness after sleep or coition. The bright rocks puzzled his eyes; twice the jerk of the pack-horse unbalanced him dangerously. Should he cut it loose? But every second of indecision brought him closer to the trees, thus increasing the proportion of time lost if he stopped. He wiped a quick hand across his eyes, brushing away sweat and sorrow. It seemed that at every momentous pause of his life time jerked him forward; action was considered only in retrospect: what did he want of Robert, his memory asked as the horse ran down the hill?

At the foot of the slope he had three hundred yards to canter into the trees. Robert would be fording the river. The trees were thin now that he was close, with space to gallop between them. He hoped to catch Robert in the water; surely he would have stopped for his mules to drink? He slowed at the thought, alarmed by the noise of his hoofs. At a careful walk, rifle in hand, he picked his way forward.

When he reached the water Robert was not there. But on the far bank he saw the deep-etched prints, holding water in the shapes of hoofs, leading into the trees. He followed them with the river dripping from his horse's belly. Where the trees faded into gloom, a large piece of paper was stuck with a clasp-knife to the bole of a fir.

It was another spread from the *Rawalpindi Times*. The pencilled writing was difficult to read across the black print:

A BIT FURTHER ON THERE'S A CLEAR SPACE WHERE THERE

WAS A FIRE. I'LL BE STANDING IN THE MIDDLE. I WON'T
BE ARMED.

Salutation and signature were unnecessary. His eyes stayed
on the paper a long time. After many years he still recognized
the style of writing, the affected tidiness of Robert's person
and relationships, peering through the clumsy capitals. The
circling hawks would have seen the paper being impaled to the
tree, the notification of defeat. Nothing is not sad, out of time
and context; even his victory was only the sands running out....

There was no hurry now, but the scenery pressed back
eagerly past him, trees and sunlight blurring his eyes. The
cool gloom enveloped him and he sank into a soft bed of pine
needles and smelled a gust of resin and dry timber. He allowed
the tiredness to gather and drain through his limbs, for it
didn't matter any more, the journey was finished.

He went on until he came to the first of the trees whose
trunks were smudged with fire. A sooty dust drifted up from
the muffled hoofs. Then sunlight showed ahead and he
emerged into a wide clearing among the sweep of burned
timber and Robert stood there waiting for him.

He did not want any advantage over Robert that he did
not morally feel, and he got down from the horse. He tangled
the reins in a bush and put the rifle back in its sheath. Without looking aside he began to walk across the ashy ground
and watched Robert coming slowly into focus. He looked a
bit awkward, such a big man in an empty space; his face was
tanned from the snow glare darker than Ernie's own, and his
smile had the warmth of years.

'Ernie. . . .'

'I've caught you now.' It sounded wrong, like a misquota-
tion.

'My God, it's good to see you, Ernie!'

'Considering your position, that's very sporting.' There he
went again. He couldn't handle scenes like this. He looked
carefully into Robert's face as if he could communicate better
that way, without words misrepresenting his thought.

'There's a thousand things I don't understand. When I saw you in the teahouse. . . . Oh God, Ern, why is it you?'

He had somehow expected Robert to have a uniform, but he wore an old pair of green woollen trousers tucked into stockings, a brown rainproof jacket reaching almost to his knees with pockets bulging. A shabby pair of binoculars swung from a cord round his neck. And yet there were the little touches—polished boots, clean handkerchief—that pulled it all together into a familiar picture.

'Ern, why is it you?'

'It was because I knew you. They thought it appropriate.' Suddenly they smiled with embarrassment, for the longer the separation the less there is to say.

'I must congratulate you, Ern. It was a damned fine effort to follow me up here—' but he stopped as Ernie flushed angrily.

'I am not a good native to be congratulated.'

'Ern—'

'Don't be condescending to me, Robert. Anything but that.'

'I wouldn't ever—'

'Oh no. . . ?'

And Robert said awkwardly: 'All right. But it's ten years ago. And anyway, who came off worst in that?'

Ernie remembered Pachai's description and said: 'Are you all right? You know. . . .'

Robert nodded.

'Show me,' Ernie said.

He didn't think he would; but Robert unzipped the jacket and pulled the shirt off his shoulders. Ernie saw the scar in his upper arm running back from the elbow. The arm was crooked all right.

'They wouldn't take me in the army.'

'I know,' Ernie said. 'I'm sorry.'

'So I went to Palestine, until they kicked us out of there.'

'They told me,' Ernie said.

It seemed to bring the first phase of the meeting to an uncertain end, for they looked at each other for a long time with nothing to say. Eventually Ernie broke his own silence.

'What does it mean, you coming here like a mercenary? It doesn't make any sense.' It was very hot, standing still in the dusty clearing; his shoes were full of dust, and his mouth too.

'I happen to believe in it,' Robert said. 'Kashmir is Pakistan's. If I wasn't serious about that I'd have handed in the cards when my friend was shot in the orchard.'

'But what right have you to umpire our battles? This is not a game of cricket. You would do better questioning your presence in Africa right now.'

'I told you,' Robert said. 'I believe in it. You believe we're doing wrong in Africa, but it's easy to moralize on other people's wars. Nobody does it to their own, though, because morality is only a justification of the will of the majority.'

He would have expected Robert to change, after a ten-year separation, but there was something more. Perhaps the change was as much in himself, his own advanced maturity, and depended on parallax. Groping for expression he found a phrase—was it the joker, Shaw?—something like: 'Only the reasonable man adapts to his surroundings.' The unreasonable man adapts the world to himself, and therefore all progress is made by unreasonable men. Robert seemed to have retreated from ideology to reason. The triumphant boyhood, the golden god of Oxford ... the images had become blunted by time and weather. If this was true then the past as seen now was a fake, and as if he had been following Ernie's train of thought Robert smiled and said: 'It's a long way from the Cher.'

'I have my morality too,' Ernie said with increased confidence, 'and it doesn't permit arming the enemies of a country that bred me.'

'I imagine that refers to me,' Robert said.

'You recognize the description?'

'No, as a matter of fact I bloody well don't. It was English-

men like my father who made India in the first place. It has
nothing that wasn't given to it. We're just not giving them
Kashmir.'

'You talk of "we" as if you represent England. But to them
you're just a thug acting against the human rights of the
Kashmiris. Or did you make the Mogul empire too?'

'All good Hindus the Moguls,' Robert said. 'Perhaps when
you get back to Delhi you can tell the Congress wallahs what
you really found up here, after peeling away the wrapping
marked Hind: a Muslim way of life so self-evident that they
don't even think to demonstrate it.'

'You can tell them that yourself,' Ernie said.

'How?'

'Because that's where I'm taking you.'

Not a muscle moved on Robert's face but Ernie was as aware
of a change as if he had been jolted with an electric shock.

'What's the matter. . . ?'

'Ernie,' Robert said at last; 'you know, you have done bloody
well to follow me up here. . . .'

He dropped his eyes and hurried on: 'And—and no one
can ever say you haven't done your best.'

Then there was such a long silence between them that when
Robert spoke again it was apparently only in an effort to end
it.

'Because, you see, you haven't had the element of surprise
since you entered the gully, and I imagine that was what you
were banking on, wasn't it? It's no good coming any further,
Ern, someone should have told you not to bring horses into
mountains.'

'You bastard! You bloody, bloody bastard!'

'But what—?'

'You bloody shaitan of a bastard, you have tricked me!'

'No I haven't. For God's sake, what did you expect?'

'You said you would be unarmed.'

'I am.' He turned and nodded towards the mules on the far
side of the clearing. A fine dust shrouded their ankles, and

one of them was trying the taste of spruce with upstretched head.

'You imagined the rest, Ern. This is as far as you can come, surely you realize that. Good God, you're not even dressed for it, you've probably got no food—'

'Robert, I think I might kill you—'

'I don't understand you, you're not a fool—but the snow is not for amateurs. But at least this route is finished for me now, that's something you've achieved.'

Ernie was shuddering with closed eyes. His legs struggled to keep balance. The sweat broke out and Robert stepped closer, watching him with interest.

'Do you still suffer from these turns. They should never have sent you, Ernie my dear. But I cannot help you. . . .' He turned away.

Ernie plunged blindly towards the horses. They were sixty yards away, cropping in the bushes and the butt of the rifle was sticking up ready to his hand.

When he had run fifteen yards Robert overtook him and club-fisted him to the ground. He lay stunned with a mouth full of grime and ash. Through the rage in his eyes he saw Robert running swiftly away to his mules, his boots exploding clouds of dust at every stride.

He got to his feet, nearly fell again, and stumbled as fast as he could towards the horse, the pain of Robert's fist thudding in his neck. He reached the rifle and jerked sobbingly at it but it was held fast and he had to stop to undo the buckle.

Robert had mounted and was entering the woods as he pulled the rifle clear. He fired the six rounds at the ball of golden hair and heard them cutting through the leafy branches, and then the thump of the mules dying away and away. A mighty stillness descended on the clearing, and only then did he remember the pistol under his jacket.

Plains

Ernie hailed his first taxi nervously and piled all his bags into the cab while the driver eyed him in silence.

'Where to, Sambo?'

He reddened. 'What?'

'Where d'you want to go?'

The Indian Hostel, Ram Lal had told him.

'The Indian Hostel, please.' Bastard.

'Where's that?'

The driver ambled away to his friends to make enquiries, and Ernie peered through the smoky windows at his first sight of London. Masses of people, more than in Delhi and all moving purposefully, going somewhere: standing in long queues for the double-decker buses, driving a moving wedge across any hesitation in the traffic. Everything was grubbier than he had expected, buildings dirty with age and newspapers blowing idly through the yard: he had anticipated something grand, like Rashtrapati Bhavan. There were the remnants of the war, the great hole in the station roof, posters still asking if journeys were necessary. He could see the taximan talking to a group of his mates round a tea-urn: the man had insulted him, automatic response to a coloured face. Well, if that was how it would be he was prepared for them, and he watched the man returning through the traffic with a surly resentment at his unpromising fare. Foreign, and not even a hotel. . . .

'Great Russell Street,' the driver said, and swung his shiny trouser-seat sideways into the cab. Only then did Ernie remember that Ram Lal had told him it was opposite the British Museum. They turned out of the station yard and Ernie watched London go by with the hope and despair of a man crossing a minefield.

He had two months before the beginning of the university year. Not a day to waste, for Ram Lal always insisted that he had gained a special place, reserved for an Indian student. In open competition, Lal said, he would not have had a chance. He did not believe him: he knew his own ability, and Ram Lal's methods. But the years of waiting had made him stale, like a runner trained to readiness for a race postponed day by day. The mind can absorb only so much without using it, and his brain felt flabby and tired as he watched London ride past his eyes.

The taxi did a U-turn and stopped outside an aggressively-curtained house opposite the British Museum. Again the driver sat stoically while Ernie pulled his heavy suitcases on to the pavement and fumbled in his pocket.

'And the rest.'

'I beg your—'

'That's not enough,' the man said roughly.

Ernie peered again at the meter. 'I have given you three shillings and sixpence,' he said. 'That is correct?'

'It might be correct, mate, where you come from, but it's not right.'

Ernie hesitated . . . any difference between the subtleties of Delhi and London English had not been explained by his books.

'You have to give more than the clock. It's the law.' The driver pushed forward a hand like a shovel and glanced only briefly up and down the pavement.

'I beg your pardon. How much more?'

'Twice.'

It was terribly expensive. An instant suspicion arose; he knew he was being cheated. But he lacked the confidence; the hand was still demanding over the lowered window and miserably he counted another three shillings and sixpence into it.

The taxi moved away from the kerb just as the door opened behind him and a white-haired woman about four feet and six inches high leaped down the step. She had to ask her question three times before Ernie could decipher her Scots accent.

'I said how much money did he charge you?'

'Seven shillings.'

The lines around her mouth tightened like knife-cuts. 'He has cheated you. They always get the new ones. Lunch is ready. There should be a law.'

His room was small, with oversized furniture, but it was the first he had ever owned. He arranged his few books on the mantelpiece and hung his only suit in the cupboard, which made it look even bigger than it was. Through the grimy sash window he could see a straggling line of schoolchildren being marched up the wide steps into the Museum while the bus-driver leaned on his cab and munched sandwiches solidly as if they were on his schedule, so many miles, so many swallows. A bulky young man sat with a girl on the steps, reading the one book over each other's shoulders, and as he watched they shifted a few yards to the left to stay with the moving sunlight.

His own room was in shadow; only now did he see the line of dusty Dickens behind glass and the Goya print over the washbasin. They could take their education so casually, like snacks at a picnic, while he had fed like a man in a desert, never knowing which meal would be his last.

During the next weeks of study his confidence ebbed and flowed like the marching up and down on the Museum steps. He was overtrained: his collection of facts had dissipated during the years, like the texture of overworked soil. His power of reception responded inversely to the proportion of hours he worked. Then he would go for a walk down Charing Cross Road or Museum Street, contemplating the ever-receding borders of his ignorance in a single bookshop window.

One Saturday afternoon he was sitting up in bed clutching

with a cold hand a book by Hobbes. He had caught a cold
during the week which was turning to flu. An early chill was
stirring the dust and an eddy of dry leaves went up past the
window. What had the previous chapter said? He was trying
to recall it while somewhere below a door banged; he heard
the Scotswoman talking to someone and then there was more
noise on the stairs and the small landing, a banging of feet
and then a rapping on his door.

'Ernie! Ern!'

He had a sudden swift vision of a tree and a black pond.
And stumbled from the bed; it was too soon, he wasn't ready.
He pulled a pair of trousers up over his scruffy pyjamas and
searched desperately for a comb.

'Ernie! Wakey wakey! I say, can I come in?'

And Robert stood grinning and delighted in the open doorway. His blond head was a new shock to Ernie; after arriving
in England expecting to find half the population with golden
hair he had only recently managed to adjust his beliefs: now
here was Robert as startling as ever.

'How was the trip? When did you arrive? And Ernie you
old dog, why didn't you get in touch? I had to write to your
father. It's months since any of us had a letter from you.'

He stood uncomfortably with his bare feet on the old
carpet with the faded yellow pattern, of a sheep or a dog. . . .
He had recently spilt his cup of tea in bed and one pyjama
sleeve hung damply over his hand.

'I have been very busy, Robert.'

'So I see.' Robert was looking with exaggerated distaste
about the room.

'If you'd like to wait downstairs—let me get dressed—'

'All these books,' Robert was saying. 'What do you do with
them? You should be learning how to drink beer, date girls,
all the important things.'

'No, it is easy for you to speak like that. I have to work.'

'But honestly, Ern, old man, you'll kill yourself like this.
Look, you're in a sick-bed already. What's the matter?'

'Mrs Maxwell called it flu. It is a cold. I have a temperature. She is my landlady,' he said, as if trying to patch up the fabric of his interrupted existence. 'She said I should stay in bed.'

Robert shivered, not with cold, and said: 'Ernie, get up. It's rotten in here. Honestly, it's warmer outside. Get an overcoat on and we'll go for a walk or something. You'll feel heaps better.'

'I don't think—'

'Mother's angry with you, I'll warn you now. You were expected down at the house. And Susan too.'

'Susan?' His face brightened; it was seven years since he had seen Susan. 'How is she?'

'She's O.K.'

'She is what?'

'O.K.'

'What is the meaning of that? It is a new word to me.'

'It means—O.K., all right, there's nothing the matter with her. She is very well. Come on, let's get out of this place, I've got the shivers.'

Robert took him to a pub near Fleet Street. 'You often see journalists in here. I saw Hannen Swaffer at that table once, doing a crossword.'

There were high-backed benches between the tables. Litho-prints of racehorses looked down on a Saturday-afternoon collection of men at the long oaken bar. A diamond-paned window separated the street outside into a dozen distorted scenes.

'All the newspapers are around here. But if you've been in London for the last few weeks you'll know that already.'

'No.'

'Gosh, Ern, it's so good to see you again. I could never forget you, always trying to be a Sarsut Brahmin or something . . . no, I'm only teasing, but you always claimed to be more Indian than British, to your father's despair. And he was more British than any of us. What do you feel about things now, things generally, I mean, you know?'

Ernie said : 'I am an Anglo-Indian. I'm not going to pretend about it while I'm here and I am not ashamed of anything.'

'No, of course.'

'And I feel close to—well, Hinduism, its culture and—language and everything.' He spoke with the puzzled uncertainty of a mathematician suddenly called upon to recite the six times table. He was not the first to discover he carried knowledge uneasily, and the more he read the less he knew. Neither was this the time to mention his tenuous connection with Ram Lal and Congress; if Robert argued about that he would find himself defending more than he felt.

'I am in England to study and I must adapt to my surroundings. I must be popular with my tutors. You know what I mean,' he said with a sudden anger at being so inarticulate. 'In England I must be English. I must work hard and do jolly well in my studies. I am determined to get a First.'

'Go easy old man. I've been up two years now and it's not quite like that. You'll soon fall into it, but it's not really done to appear to be working too hard.'

Ernie frowned, and Robert said: 'I mean it's not, well, friendly—you don't know what "done" means, do you? I mean it's not . . . well, it's like in cricket you don't jeer at a man because he's out . . . oh, bloody hell,' he said, and laughed. 'We've been apart too long, you don't understand my way of speech. You've learned your English with a textbook and you've learned how to behave at university from a textbook but in real life they're both different.'

Ernie took another tentative sip of the beer glass and then set it down and looked at it in a puzzled way. A line of foam had formed a second edge to his mouth.

'I understand you, Robert. But I must do better than everyone else. Did you ever inform me what you were reading?' He just stopped himself saying 'studying'.

'Oh, history. You've got to find something. I'm specializing in the Indus Valley as a matter of fact.'

'That is very interesting, of course. A most ancient civilization.' In every way Robert's arrival had caught him off guard; unconsciously he had retreated to the formal Indian phraseology, the old-fashioned slang.

Robert took a long pull at his glass. 'It's beginning to look nasty out there, isn't it?'

A passing bus shattered itself against the diamond frames, then realigned at an open window and passed on up the Strand. 'Out there. . . ?'

'The Punjab, Partition, everything.'

'But Robert, I beg to disagree. I think we will achieve independence very soon now and—'

'I didn't mean that. I don't actually see us giving in so easily. But I mean if it does come, it's beginning to look bad for the Muslims.'

'But why, Robert? The Muslim community have the same interests as us. We are all Indian. Gandhi—'

'Yes, yes,' said Robert irritably; he wasn't used to an argument getting away from him.

A bunch of men pressed past and Robert lifted both glasses clear of the rocking table.

'Here, you're not drinking. But they're going to have a raw deal and you know it. And Gandhi and his boys all know it too. They're kidding themselves. The Muslims won't take it.'

Ernie said: 'The British Government will no doubt use that as an excuse.'

'Oh, shut up Ern. You know as well as me . . . but dammit, why do we argue?' He cupped both hands around his beer and regarded Ernie intently for the first time. He saw a man unexpectedly fragile-looking, but with an occasional swiftness of reflexive movement like a nervous deer. He had large round eyes like a girl's and a skin duskier than he remembered and very smooth; he probably hadn't started shaving, Robert thought, and his hands were smooth too, with bony knuckles. It was odd; one expected an older version of the boy, but there was a different type of change too, other qualities tacked on

like extra limbs, a growth horizontal, as it were, as well as
vertical.

'I want to help you,' Robert said. 'You've got a tough time
in front of you, in a way. I didn't know what to expect, or
if you'd want to bother after all these years, but I feel as close
to you as ever.'

'That is very good of you.' He took another tiny sip of his
drink and put it down quickly. 'Robert, did you say this was
bitter? I think it is gall.'

Robert laughed. 'It's an acquired taste. Like—' he was going
to draw a comparison with something Indian but he hesitated,
and they smiled cautiously at each other, still unsure.

'You've got to learn to like that stuff,' Robert told him.
'Now that's much more important than Hobbes. No more
Hobbes until the term starts. Promise? All right, don't
promise, but I'm giving you good advice.'

Ernie had never seen anything quite like this pub. He had
heard about them, places where anyone could go and drink,
but he had always been too nervous to try. The inhibitions
of class were as clearly defined here as in Delhi and he could
have made a dozen mistakes in merely walking in and asking
for a drink; and he would not have known what to ask for.
Now he looked about him like an older boy at his first panto-
mime, impressed but not wishing to admit to his inexperience.
A party of men and women in evening dress, the ladies with
furs around their pale shoulders, made a noisy group round
a tray of sandwiches; while beside him at the beer-swilled
table an old man marked the racing results with a stubby
pencil, coughing into his handkerchief.

'Mother was expecting you at the house,' Robert was
saying.

'Robert, how is your family? Why haven't I asked before?
It is very rude of me. I heard from your mother, I think, in
March.' He searched his memory for an item to comment on.
'She was collecting clothes for someone. . . .'

'Oh, that's Ma all right. The grand dame of the W.V.S.

They're frightfully intense about Polish refugees being properly dressed.'

'How is Susan?'

'Susan and Rowena both want to work but Ma thinks it's not quite nice to do it for money. They keep saying they'll move up to town and take a flat. Ernie, that reminds me. Where will you be living? In college?'

Ernie picked up the unwanted glass for another attempt. 'No, I don't think so.' His grant did not cover that sort of expense: he had thought vaguely about a cheap hotel.

Robert said, after a long hesitation, 'Left it too late, did you?' but Ernie knew he must have guessed the real reason and wondered why Robert should make it an occasion for a show of reticence.

'I'm not really surprised,' Robert said. 'The place was stiff with ex-servicemen last year, descending on the place with middle-east sun-tans and gratuities. I was lucky to get in college myself. I hope you've got digs then, or it's probably too late now, of course.'

'Digs?'

'Lodgings. Hasn't anything been fixed up for you?'

Ernie's face dropped, like a man who reaches what he thought was a mountain peak and then sees the whole range scaled up before him. As if entry to university wasn't enough, he had to learn all the new way of life: digs, stale-smelling beer, what things were 'not done'; how to pay off taxis, and move around. He said: 'I meant to go up there a few days before the start of term.'

'It's not your fault,' Robert said. 'You couldn't be expected to know. But you'd better get up there right away. Then I'll come back a day or so early and show you around. If you're not reading Hobbes.'

Robert finished the last of his pint and looked at his watch. 'I've got to see a bloke. You can come too. We've got time, though. Another?'

'Another—what—?'

'Another drink,' Robert said patiently. 'Another pint of beer. Would you like—?'

'No, thank you, Robert. Definitely not.'

Robert chuckled. 'You will. You'll be more English than any of us within a year. Hobbes, Christ!'

Robert tapped on the heavy oaken door, then pushed it open and gestured Ernie in front of him. The room was much smaller than the door suggested: Ernie had half expected a staircase, doors leading to other rooms, a balcony of bookshelves as he had seen once in a film. There would be a large globe and perhaps a polished brass sextant. . . .

The absence of all this caused him to hesitate uncertainly in the doorway; and this man couldn't be the Master?

Robert said: 'Professor Scobie, this is Mr Maher, from India.'

The Master said: 'How nice of you to come and see me.'

But he had been summoned by a written note delivered the day before. Was the man making fun of him?

There was a large, littered desk under the window, with a typewriter and some battered wire trays. Did the Master do his own typing? A sheet of paper was in the roller, with the grey look of having been there for some days. Above the desk, another surprise, a photo of the Khajuraho temples. He switched his mind from it, for the Master was addressing him; but it would be a talking point when he needed it.

This was the moment he had been awaiting in fear, an intellectual confrontation with the Master of the College.

'You must find it rather chilly here.'

'No.'

The Master raised his eyebrows, his little spectacles came up with them, and Ernie said: 'I mean I have been here for some weeks, in London.' He wondered if he should mention he had stayed near the British Museum.

'It's going to get colder yet, I'm afraid. Though it always seems to be warmer here in the city than a few miles outside.

Perhaps the buildings keep us warm, like clothes. Well, sit down. I hope you have no oriental scruples that prevent you accepting a glass of port.'

He didn't know what port was, but hoped it would be nothing like Robert's bitter. He had drunk a lot of it since his first glass in Fleet Street but still the smell of it made him feel sick.

The Master pulled open a filing drawer and lifted out a decanter. Glasses clinked pleasantly as he poured. He was a big man, in the small room, as tall as Robert but with a fragile look about him nevertheless. His large hands were gentle, and his heavy jowls looked as if they could be comfortable only while resting on a violin. His clothes looked untidy and wrong, as if made for someone else; only when he sat down did they tailor themselves to his shape.

'Cold in temperature but not in atmosphere, I hope, Mr Maher. You are the only Anglo-Indian here but there are several of your countrymen and I am sure you will quickly make friends. Do you play any sport?'

He felt sure it was a trap. If he admitted to liking sport too much it would be a mark against his academic record. He said: 'Oh, I used to play a bit of hockey, sir,' but then he could not control the temptation to add: 'I was captain of my college in Delhi, as a matter of fact. And, er, I played for the State a few times.'

'Who is captain of hockey this year, King?'

'Harry Patel at Balliol.'

'I expect you'll be getting a note from him. Anyone from India seems an automatic choice for a trial, don't they? And what about you, King? It was nice to see another rugby blue in the house last year. What are you going to do this season?'

The Master handed the port around, and with a little gesture to Ernie raised it to his lips. The ordeal would start any moment now; he wondered if it was time to mention the Khajuraho temples. But the Master and Robert were talking rugby now; words like 'touchdown' and 'scrum' fell uneasily on his ear. He heard his school-leaving report rustle in his pocket as he fidgeted in the chair; he had hoped the Master would ask to see it but he seemed preoccupied at the moment with something called drop-out.

He took another little look at the tiny room. A bag of golf clubs lay on top of the piano: a piano—he hadn't noticed it before because its lid was covered with seedboxes, and a green tendril was curling up the music stand. On the mantelpiece above the gas fire was a framed picture; he recognized the same print as hung above his Great Russell Street washbasin.

'Mr Maher.'

Ernie jerked up. 'I'm sorry sir—'

'You were engrossed in the Goya. King and I were talking about the army as a life for a thinking man. It would seem to me a little innocent of opportunity for intellectual activity.'

'No,' Robert interrupted. 'Excuse me, but it's like the difference between football and rugby. Now, rugger is more scientific—'

'It depends how you play it,' the man interrupted in turn. 'Someone once told me that draughts is more scientific than chess.'

It put Robert off his stroke and Ernie saw him flash an annoyed glance to the floor.

'But, of course . . .' the man encouraged him.

'Well, at least there is more variety of action, more ways of scoring. Well, army life can be uneventful, of course, but I say there are times when a general needs every ounce of intellect he can muster.'

He started to talk of Wavell, his current hero. He had beaten Aosta and the others because of his superior intellect. He was not especially a soldier, he was a thinker.

It was doubtful how much Robert had understood of the subtleties of the North Africa fighting but he certainly had a command of dates and personalities. But Ernie found himself listening coolly to his argument and rejecting it. Perhaps it was unfair to judge a man's argument about intellect when . . . well, when he did not, for Ernie felt it while he listened, he did not have the intellectual capacity himself to present it effectively. Oh, Robert was brilliant and dangerous, he would make a fine soldier and his life had been charted from birth like a roster of promotion. But Ernie began to feel the heady arrogance of the pupil who has overtaken his master.

'And what do you think about it, Mr Maher? Do you think a man is a better soldier for being a thinker?'

He had been sipping the port again; he liked it much better than the beer. Now he swallowed it too quickly and had to swallow twice more before speaking.

'Yes sir, I think that's true. But I think a man is better at anything if he applies an intellectual approach to his work. It's not especially true of a military career and many successful generals haven't been thinkers at all. Some of them have been illiterate.'

He saw Robert stiffen and the Master smile before saying: 'Ah yes, the Mongols.'

'Yes sir. I don't suppose any of them were great thinkers, but if the size of their conquests is anything to go by . . .' and at this point he felt his argument beginning to tail off, but the Master rescued him and after a while the conversation turned aside.

When would the Master begin his interrogation? His mental agility had been on the boil as he stood outside the Master's door, but now he felt dull and heavy. He had expected stern questioning of his scholarly accomplishments, a lecture on academic responsibility and the traditions of the college. Or . . . something. But once again the man was talking about sport. Was it really as Robert had said—once you were through the door, the heat was off? His world was shifting again; he knew he could establish his identity in competition. But if the struggle were to take place only in social and sporting worlds where he was a beginner . . . he felt the hopelessness stealing over him, out of the Indian past.

'We're expecting great things of you, Maher. We haven't had a good hockey player in the house for years. Mr Archer in Delhi has told me something of your record and it gave me a lot of pleasure to hear it.'

'But,' Ernie said with some irritation, 'I have come here to work. I cannot waste time with hockey, much as I enjoy it. My work comes before everything, and I am determined to get a First.

'I shall be working in all my spare moments,' he added with growing desperation at the Master's apparent lack of enthusiasm. 'I shall be a credit to my tutors. But of course, I shall take an interest; I will watch the games so long as they do not hinder my work.'

The Master held up his glass and studied it closely against the light as if he expected to find a creature swimming about in it.

'Your path to enlightenment is the contemplative, eh?'

It struck a little chord in Ernie's brain.

'You cannot achieve freedom from activity by merely abstaining from action. Am I being frivolous? It is deception to let your mind dwell on the objects of desire from which you abstain.'

'The *Bhagavad Gita!*' He was delighted; this man was a student of Indian literature or theology. Who had he read: Swami Prabhavananda? Radhakrishnan? Isherwood?

'Ah, I can see you know it too. Go on from there.'

'I can't, sir.'

The man smiled. 'Neither can I! You've called my bluff. It's something about activity with self-control being more truly enlightened than mere inertia, even though action is despised. Well, not despised.'

'Where did you study, sir?'

The Master looked startled for a moment. 'Study? Oh no, nothing like that. But I read quite a lot. I'm a jackdaw. It's good to be a jackdaw, you don't have to collect too much of any one thing. And it's more fun. Don't shut yourself off from all interests but one, eh? Well. . . .'

Ernie found himself left behind. The Master had glanced at his watch and Robert was already on his feet. He stood up hastily: were they to go? Nothing had been said. He looked for somewhere to put down his glass and then, thinking it might be rude otherwise, paused to swallow the last of the port before setting the glass down among the seed boxes.

As they walked down the passage the door opened again. ' "Duty well done fulfils desire." That was the bit I was trying to remember.' He looked as pleased as a schoolboy for a moment; then: 'Not particularly relevant, I suppose. Oh, well!' and the door closed again.

They walked down the passage and out into the cold sunlight; the sky was a very pale blue above the roofs of the stone buildings. The gravel path crunched like a beach as they walked towards the playing field.

'Fancy old Scobie quoting that stuff at you. Jackdaw's the right word. He once spent two hours telling me about the campaigns of Geronimo, the Red Indian. But he didn't seem to know anything at all about Napoleon. He hadn't even heard of Ney.'

'He is very impressive,' Ernie said thoughtfully; he was not sure yet if the master was impressive, but imagined he must be. He had expected someone more imposing, more . . . well, not a man so untidily dressed, with seedboxes on his piano and the shabby bag of golf clubs.

'He's a clever old stick,' Robert said.

'That seems to me very disrespectful. He is a professor, Master of our college. And this is the greatest university in the world.'

'Well, yes, all right,' Robert muttered uneasily. Two

students had passed by, near enough to hear Ernie's last words, and they were looking back and grinning.

Robert took Ernie's arm and guided him down the long path to the rugger pitch. 'No need to broadcast things like that,' he said quietly.

The college second XV was playing a visiting R.A.F. team from Abingdon. As they approached, a high kick for touch bounced off a car's roof and was caught by one of a dozen pairs of upstretched hands in the stand. There was some desultory clapping and a mufflered touchjudge guessed the place and waved his handkerchief.

'How did your meeting with Aiken go?' Aiken was Ernie's tutor on the P.P.E. course.

'He is rather young,' Ernie said disappointedly.

'He's thirty-four or five.'

'I expected someone with more experience.'

'You mean like Professor Scobie?'

'Yes, that is what I thought. He is a man of great experience.'

'Too much,' Robert said. 'I've attended some of his lectures. He's a great entertainer, but if you want a degree you better stick to Aiken.'

A scrum had formed ten yards in, and a moment after the ball came flying out the front rows collapsed. The three-quarters went diagonally across the field, and when the scrum had cleared there was one man left lying there. The whistle blew after a while and one or two players strolled over to see to the injured man.

He had been watching rugby with Robert for two weeks now and the game seemed as far removed from reality as the rituals of Diwali. Were all these fellows studying for degrees? Suppose they failed, they would curse the waste of time.

'Symonds has invited us to a party in his room. It's his birthday and his father's given him £50. You remember Dick Symonds with those sideboards, don't you?' Robert was talking without taking his eyes off the field.

'I would like to go,' Ernie said doubtfully. He was still very shy, finding unfamiliarity beyond every door, social difficulties waiting like examination questions.

'There'll be some girls there,' Robert said.

'What sort of party?' he asked uneasily.

'Just a party. Drinking and that. Talking, whatever you like. A chap's bringing his saxophone, perhaps there'll be some dancing. It'll be your first party here, won't it?'

It wasn't that the other students didn't try to be friendly, but always he found himself looking for what lay behind it. It had been as Ram Lal said: in Delhi he was a respected man, here he was a schoolboy again. On his first day at Oxford Robert had taken him to Dick Symonds' room, and he had made a complete fool of himself; he was sure Symonds would never forget it. Symonds had been down on his knees in front of the gasfire, toasting a crumpet at the end of a fork held in a leather-gloved hand. He wore carroty muttonchop sideboards which turned dark at the edges, and his red face was shiny with heat as he looked up to shake hands.

'Excuse the glove.'

'How do you do, Mr—?'

'Dick.'

'Mr Dick—'

And he and Robert had both laughed and the greasy crumpet dropped off the fork and rolled under the bed.

Remembering this, Ernie said: 'I think that I should work tonight. Mr Aiken wants my essay by Friday and there is a lot of work in it.'

'Oh come off it, Ern. Today's only Saturday. You must make an effort,' and the irritation in his voice made Ernie decide to attend the party. But:

'How should I be dressed?'

But Robert was engrossed in the play. The ball had just been squeezed from a tight scrum like a bar of soap from a hand and the college fly-half had taken a bad pass and sent the ball out to the wing. The man handed off the Abingdon winger so fiercely that his nose spurted blood and as he came up to the full-back everyone knew he was going to try a handoff on him, too, to be the one across the goal-line. But the full-back went in low and Ernie heard the little crack as the winger's knees were banged together and then the thud as his shoulders hit the hard October ground. It was astonishing the way these people played their sport. He had seen a documentary film about the war just before leaving Delhi, and now these jerseyed youths were fighting over a ball with as much intensity as the black and white images had struggled to kill.

He went to Robert's rooms that evening at seven o'clock. When Robert answered his knock, the lower part of his face was covered in shaving soap except for a hard line around his mouth. An expression of surprise and anger seemed to slip out through the widening door-gap.

'I thought I'd see you at Dick's place.'

'I don't know where it is.'

'But you've been there.'

'Well,' he said, 'I'm not absolutely sure. . . .'

Robert stood on the step holding the razor half-way to his chin. 'Oh, all right. But I can't wet-nurse you for ever, you know. Still, your first party. . . . Come on in.'

'But I say, isn't it late?'

He followed Robert into the room; there was a kettle steaming on the stove and the mirror was running with damp. That was the only disorderly thing about the place; clothes and books were arranged with military precision; the towels hung neatly, and furniture was square with the walls. Half a dozen magazines were arranged fanwise on a table; he happened to knock them awry as he passed but Robert paused to restore them to their pattern. It reminded him of Robert's room in Delhi, the rigid tidiness of desk and shelves, the bed made up even before the bearer could reach the upper landing.

'Aren't we late?' Ernie asked again.

Robert had finished the downstrokes and started to relather.

'You don't turn up on time here. What have you got that spiv suit on for?'

'I wished to look smart.'

'It's all right for a board meeting. Or perhaps for a charabanc outing to Brighton. Here we tend to take things a little more casually.'

And there it was again: the striving for effortlessness, the bottom button of formality so carefully left undone. Not even to *be* more casual, he noticed, but to tend to take things more casually. It wouldn't have been quite casual enough, of course, actually to *be* casual. All their passion was reserved for irrelevancies—sport, and oddities of tradition and knowing which beer no one ever drank.

But some of these things had already become clear to him; he was beginning to understand, and it was all very different and strangely influencing.

'What can I do?'

'There's a jersey of mine in the cupboard. Help yourself. Leave your jacket behind.'

'Robert, I think I am going to like Oxford.'

Robert smiled at the mirror, then bent to splash water on his face.

'And I'm so much looking forward to meeting your mother and the rest of the family again,' he said happily. 'Susan and —and everyone.'

But Robert didn't respond to that, perhaps he hadn't heard; and a few minutes later they walked over to Symonds' room. Through the open door he could see the gas fire and the glow of candles. He was accepting almost everything now, whether or not he understood, as the Oxford way of things. If undergraduates didn't use their electric light at parties then that was quite all right, and he must discover, without actually asking, why it was so.

It was warm inside the room. Someone pushed an empty glass into his hand, but the offer of a drink didn't follow and Robert was no longer beside him, so after a while he shyly

walked over to help himself. There were bottles and glasses
on a long table, and in the sink were more bottles submerged
in blocks of ice.

'Can I help you, sir?'

A young man in a gaudy waistcoat and chef's hat, like a
character in a Christmas charade. 'What can I get you, sir?'
and Ernie was sure he had leaned just a shade heavily on the
'sir' the second time around.

'I will have some port.'

The young man looked startled. 'No. No port. Sherry?'

But Ernie didn't know sherry. 'In that case I'll have a beer,'
he said firmly. The man looked startled again, but lifted a
brown ale from the sink and jerked off the cap. Ernie poured
clumsily and got the froth over his trousers.

The room was growing fuggy with cigarette smoke, hanging like veils between the glowing candles. He saw Robert's
blond head pass through a patch of light, then heard a general
laugh and a clashing of glasses. 'Dance?' a girl asked him. He
had not seen her before, but now she stood peculiarly demanding, swinging her brown hair. 'No, I'm drinking beer,' he told
her nervously, and she giggled and moved away. Symonds
waved and grinned to him from across the room so he struggled
through to find him, but when he reached the spot Symonds
was no longer there.

The saxophone had now started, like a lost animal telling
its loneliness. Behind him three men were arguing heatedly,
dodging the saxophone's note by speaking now above, now
below it; something about a horse race. One of the three turned
round and to his delighted surprise he recognized Aiken. A
tutor at a party! He was beginning to understand the Oxford
scene, a thousand peculiarities but with one embracing pattern
like a jigsaw.

Three girls were dancing by themselves in a corner, and
one of them came over to ask Aiken to join them. He did so,
dancing with a strange limp shuffle, beer glass in hand, hullo-
ing Ernie with his eyebrows as he turned in his view.

The party's noise reached its early climax and then began the long return, down muted bars of music and the slow wash of the beer. He was beginning to feel a little bit lonely; if the brown-haired girl came back he would risk dancing with her. But it was a blonde-haired girl he was thinking of when Symonds came back again, pulling another man by the sleeve.

'We're thinking of ducking out,' he said. 'Care to join us?'

'But Dick,' his friend was protesting, 'you can't dodge out of your own party.'

'Why not? Who'd notice?' Symonds was a bit drunk; the long sideboards wavered as if engaged in keeping his head carefully balanced. 'I'm twenty-one now, I can do what I like. Who's for coming on the river? Ernie?'

This was exciting? He looked round for Robert.

'There's a pub down near where they hire the boats,' Symonds said. 'This party's got away from me.'

'Is Robert—?'

'No, he's occupied.'

What did it matter? His head buzzed with a peculiar excitement: he and Symonds and two others. They left the party and walked raucously through many small streets with the cold making his ears sing. They told jokes and sang snatches of limericks; he understood little but laughed in all the right places. They played football with an empty tin can, barging each other and calling for offside. Symonds was singing drunkenly: 'On Gibraltar Rock, So high and steep, A fair young maid lay down to sleep. . . .'

Soon they arrived at the river. The boathouse was closed, but they took one of the rowing boats and pushed it across the shingle into the water. Symonds got his trouser leg soaked and the others laughed and Ernie laughed too. In they all clambered, as a man came running out of a nearby house, but they splashed him with the oars and pushed on out into the river. Symonds had one of the oars but couldn't work it properly: after scything the air a few times he lay back in

the boat, crooning gently. 'And as she lay, In sweet repose,
A gust of wind blew up her clothes. . . .'

Ernie picked up the discarded oar and pulled on it vigorously. His opposite number grinned and winked encourage-
ment. He gripped the oar eagerly, and heard the boat's owner
calling empty threats from the shore.

A public house with a veranda overhung the water on the
opposite bank. They pulled chairs up to a bench against the
railings and Symonds got out a pair of dice. They explained
the game to him: you had to throw for double-sixes. The first
man with a double designed a drink, not more than three
items and ten shillings maximum cost, but within these limits
the most loathsome mixture possible. The second double paid
for whatever the glass contained; the third had to drink it.

Symonds chose the first mixture, and ten minutes later
threw the third double and had to swallow it: gin, pernod
and beer. He staggered across the veranda and pretended to
tumble over the low rail into the water; he nearly did go
over, for he cut his hand on the broken glass, and for the rest
of the evening left a stickiness over everything, dice, glasses,
the wooden bench-top.

Ernie was delighted when his own turn came; he drank
manfully and retched into the river. And when at the end
they threw their glasses far out into the water's darkness his
was the farthest throw, the last of the four distinct splashes
which made them all laugh so very much. He had forgotten
the taxi-driver, the young man at the party. He was among
his fellows, and the social tricks could be learned like any
habit. Robert, the Master, Aiken, Dick Symonds and the
others, they had all accepted him into their wonderful world.
He woke next morning with his first hangover and lay savouring it like a wound gained fighting for a woman he loved.

A week before the Christmas vacation he received a letter
which made him feel excited even before he knew who had

written it, for recollections of happiness lay patterned in the sloping letters. Memory works faster than perception . . . and from out of the drift of time the handwriting held a promise unrealized until he had unfolded the stiff blue paper and stared for a long time at the words.

Dear Ernest,

How naughty of you not to come down to see us. We were expecting to hear from you every day, after you arrived in England, but Robert has told us you were working very hard at that time, as indeed you have apparently been doing ever since.

How are you, my dear boy? We have been following your progress, as reported by Robert, with great interest, and are delighted to hear you are doing so well, and have settled happily into a world which must be so very strange for you.

We are rather an old-fashioned family, and like to be alone at Christmas, but I do hope you will come and stay with us afterwards. May I suggest January 2nd or 3rd?

Rowena and Susan send their love, and look forward to seeing you again. Won't it be strange! They're quite little ladies now, 19 and 20 last month.

Everything is under snow here (just like Kashmir! Do you remember?) but I don't think you've had it in Oxford yet. I do hope you have a nice Christmas, wherever you are, but afterwards I want you to drag yourself away down here. Best wishes, my dear Ernest.

Affectionately,
Gladys King.

He knew it was ridiculous to turn dreams into hopes. He could not even remember her face properly. After seven years, and the changes in her life, she was probably less like his memory of her than many other girls were now. The girl at Symonds' party . . . she had been a bit like Susan, a bit like Susan had been seven years ago. And he had changed amazingly himself. If he loved what he remembered, could he possibly love what she was now; or was time too active a catalyst?

In the train to Turley he had to keep wiping the condensation from the damp window to watch the passing country. Thaw had slackened the grip of cold on the earth, and discoloured ribs of snow lay in the hollow places and the north side of the hedges. Little hedged fields had wheel-tracks of brown water at the gateways. On the hills were blue shadows of forest with cows grazing ankle deep in the wet grass beneath. The crows had built high that year and the boughs bent like shipmasts before the rain. A band of cyclists passed under a bridge as the train clattered over it. Their yellow oilskins swelled with wind and alarmed a mare with its cartload of steaming potato sacks, and a dog ran out from a yard and barked and barked.

Closer to Turley the rain eased; a woman walked with a heavy pail from a barn to a place made mysterious by the train's swift passing. The train wheels changed rhythm past a schoolyard, a garage with a red roof . . . a double-decker bus was overtaken, hesitated then drew ahead, and the long station slid slowly past his window. On the platform a farmer waited solidly with baskets of chickens, twice himself in coats and wellingtons.

He had sent a telegram only that morning, forgetting to do so the previous day. It was his own fault that nobody waited to greet him. He carried his suitcase out of the station and along the dripping main street, looking for someone to direct him to a bus. Then he felt his arm grabbed.

'Ernie, it's you!'

He turned to stare into a young woman's face and tried to recognize it as Susan.

'Ernie, don't you know me?'

And far back he felt a thud of disappointment.

'Yes,' he said wonderingly. 'Of course I remember you.'

And began the long search back through boyhood to establish

the girl of the cantonment. Blue eyes. Brown golden hair, and soft mouth. And then he carried the picture back to the present and identification hovered at the surprised edges of his memory.

She said something as a bus moved away from the kerb, and he watched her mouth moving. She wore a brown raincoat unbuttoned over a tweed frock. They stood in the middle of the narrow pavement as shopping bags nudged them.

'Come on,' she said again. 'Robert's at the station. We went for petrol and missed you.'

With his suitcase under one arm, Susan in the other, he stumbled back up the narrow street to the station. He stole furtive glances at her long hair, the disconcerting bosom under the raincoat. He found only a mature and confident young woman; but then memory reasserted itself in a rush, and he saw it happening to her as well. She said: 'Oh Ernie, it's such fun to see you,' and the childish eyes peeped out from behind the confident smile.

Robert called from the station yard; a Bedford utility was parked against the wooden building.

'You travel faster than your telegrams. We came straight down.'

Ernie sat between Robert and his sister; they turned out of the yard with a noise of wet gravel and began to climb uphill away from the town.

'We've hidden all the books in the house,' Robert threatened. 'The ones on economics are buried six foot deep. So you'll enjoy your holiday, like it or not.'

He enjoyed this banter, for it would remind Susan how hard working he was. A moment later he dared to catch sight of her eyes and she smiled and turned her head to the window.

They travelled uphill for a mile, then turned down a narrower road where woods of holly and oak pressed in against the road's high earth banks. A tall drystone wall cut firmly through the woods towards the road, then turned alongside so that the car was in its shadow for the next five minutes.

'This is the edge of our place,' Robert said. 'On the other side of that wall.'

'All of it?' Ernie asked, amazed.

'Yes. But it's all mortgaged and leased out and so on. It's ours like a company belongs to its biggest shareholder.'

They came to a pair of lonely gateposts ('We sold the gates,' Robert said) and turned in between them. Ernie had a swift view of a large house at the end of a drive before a clump of rhododendron hid it from view.

'It was built about three hundred years ago,' Robert said. 'But about the only part left is the plumbing. It's had bits added on at all the wrong periods.' He tried to speak casually, but could not keep a sort of pride out of his voice.

Behind the house was a kitchen garden, and then sloping grass fields leading down to woods.

'We go shooting there,' Robert said. 'It is ours, actually, but we rent it out. We even rent ourselves out. I worked on one of the tenant farms last vac.'

'It is all very beautiful,' Ernie said. He was still overcome at the size and richness of it. They had never spoken about this; he had expected a nice house and perhaps a few acres. But they were rich; Robert and Susan and Rowena had grown up in a background incredibly beyond his expectation.

'You never told me,' he said.

'What? About the shooting?'

'That you were rich.'

'It's not the sort of thing one talks about,' Robert said with a touch of severity. 'And anyway, we're not rich as you call it.'

And he thought again of the children in the cantonment, football on the 'green', the shabby bike on which Susan had accompanied him on their rides beside the canals. It was as if they had always deceived him, and even the Major's house in the cantonment must have oppressed them with its smallness.

And now he felt an excitement in their company, an extra pleasure in their acceptance of him. He had been enjoying Susan's warmth pressed against his left side and was disappointed now that the ride was over. Once his hand had touched hers and she had not shifted it away; their fingers had lain together like an embrace.

There was a servant woman to carry his suitcase; and Mrs King waited at the top of the steps.

She had not changed at all. He looked for signs of widowhood in her face but found nothing. Perhaps she was a little calmer, that was all.

'Ernest, my dear boy. How beautiful you have grown! And you're doing so well at university, I'm very proud of you. Robert, ring Elma for tea. I'm going to have him all to myself for the first hour.'

But Mrs King went to bed early, and that evening in the firelight of the library, the only part of the house to match his first impression with its Meshed carpet and dignified rows of books, he talked to Robert and the girls till midnight. It was wonderful to be sitting opposite them again, reminding each other of happiness and catching up with the news of years; yet he could not shake off a feeling of oddness. It was a shock to realize that, to the girls, he was a curiosity. They wanted to hear about events in Delhi; who was living in their house now, had they built the new swimming pool yet? When they did talk of his work at university it was with a sort of slanted curiosity that made him feel like a conjuror performing a trick against odds, instead of a genuine student. Robert could chat about his rugger and his parties, but Ernie was permitted to be only a student from abroad. Even while talking of his home they asked not about his father but about Gandhi.

'Have you ever seen him?' Susan asked. She collected information from him like a jackdaw grabbing interesting but unrelated objects.

'Have you actually seen him?'

'Yes.' He was guarded; he didn't want to spoil anything, before he knew her well enough. And anyway, how unimportant it all seemed now, his relationship with Congress like an old friend who no longer bothers to write. It had flattered him once; and Congress was in the right, of course, but he had his own life to live. Oxford was expanding his ambition beyond a lifetime in the Indian civil service.

'But why,' Susan demanded, 'didn't they help us in the war?'

Strangely, it was only since his time in England that he had become ashamed of that part of Gandhi's policy. It had seemed right; they were fighting for themselves, not a Government that could turn on them afterwards.

He said cautiously, and a little shyly: 'It is a very complicated matter. It is not always easy to decide between one action or the other.'

'But it was the Germans,' Susan said. 'Surely they could see it was right to fight the Germans.'

'Well, the Germans did bad things, of course. But I expect they think we did bad things. Perhaps—'

'We?' asked Robert.

'Yes. I mean—the English.'

'Oh, I see.'

'But no,' said Rowena.

She had been quiet (and now he remembered she always had been) but her passionate tone reminded him of her strong personality.

'You cannot be so woolly about principles,' she said. And then stopped suddenly as if talking was forbidden.

'Yes?'

She seemed unwilling to expose herself. But: 'It's just that the apologists make me angry,' she said. 'Already you can hear people say they were forced into the war, that Germany was a poor little victim.'

He felt on firmer ground with Rowena. 'You can't look at these things in isolation,' he said smoothly. 'The economic situation in the thirties—'

'Oh, stop trying to be so cold-blooded. You're not cold-blooded at all, it doesn't suit you. Just because you're studying politics. But politics excuses nothing, it doesn't explain torture and genocide and if the world ever forgives them or pretends it didn't happen then it's gone just as mad as they are.'

'Rowena's very passionate about people, and cruelty,' Robert said, into the sudden quietness.

'And just because it did not affect you personally—'

'I'm sorry,' Ernie said inadequately, and remembered with awkward sadness what he had been told of their father's death.

Robert said: 'Yes, we're getting too heated, what about a drink for us all.' But because Rowena was normally calm her emotional words now hung in the air like an uncomfortable echo. It jarred him because his own confidence about things had surrendered so recently to the rules of logic and investigation, and he was still groping among all the theories for a point of view. He remembered one of his tutorials with Aiken, half-way through the term, when he had been greeted by a bellow as he approached the door.

'Come in, O Thou of the mysterious East!'

He had hesitated with his hand on the door. What on earth was Aiken doing?

'Ah,' said Aiken as he entered. 'There you are, you lazy wog. Have you been consulting your horoscope to see if your wife will commit sati?'

He flushed angrily. 'What—?'

'But I see a goad in your skinny hand, you've just returned from a tiger-shoot on your diamond-encrusted elephant.'

He had a quick intuition of what Aiken was doing; but fear of ridicule showed on his face like pain.

'What's the matter? Isn't that an *accurate* description of you. Have I perhaps listened only to the popular *clichés*.'

Aiken was a short, soft man with an unmemorable face, and a personality blurred at the edges. His voice was a shade high-pitched and he tried to compensate by mentally underlining too many words.

'No, it's not accurate,' Ernie said coldly. 'Can't you just tell me what's wrong? Is it my essay on the causes of communism?'

'Now why should you think that?' Aiken said. 'You use all the proper arguments from the *Communist Manifesto. The German Ideology, Das Kapital*—and I detected three barely-concealed quotations from *The Condition of the Working Class in England.*'

'It's all relevant,' Ernie muttered; 'the causes are still the same today.' But he knew Aiken had got him.

His tutor was flicking through the pages. 'Under-privileged masses . . . imperialist lackeys. Incidentally, do you know what a lackey is?'

'It's . . . someone who opens carriage doors.'

Aiken looked at him. 'Do you know even what *communism* is?

Ernie shrugged. 'It's a bit complicated actually to sum it up.'

'Precisely,' Aiken said. It was somehow an incongruous word for him to use; he was such an imprecise person himself.

'Precisely,' he said again, and thus, the repetition of the sound weakening its effect, restored his own personality to the word.

'You could perhaps define it in Russia as Marxist socialism, where possessions are owned not *personally* but *collectively*. But would that do for China? I foresee a very different type of communism arising there because they're very different *people*. The Russian revolution was an *intellectual* one, that's what so many people disregard. It all means you must not put labels on things and thereby pretend you have defined them. You know what I mean by *labels*—Trotskyist, revisionist, capitalist. They are designed, not to im*part* information but to con*fuse*, to stop you thinking. And, by God, they have.

'I want you to write that essay again. And I'm making a list of words you are not to use. And for Christ's sake don't put anything in like that again.'

'Then please tell me some of the points I should make.'

'No fear,' Aiken said. 'I'm not paid to *work*. I don't give answers, only ask questions. And my question for you this week is, can you describe the causes of communism without mugging up your Engels. Think of your own country, Ernie. Describe it as *you* see it.'

He had complained to Robert that Aiken wasn't positive enough. He had been disturbed, on receiving back his first essay, to find not a mark on it. It was perfect, then? But after the half-hour tutorial with Aiken he came away knowing it had been an uninspired piece of work.

What he wanted were the pencilled annotations: '1863, not 1864. . . .' 'No, this is wrong, re-read pages 188-209 of *The Economics of Socialism*. . . .' and perhaps the occasional 'A very good paragraph.' He wanted to measure his progress against recognizable data, like a horse jumping fences. But Aiken would never tell him he was *wrong*. An ill-scrawled 'But don't you think governments try to suppress politics?' was the closest he had ever got to a positive statement.

Now he was learning Aiken's quiet wisdom and he tried to use it on Rowena as if it were his own. It was like buying a new suit and becoming rather ashamed of the old one; he donned the new suit now with a disregard for the thought that he had ever worn anything else.

'You cannot be so definite about things,' he said to Rowena. 'In political science there are no rights and wrongs and there are few clearly defined problems. It is a science of observation rather than accomplishment.'

'Well, keep watching,' Rowena said warmly, 'and in another ten years or so you'll be able to exercise your talents again.'

Then Robert stood up and put a hand on Rowena's shoulder. Immediately she turned and smiled, and touched him back, and there was no anger in her eyes as she said to Ernie: 'We must talk more about this, if you like, but not until I'm in a politer mood.'

Then Susan stood up and kissed Robert's cheek, which gave Ernie an unreasonable moment of jealousy.

'It's terribly late. Who's coming riding tomorrow? Ernie, will you?'

'You have horses?'

'Three. But Robert and Rowena enjoy their beds too much. I go by myself every morning.'

'I haven't ridden for a long time,' he said.

'You'd better be early,' she warned him. 'I don't wait for anyone.'

On the third morning they changed their normal route. The rain had dried and a new snow lay like dust on the purple rows of winter cabbage. On the far side of the frosty fields was a thicket a few yards deep, and then a narrow lane on which they could trot, ducking often to avoid the low branches.

He had not noticed, before riding with Susan, that it was an uncompanionable occupation. Moving behind or ahead of her there were few chances for speech, and silence lay on him like a burden. But on the return journey they walked their horses side by side through fields he had not seen before. He noticed a greenhouse standing in a curve of the river a half-mile away and immediately said: 'That's the greenhouse you told me about . . . in your letters.'

'Which letter?' she asked.

He was about to tell her, when she said distantly, 'That's Rowena's greenhouse,' and rode on.

He was disappointed, but did not pursue her meaning, and the unasked question slipped forward into the future. He wondered how much she did remember, and how much of her feeling for him was lost in their Indian childhood. So much of early life is uncertainty and despair . . . and one of the few memories he carried of her afterwards, like pictures in a wallet, was of himself creeping from bed an hour too soon on the morning of their first ride, afraid to miss the beginning of something that had ended at his birth.

Mountains

The six shots re-echoed in his brain as the strength-giving anger drained out in despair. The next table at Baramula, a rifle-shot away at Sopur: when Robert was closest he was most unattainable; and now he was only a hundred yards away, bouncing on two slow mules. But in the time Ernie could have turned to his horse he sank down instead to the ground, in slow submission to his hurt.

The pain of Robert's fist throbbed in his neck as he thought back to the notice on the tree, trying to recall the words: 'I shall be waiting for you . . . I won't be armed. . . .' No, Robert had not actually said he was giving himself up but . . . he had always been clever like that, setting decoys, leading his attackers into their own fire.

It was very hot, even under the trees, and without standing he struggled out of his jacket. There was water in the panniers, and when the strength returned to his legs he went to wash his face and splash water down inside his shirt. His body was covered in a fine grey dust even inside his clothes and boots, and the water ran down his skin in grimy trickles.

Then he sat down again and watched a leg muscle moving to and fro in nervous tension like a horse refusing a jump.

Ever since their childhood Robert had fed on scenes like this: the banyan tree, for instance; the gentle bullying of his mother and sisters, always with those he loved as if love was measurable only by its degree of submission.

It didn't matter, he decided after long thought, that Robert had fooled him again, for he was only delaying what was inevitable. He had to be off his guard at some time and the advantage always lies with the hunter. He would be coming from behind, choosing his moment; even Robert had to sleep.

The clearing was hot as he crossed it. He had thought of going back to water the horses in the stream, it was only a few hundred yards behind him. But he couldn't risk it, Robert was already racing ahead and his mules were slower only in easy country. In the steep hills and the snow the horses would be at a disadvantage; he might even have to abandon them. He could not afford to play a waiting game.

As he passed into the trees he felt a small but instant drop in temperature. He pressed on quickly; the belt of trees was only a narrow one. He could not afford to have Robert for long out of sight.

He came out into the sunlight and yes! there was Robert, far up the slope among the boulders, goading his mules from behind. For a second he thought of concealment until Robert had crossed the skyline. But then he followed, letting the horses pick their course until the slope increased and he had to dismount.

He had shot at Robert, meaning to kill. His anger returned, reversed on himself : he should have immediately mounted his horse and chased after Robert and run him down. Now Robert was disappearing over the hilltop, the few seconds advantage multiplied a thousand times. But the trick would not work twice; to throw the spear is to disarm the thrower.

He had to stop and rest many times on the hill and at the top he had a nasty shock. Unfamiliar with mountains, he had expected a general, continuous rise to the peak, as it had seemed from the other side of the river. But now he saw a downhill stretch of scrub and boulders, another incline, and beyond it another and another . . . shoulders of loose shale reared in his path and spiky bushes spread their carpet in stretches a thousand yards wide. He was sweating hot; the dirt covered him like a second skin and it became a conscious effort to take each succeeding step, as if his will were situated in the base of each aching thigh. The snow peaks were ever as distant as before, on another plane in the sky . . . and during the rest of that day he could feel, stumbling over the mountains behind, drawing over him like a cloud's chill shadow, an awareness of what he had taken on.

That night he camped in an exposed position on a hilltop, constantly reawakened by the noise of the horses circling each other for the lee of the wind from the snowfields. The dark had overtaken him with surprising swiftness. With the daylight still lingering in the air like a fireglow he had been tempted to carry on, but then all the light had suddenly drained away down the sky and without time to find a good place he was groping in the dark for food and blankets.

It was so cold the next morning that his limbs lay stiff in the sleeping bag. He had to go for a run to thaw out, stumbling among the stones and small bushes, and when he returned he noticed both the horses were coughing. He had forgotten to rub them down the night before, that would be part of the reason. A small thing, but the mountain conditions magnified the offence.

He looked for smoke from Robert's camp but it would have been obscured by the mist drawing up all the valleys as the sun's first rays struck through to the ground. On waking he had been able to look across the top of the mist to the neighbouring hilltops in a clear dawn light, but now he stood enveloped in the fog and not till mid-morning did he see the hills again.

Three hours after starting he came upon a small stream flowing from right to left across his path. Deodars and spruces straggled along its banks and flatter open country lay upstream. He could not see an obvious way to advance; the mud at the water's edge showed no revealing prints. Faced with a decision, another layer of doubt settled slowly upon his shoulders. He had been travelling by compass direction since the early morning; without Robert in sight there was not much else to do. It was guesswork but the map was almost useless in the tiny scale of reality. A single contour indicated the hill he had taken half a day to cross; the hundred-foot gullies, the broken scree patches which the horses would not walk on, were not marked at all. The obstacles ahead were unguessable, and without Robert as his guide. . . .

But Robert knew these mountains and could well have started in quite a different direction that morning. With a degree or so off course, an inch or two on his little map . . . a mountain could already separate them.

If he didn't find a sign, footprints or a cooking-fire's remains, he would go back to Khadzil. . . .

He splashed through the water and searched downstream first, but began to feel helpless before he had gone half a mile. It wasn't like searching a road or path, for a vehicle that could not leave it. The stream twisted haphazardly, thick reeds clogged the banks, the low branches turned him perhaps one way instead of another. Even a small rock presented a decision, to pass it on the left or right. The alternatives doubled and doubled while the evidence might have been passed a half-hour back, hidden by ten yards of grass.

He forded the stream and began to work his way back, already resigned to the humiliating return to the silkworm breeder. At least he had tried; there was no dishonour in being beaten.

A shadow flicked across him and the golden sand, and looking up he saw a circling hawk a great distance off. With an abject cynicism he allowed his vision to shift so that it was there, in the bird, looking down at the tiny speck of himself in the vastness.

At least Robert knew he had tried. He had challenged the mountains on equal terms and Robert could never claim that he had funked it.

Back at the starting point he saw a movement in one of the trees on the bank upstream. He would have noticed it before if he had looked from this spot, a few feet higher than where he had stood before. All the trees were stirring in the slight

breeze and his gaze had brushed past and across the river
before a reminder of the movement's shape, a difference,
brought him back to this particular tree and the thing hanging from one of its branches on a cord. . . .

It was the remaining portion of the *Rawalpindi Times*,
bunched into a ball, swinging from a low branch and pointing
the way to the temple and Pakistan.

He nearly felt the sickness upon him, fury without release.
Robert would never have cheated and that was the angriest
thing of all. He had to follow the sign because it told the truth;
Robert had not crossed the river, he had travelled up the right-
hand bank, into open country. With a sad fury he obeyed.

The next sign lay in the mud two hours journey upstream.
A line of white stones in the shape of an arrow pointed to the
high ground above the water. A fluttering white handkerchief
on a stick underlined the message, and the fact.

The river bank ran sheer at that point, the slope of the
ground carrying him away from the water's edge. It would
have been a choice between the high ground and crossing to
the opposite bank, if Robert had left him a choice.

For another three hours into the afternoon he followed the
stream on steadily rising land. Robert would not be leading
him into a trap; the Englishman had mastery all along the
line, and needed only to leave him alone. No, his motives were
more complex, as always. It was a challenge, and a punishment; the carrot dancing before his nose.

But humiliation is a devaluing currency: the wave from the
hillside, the buying-up of the mules in Khadzil, the game of
surrender in the burnt glade of the forest, and now the
insolent token of aid. . . . Now it had started it had to continue until Robert was overreaching himself, inviting danger,
his own hand steadying the rifle as it fired.

The land bent upwards and he was moving into hills again.
An hour later the stream turned away through a grove of

juniper and ahead of him across a grassy incline was the vast
stretch of pine forest he had viewed from the escarpment the
day before. It hung across his vision like a thick green curtain,
rearing up and back into the anonymity of the midday haze.
Here and there the forest was broken by an area of sandy
rock, and an occasional burned area appeared as patches in the
curtain.

But at his feet was a circle of stones; in the centre an empty
butter tin. From the tin Ernie took a sheet of notepaper and
smoothed it out. Robert apparently caught up with his corres-
pondence on these trips; the message was written with a
fountain pen and without much difficulty he could picture
Robert deliberately filling the pen from a new bottle of ink,
screwing the cap on carefully before settling down to write
in his neat, feminine hand: 'From this point you must go
directly S up through the trees, about 12 hours climb. Thereafter the temple is roughly S by W, but the direct route is
impossible, you must work round just above the treeline. Good
luck.'

It would all be repaid. He stared with tired and dusky eyes
at the neatly-written message and remembered the banyan
tree and the flight from Turley, Wilts. Whenever his cup of
hate ran low he could trust Robert to refill it.

He could actually smell the difference as he approached the
vast area of green vegetation. The forest grew like a plantation within its self-defined boundaries. The light brown dusty
ground inclined steadily and then disappeared behind a wall
of timber. He moved forward against the edifice, and just as
he was about to step into the forest he glanced up and saw
the snowfields, near at last, hanging like clouds beyond the
trees.

Once into the forest it was not so thick as he had feared.
The trees stood yards apart amidst the columns of sunlight. It
was the ground's inclination that gave the appearance of
density, for it reared up always a few feet before his eyes and
he had to tilt his head back to look up and towards the light.

Generations of decomposition covered the broken rocks, almost smoothing the ground, like one fresh sheet laid over a rumpled bed. Compass always in hand, he struggled to maintain a course directly south. The ground was too steep for the horses; he was on his feet again and he could hear the two animals panting and bumping their heads in the gloom.

For seven hours, until dark, he toiled up the steep slope between the trees, on the brown pine needle floor of the forest. He adopted a rhythm of climbing for half an hour, then resting five minutes, and climbing again. Without that rhythm repeating in his brain he was sure he could not have done it; his body could not have managed the climb alone.

At dusk he fed the horses, washed them down with bunches of damp grass, and covered them against the chilly air. He was so hungry and so exhausted that he watched his behaviour curiously, like a third person, to observe which desire would overcome the other.

He crawled into the sleeping bag with stale chapatti in one hand and an apple in the other, and woke long after sunrise still holding them in his hands like an offering to the dawn.

Half an hour of pain, five minutes' rest; then another half-hour. Afterwards that was all he could remember of the climb, the rhythm of effort, thirty minutes and five, that seemed to take hold of his body throughout the day and force it along with its own momentum. At first he felt pain in his body and had to fight against it, but later his sensibility to pain was too dulled to respond with more than an observer's interest. So that when evening began to spread across the hill he was almost reluctant to stop, for it spared his body nothing.

Then he did feel the pain in his thighs, stiffening his muscles so that they felt like spears breaking through the skin. He noticed that the sweat had chilled on his forehead; the horses were pumping clouds of frosty air from their nostrils. He knew he must eat, and he lit a fire to heat a can of beans and eat the last of the chapatti which tasted like strips of thin leather. For the horses he spilled a bag of oats on the ground;

then he drew off his shoes and lay the sleeping bag on the groundsheet and crawled down to a dark oblivion. At the last moment of awareness he remembered the horses, he had not rubbed them down or put on their blankets. . . . He carried the thought like a burden into his sleep.

In the morning only the packhorse stood by him. When he went to look for the bay he found it forty yards off, lying with head downhill. A cold dew clung to the ruddy coat and flies were already stitching a delicate pattern in the air around its muzzle.

Warm now, with the sun touching his face, it was impossible to remember the fear of last night.

He transferred the saddle to the packhorse, and made up a meal of hard-boiled eggs and chocolate. There wasn't much else; that was another concern which when considered in relation to all the others, did not matter so much. There was no excuse for his behaviour. He had satisfied his own needs and now a horse lay dead.

He moved up the hillside, nursing the areas of pain. Almost at once the first grey patches of snow started to appear in shaded places. They were few at first, with acres between, but after an hour they lay like long grey sheets between the trees. When he trod over them they felt as hard as the rocks; having lasted so long they would now remain unthawed till next winter. It seemed to grow colder every minute. He stopped to put on all the clothes he had.

At ten o'clock he was suddenly clear of the trees. They finished as abruptly as they had begun. He saw gaps of light ahead—only minutes later he walked out from the forest edge into long bare slopes of melting snow. The mud sucked at his boots as he turned to look at the entire length of the forest stretching away on either hand, as if the first line of trees were a fence to hold them back.

This was the edge of India.

He set his map to the compass and started up the melting slopes in the direction of south by west. The clear light before his eyes, the loosening of the constriction of trees, seemed to give him air to breathe again, space for action within the thought . . . Ernie Maher of the Calcutta office, grade two officer at the ministry, standing in the hills of Kashmir. His identity re-established itself in the body tautened with pain: he had climbed a mountain. He had climbed a mountain.

A sheet of paper crackled in his pocket and he took it out into the light: '. . . the temple is roughly S by W but the direct route is impossible, you must work round just above the treeline.' And then the mocking salutation, Robert grinning up through the words; and back on the hillside the bay mare lying under a shroud of ants.

The snow slopes before him travelled on and up until his eyes strained at the grey glare. Away on his left the wall of green-black pines arced round the lie of the hill like a contour, the carpet of snow turning from white to grey in the melting patches. He began to trudge along the perimeter of the trees, pulling the horse behind him, the mud sucking at all their feet.

An area of soft, powdered snow lying above the mud caused him to turn into the trees and he moved along fifty yards inside their shelter, the horse stumbling among the juniper roots. A thin rain began to fall and a white mist drifted through the pine boles, turning them black and wet.

Once he gasped as his foot sank almost to the knee and a root tore at his leg as he pulled it out. He stumbled forward again, pulling the dragging horse hard, and heard a loud crack. The rein went like a steel bar in his hands and he turned to see the horse flopping like a fish on a line with its leg trapped far down in the mud. Then the horse screamed and he knew what the crack must have been.

The screams drove him far into the trees, running for shelter. A huge strong animal screaming with pain, it was worse than a leopard's howl. He ran back sobbing, tugging at his pistol, wanting only to stop the noise. He fired blindly and hit it somewhere unnecessary. Then he steadied himself

and the pistol and fired at its head and then a last time as if to
stifle even the groans of slow dying.

Now there was peace and death. He could turn the gun on
himself for all the chance he had now.

He began to cry . . . as involuntary as the horse's screams,
the snow's whiteness. The horse lay on the pine needles,
visibly shrunken, the foreleg reaching down at a strange angle
into the mud. Nothing lasted long—a horse, a friend; he
thought of the Sikhs who had offered him something he had
never known, and he had rejected their company for a reason
he could not even remember.

He hadn't known, while it was alive, that the horse was
his friend. The mist dripped from the trees in silence and the
wind moved quietly on the surface of the snow.

It was a thought he could not entertain: there was absolutely nothing now that he could do.

Or just one thing: he could make a fire. It did not get him
anywhere, but he could make a fire.

The ground was wet, but he could break off dry branches
from the trees. Some of his matches were damp and the
sulphur flaked off on his boot. When a match finally caught
he had no paper ready and he had to let it burn out again.
He got the fire going at last, sat and watched the smoke
drifting through the trees, sat and remembered the Sikhs, and
the Pathan on the road, and the water bubbling in Mahbub
Ali's pipe.

The fire burned low as he sat hunched over its presence. He
must move away and fetch more fuel if he wanted the fire
kept in, if there were any point. . . .

A horse's leg broke out in the snowfields, or a rifle shot . . .
there followed the noise of a tree falling, and that would be
the echo banging between all the hills.

He was on his feet, and stood rigid as the echoes rolled away
into the valley. That had been a rifle shot and it could
mean—it could only mean—that Robert had signalled to
him.

Another decision awaiting. How lucky those people whose lives were circumscribed from birth towards success or disaster. He had to bear the burden of choice each time, the long train of alternatives stretching away down roads of endless terror or pain. Even now: retreat or advance? And then the next pair of imponderables: retreat, how? advance to what, and why?

He stirred the fire to life with his foot and put on more fuel, to help him find the way back; and then he knew he was going.

The white smoke had drifted far from the fire, hanging low to the ground, and mist was dripping from the wet boughs. He moved through it, body aching, into another area of whiteness where the snow inclined away to the sky. He paused to get his bearings, to think himself back to the fire and remember the direction of the rifle shot, then moved tiredly up the hill, his feet sinking in soft powder. Grey sky, white snow . . . and away up the hill a black spot like a pinprick in the white sheet. He narrowed his eyes, bringing the spot into focus. It grew larger quickly; it had been only a few hundred yards away, he was losing his sense of direction and distance. As he drew close, as the shape assumed substance, he cursed Robert with tears on his face, and for the first time felt afraid of the man who, after the banyan tree, after Islamabad, after Wiltshire and Sopur and the glade in the burned forest, was once again offering him the awful burden of a release he had not the courage to take.

He had never ridden a mule. It looked a lesser animal than a horse, with its lopsided face and thickness in the wrong parts of the body, chewing slowly at its tether as if savouring the taste. When Ernie put his hand on the bridle it laid back its ears and stared from a flat, dark eye.

He had to return for the panniers but he was weaker than he had realized; he could manage only one at a time. When he

returned from the second journey the mule had already tried
the taste of the first, the canvas was teethmarked and damp.
The mule shifted grumpily as he tied on the panniers; it
sneered and farted and dilated its belly against the saddle
straps. It would not move until he returned to the forest a
third time for a stick to goad it. Each time he went back he
had to move close to the horse. Its dead eyes reflected the fire,
and the woodsmoke glowed in the columns of sunlight.

Had Robert meant him to go back? It seemed almost certain,
and yet . . . he must be close, very close; he must have heard
Ernie shooting his horse, returned to see, gone back to stake
out the mule like a leopard's decoy. Would he have gone without saying goodbye?

It remained a question. He did not know Robert's mind; he
realized now that he never had known, that in the moments
of closest intimacy or clearest understanding it had been only
the relationship of the wolf and its keeper.

When the mule finally started he had to cling to its tail to
keep up. It waded powerfully through the soft snowdrifts,
stepping over the rocks like a dancer. He was tempted to
mount but he was not going to waste another chance. He was
back in the race again : he was rested and fed and Robert was
only a half-hour ahead.

It made no difference to his triumph that Robert had aided
him in the chase. It was all part of the game which Robert
understood very well. The help was like a gift of poisoned
meat; it was for his enemy's benefit, not his own. If Robert
lost the game by giving away the wrong sort of trick, then he
had underestimated his opponent.

The mule scaled the hillside as if a meal were waiting on
top. A warm wind was blowing across the slope and every few
minutes they splashed through melting snow. A fresh bright
grass grew in the clear places, and twice he found a pale blue
flower poking up through the mud. They were moving up and
round the mountain. After an hour of climbing they reached
the hard snow on the north face where the sun did not reach,

where the snow never had time to thaw before the next winter gripped the earth. What perverse desire was it of Robert's to lead him on, to tempt him either way? He was too tired to think; pain dulled the edge of his senses and he moved through dark periods of incoherent thought and woke to the hard glare of the passing snow.

He was searching for footprints, and the black shape of Robert's mule in the snow ahead. Would Robert still be making for the temple? It was only six hours away, he would be there by sunset, they could both be there. Beyond that he did not think.

He moved on for another two hours round the mountain. Then the last turn of all round the slopes brought him out, facing the sunlight, facing south to Uri forty miles away on the Jhelum river. As the crow flies, he was very near Baramula and Inspector Mokerjee; he looked forward to telling the stupid babu that the arms entered Kashmir not through Tibet, but a few miles from his office.

The ground was treacherous with pools of icy water; sometimes his feet slid in mud, and a moment later he was floundering in knee-deep powder snow. Then a sheltered place would be hard with ice. Here and there large black rocks stood up from the level whiteness; one of them appeared to be moving. . . . Joy and fear gripped with simultaneous hands as he saw it was the mule.

But there was something strange. It stood a hundred yards away; the reins swinging from its neck like Robert's binoculars. There was nothing else, no sign of Robert. It could be a trap. . . . At last he moved cautiously forward.

Beyond where the mule stood, the ground fell steeply away into a rocky gulley. Fresh grass lay gleaming and flattened on its brim, not yet arisen from the months-long snow burden that had, in the last hour, slid to the bottom of the slope. The black shapes of rocks lay exposed by the avalanche and beside one of them lay Robert, his karakul knocked awry, one side of his head darkened with a heavy, purplish bruise. His face wore a look of angry surprise that he should be frustrated by a snowslide at the eleventh hour.

More snow tumbled wetly from the gulley's brink and Ernie started down in guilty triumph.

He had seen, in films, an unconscious man carried easily across a saddle, weight distributed either side of the horse's back as it galloped along. It had looked very simple and obvious, but it took Ernie half an hour even to lift Robert on to the mule's back. Then the inert body kept sliding off one side or the other. He had no rope. He improvised as he went along; his first idea was to wedge both feet into one of the panniers, pulling the drawstring tight over the ankles. He tied a blanket across Robert's shoulders and under the mule's neck, fastening it in a large knot which kept working loose. Movement of walking caused the body constantly to slide off and he steadied it with his shoulder as he walked and stumbled at the mule's side. He had had to fasten the reins of the second mule to the front mule's saddle so that they walked too close together and kept turning to bite and quarrel.

The temple stood like another black rock in the wilderness. Snow lay a foot deep on the roof but, looking up the slope, he spied the black shape of the square stone walls.

A half-hour later he was inside. It was very small, perhaps enough for twenty men to kneel close together. Square on three sides, the fourth wall curved round a stone plinth which must have contained the receptacle for the Hair. A piece of rotted, colourless fabric still hung on the plinth. Two incongruous petrol tins stood rusty in one corner. A fire had been lit in the room within the last few months; there were charred pieces of wood and smoke-blackened bricks torn from the temple wall. Scattered droppings of goats' dung covered the earth floor.

He brought the two mules in with him, squeezing their ribs through the narrow opening. With his last strength he dragged Robert in by the lapels of his coat and pushed him into his sleeping bag. He could not light a fire for there was no wood, but he found candles in Robert's coat pocket and lit them against the encroaching gloom. Outside the rain had started to fall into the silent snow.

He broke off the top of the petrol tins and filled them with snow. When it had melted the mules drank from one and he scooped with his hand from the other, wincing at the cold on his teeth. He had no more food of his own, but Robert's bags were well stocked and he ate hungrily of onions and peppers and chocolate. Robert's wound was weeping; the broken purple lump looked terrible, and his fingers were stiff and cold. He had heard how people could die from cold even in half an hour. It was icy in the temple even though he had stuffed the doorway with one of the saddlebags, and the mules were blowing their breathy warmth against the walls. He pushed down into Robert's sleeping bag all the clothes he could find, and wrapped a jersey round his head like a balaclava. Then he blew out the candle, lay staring through the doorway, and after some minutes the stars twinkled out through gaps in the rain. . . .

Much later a noise brought him instantly awake. It was three o'clock by the luminous dial of his watch. He lit the candle and saw Robert struggling feebly to pull the jersey from his head. The candle-flame trembled in the space between their eyes. A subdued wonder replaced the anxiety in Robert's face, and then he slowly lay back again, and as his eyes closed Ernie joined him on the pillow.

In the morning Robert was already awake. He gave Ernie a small grin and muttered that his head ached. The sky seen through the doorway was bright and grey, suspended between rainstorms.

'Can you walk a few hundred yards?'

Ernie said: 'Why, is there wood?'

'They planted pine groves to mark the road to the temple. The first one is about half a mile down.'

'It's been raining all night.'

'If you pull branches off the trees,' Robert said, 'I think they should be dry enough.'

Outside the stiff wind was whipping off the top layer of snow and carrying it at knee-height across the slopes. Dark wraiths of cloud drifted low over his head, but in isolated patches he could see beneath the clouds far down the valleys, spurs of whitened rocks to the west and darker patches of vegetation down towards the Jhelum. He took the only rifle with him, Robert having lost his in the fall.

The pine grove stood like an oasis in the white desert. He gathered as much wood as he could carry, and with a few rests returned to the temple and lit a small fire in the doorway. Working quickly, for the wood would not last long, he fried strips of eggfruit and heated a tin of beans. He knew his way about Robert's kit pretty well by now. He brewed coffee and filled one of the rusty petrol cans; it was cold within minutes, but it would at least be tastier than snow water to drink during the day.

Robert watched the preparations without comment, and after wolfing the breakfast lay back again exhausted. Ernie bathed and dressed the wound without disturbing his sleep.

He woke again in the mid-afternoon looking much recovered. Ernie warmed the coffee with the last of the wood, and Robert smiled broadly as he took the cup.

'This is a funny business.'

Ernie didn't answer, and Robert said: 'I'm a gunrunner and you're the law.'

He drank the coffee in a few long swallows and handed back the cup. 'It's a stupid, dangerous life,' he said. 'And yet, if you were to ask me why I do it, I don't think I have one good reason.'

'You like it.'

'No, you're wrong. Oh, it's healthy, outdoor work, etcetera. But I'm not just a bunch of muscles.' He pressed his hand to the bandage and held it there as if trying to draw out pain.

'What you do has always been a mystery,' Ernie told him. 'But why are we talking? I'm not interested any more. . . .'

Robert stared into his refilled cup as if an answer lay somewhere in its depths.

'The motives for what we do are often hidden. Or they're hidden from every angle except one.' Before Ernie could say anything he went on: 'Did you ever hear about a boy called Jack Cornwell?'

'No.'

'Well, he was a gunner at the battle of Jutland. He was sixteen or something. He earned the Victoria Cross for sticking to his gun when the rest of the crew was dead.'

'Why are we talking about the battle of Jutland?'

'We have to talk about something, don't we? There's a long afternoon ahead and there's not much entertainment up here. You know, this boy went on firing blindly long after all his mates were dead. He was injured himself, fatally. Silly, wasn't it. He didn't really make any difference to the battle. They didn't give him his gong for what he did, but for what he was. It was unnecessary, but it was magnificent.'

'And—?'

'And,' Robert interrupted, but then resumed his solemn flow. 'Who is to say how many other large and small battles he might have won? If a boy stuck it then you have to stick it don't you? Perhaps in the next battle a dozen men thought of Jack Cornwell when they were tempted to give up.'

'Are you identifying yourself with him?'

'No,' Robert said shortly. He looked closely at Ernie and said: 'You came after me for revenge, didn't you?'

'I was ordered—'

'You wanted my humiliation. But if you had just used your eyes . . . perhaps to observe this sort of thing is really more to the point than being the cause of it.'

'If you don't like what you're doing,' Ernie said, 'then you should be doing something else. But I thought you enjoyed it.

You're arming the villagers and making arsenals for the next war's infiltrators. You believe in it, you have said so.'

'But the next war will be a bigger one. They always are. Next time the Pakistani Army will come in and what difference do you think my few rifles will make?'

'I don't know,' he said with sudden sympathy. 'Propaganda, I suppose.'

'Yes, that's it, more or less. It lets the people know they are not forgotten. It makes them feel involved, and when the army comes it will not be fighting its way through hostile territory.'

'I can see the sense in that.'

'Have you noticed something?'

'What is that?'

'We're talking to each other.'

Outside the dusk had crept up the hill and now squatted near the door, peering in at the disorder of panniers, cooking pots, the rusty tin of coffee standing on the plinth. The walls were damp from the condensation of their breath, and it had turned suddenly very cold; they spoke softly as if only just aware they were inside a church.

'This, what you are doing . . . it does not satisfy you. . . ?'

Robert picked at a thread of his old jacket. 'My father and grandfather and three of my uncles were in the Indian Army. A relative of my mother's was one of the first holders of the Victoria Cross. But the British Army doesn't want me. No one wants me. . . .'

'I must get some more wood,' Ernie said, 'before it gets dark.'

'Yes, yes, you'd better, it's getting chilly.'

And Ernie turned quickly out of the temple and ran down to the pine grove with the bitter tears freezing on his cheeks. Robert had been like a Greek god in his statue of a body, but perfection is weakness; too delicately poised, a small jolt caused it to overbalance and break.

It was dark when he returned, and Robert had the candle lit. He had changed his clothes and washed in the snow.

'You feeling better?'

After a moment of hesitation Robert said, 'No, my head hurts still. I'm very weak, perhaps another day's rest. . . . What's on the menu for tonight?'

Ernie smiled and said: 'I thought we wouldn't bother to dress. If you lay the table I'll rustle up a fondue of something.'

They chuckled, as if with joy after long separation. While waiting for the water to boil they reminded each other of things in the dying past.

'Guess what happened to old Symonds.'

'Who was Symonds?' Ernie asked; and then began to fit together the memories of an evening party, a drunken river crossing, and a vulgar song to the tune of the *Marseillaise*.

'He became a priest.'

'I don't believe it.'

'I didn't at first,' Robert said. 'But stranger things have happened. He was perverted or converted or whatever they call it. Now he thinks in Latin and considers God is edible. The bloody silly little bastard,' he said with a sudden shocking bitterness. 'My father was captured on the first day of the Singapore invasion and he starved to death in Changi Jail. What part of God's grand scheme was that? He was a soldier.'

They ate the food and threw the empty plates out on to the snow, then rolled out the sleeping bags and Robert tried to stir up a glow from the embers on the floor.

'I'm very sorry about your arm,' Ernie said.

There was a silence as their minds adjusted to the memory of ten years ago. Each of them avoided a part of the truth, and they referred to it all obliquely, like priests discussing the act of love.

'I seem to remember now,' Robert said, 'that you shouted something. . . . It's as if I didn't hear it said until some weeks after. Then I wasn't sure. . . .'

Ernie looked through the doorway and down the long hills of snow. 'I remember, too. . . .'

'What was it? . . . you don't have to tell me, of course. . . .'

'I said, "Tell them who did it. Tell them it was me." Something like that.'

Robert looked interested. 'Were you proud of it, then?'

'It was the worst, stupidest thing I ever did. Even at the time I knew that. But I don't think you—I don't think I was left any choice.'

But that brought them both to their private barriers, and they moved carefully away as the fresh rain began to fall outside.

'What is it like in India now? For you, I mean?'

'Same as ever. They still hate us and they still need us.' The area of light closed in around the guttering candle. 'And we hate them,' he said. 'When you people left you took away the better part of our lives.'

He felt Robert's surprise as something tangible in the dark.

'I have stopped pretending,' he went on. 'I'm sick of pretence. I am an Anglo and I know it now. What I felt when I was a boy and even when I went up to Oxford was what all men of good will wish to think. It made me feel morally dirty to consider myself superior to a darker race. But it's true—in my case at least. I'm sure you know what I'm talking about,' he said with a sudden bitter anger, and looked directly across the candle flame but could see only the outline beyond it.

The mules shifted, blocking the last gloomy light. They could hear the wet champing of their lips, and the falling rain. After a few minutes their eyes adapted to the new conditions and the outlines of head and shoulder were repeated faintly on the broken wall.

'Did you tell them, by the way?'

'Tell who? What?'

'You know—'

'Oh! Well . . . I didn't as a matter of fact. I told them it was an accident. There was—and there was my mother. And all the chaps. I didn't know you'd run away, back here. I had to make up something.'

Ernie's words came accusingly out of the darkness. 'So you didn't even allow me that? I told you to tell them.'

'They found out in the end, of course. And of course she, you know, she knew all along. It wasn't a case of not telling them, I wanted to give you—' but the dangerous word made the shadow turn suddenly and Robert said: 'It all happened too quickly. I didn't know what you wanted.'

'Yes you did. I told you plainly enough. Where is she now?' he cried, and at last the burden was lifted from them both and sent out of the doorway and rolling down the long valleys of snow.

'In London,' Robert said. 'She's got a job and—'

'Is she married?'

'Yes!'

'And what other happy family events have taken place? But no touch of the tarbrush, I hope.'

'Ernie. I want you to know—I don't know what difference it makes to anything now, but—I'm different. I'm not just saying it . . . but it was ten years ago and this probably makes it all even worse, what I'm saying, but I just mean that if it were happening now it would be different. I wouldn't stand in your way. We change, in ourselves you know, as much as we change towards each other. You see,' he pressed on, as if walking far enough in the wrong direction would eventually bring him back to his destination, 'it's just a matter of time. It all happened too early for all of us, and that's the whole tragedy of it.'

Ernie realized at last that the damp on his face was not the wall's condensation or the powdered snow. He pulled the blanket above his shoulders and turned his face to the wall.

Later, he heard Robert climbing back into his sleeping bag on the floor. Typically he had remembered to bring in more snow in the petrol cans and block the bare doorway with one of the panniers.

There was much more he wanted to talk about, but not now. They had reached, at last, a state of frankness in which all questions would be answered, every question could be asked. They had come a long way to reach it and it must now be taken slowly. For the moment he wanted to be alone with the memories of love that had leaped across the span of lonely years. He crouched down further in the sleeping bag, hugging the long rifle to his chest. He would not have changed his sadness at this moment for any comfort. And he wanted no more memories tonight; the next morning would be soon enough for all he wanted to learn.

But next morning Robert had gone.

Plains

Robert stepped into the changing room and dropped his boots on the floor, scattering mud. 'Ernie, if you've nothing better to do during the vac you might drop in at the old place. If you feel like it.'

'That is very kind of you, Robert.' He added quickly: 'When may I come?'

Robert raised his eyebrows. 'That's a change, coming from you.'

For Ernie had been twice to Turley since Christmas, at Easter and in the summer, but never until the last fortnight of the vacation. He studied hard in his room, drawing much of the moral strength to do so from the pride and pleasure which greeted him on his arrival, which Robert knew so little about.

Robert said: 'Don't come too soon. There'll be a few of the other fellows down there later on. I'll let you know when.'

'That is very kind of you,' he said again. He spoke quickly to conceal his disappointment, for he had meant to go down right away this time. What was this he felt, stronger than pride in his scholarship? His mind saw a familiar rush of pictures, the Wiltshire fields in snow, the hedges and the fat clean cows, the coal fire in the library; and in each one of these pictures was the hair and pale arms and look of serious trust.

The water rattled on Robert's wide shoulders as he stepped under the shower. 'How's the hockey going?'

'Oh, pretty well.' Ernie regarded his hockey casually, considering it unimportant and actually preferring work, but already he played for the college; he was brilliant without trying.

'I suppose it's because you're half-Indian,' Robert said slyly. 'They're just naturally good, aren't they? World champions or something.'

Ernie said: 'I hardly think so.' The shoelace broke in his hand and he flung it down.

Robert grinned and stepped out of the shower, scattering water over an unnecessarily wide area. 'I'm a ghost from your past, Ernie. A ghost with a memory. All things are known to me.'

'Not quite all,' he muttered, thinking of Turley. His blood quickened to a memory of a walk in the fields of wheat. 'When can I come?'

Robert stared. 'You just asked me that. And I said I'd let you know.'

Ernie left the changing room and walked through the town to his digs. The house was all grey stone in front but, inside, Victoriana, flowered wallpaper, and ornaments on small tables. His own room was the barest in the house: bed, chair, table, another chair, cupboard; books on a shelf, her photograph on the wall. Robert could not come here.

The mantelpiece was magnificent, but underneath it was only a small gas fire hungry for sixpences. Lots of these old buildings were sham. Even the house in Turley had veneered furniture, and they had been shoring up the oak rafters with metal bars when he had been down there in the spring. Susan had said, watching them at work: 'Those rafters came from an old ship, Daddy said. It fought at Trafalgar or something. It seems such a shame.'

A shame to keep the roof up. Her mind was receptive only to the romantic. It was strange how the three of them were so different: Susan pure and insubstantial; Robert brilliant and strong; and Rowena a common factor to them both, but her pureness and strength quite apart in substance, the third side of the scalene triangle.

When Susan moved away Rowena said to him: 'Don't look so disapproving.'

He was startled. 'I don't know what you—'

'Truth isn't so narrow as you think. Each point of view can show a different truth. You should know that,' she said, 'if you study politics.'

She hadn't forgotten their first meeting when he had spoken about the causes of the war. She was always so disturbingly sure of herself. Suddenly he wanted to speak to her about what Susan had said to him on his previous visit but that would have been terribly—disloyal was the word he doubtfully decided on. He remembered their conversation on one of the morning rides. She had said to him: 'Ernie, pet, don't. Don't say words like that to me, you'll spoil everything. It's so nice as it is. I don't want to get all involved, honestly. . . .'

'Don't you love me, Susan? I love you.' He remembered the words glancing off her like sunlight.

'I'm still very young, Ernie. I like you awfully but I don't want to get all intense. We're friends, it's nice like this, all of us together. . . . Ernie, don't look like that, I'm terribly fond of you, but I just. . . .'

He had not ceased loving her after that, but for the first time anxiety rose up like a deep sea monster parting the surface; he was pursuing something that could, like everything else, lead to the lonely grave.

He said to Rowena now: 'You are always making fun of my studies. As a matter of fact economics and political science do not show different truths. They offer a lot of different problems and a lot of different answers. They do not try to present an opinion.'

They were walking away from the house. Rowena said: 'It is probably just my ignorance, Ernie dear. But to me economics is just an intellectual exercise. It's an occupation, but what does it do? Look at your own poor country. Millions starve. But food is ploughed into the ground because it is economic to do so.'

'Not in India. And economics is management of what exists, not miracles. Economics can't make the rain fall.'

'It doesn't change my mind,' she said stubbornly; her strength was, after all, built on the same dreaminess that her sister and mother had brought out of the Delhi cantonment. 'If economics is meaningful it does not permit food to be short in one country and wasted in another.'

She had no thought for realities. 'You're speaking of far more than economics,' he said. 'And you're idealizing, just like a woman, you're talking just like—' But he held back the name; they understood each other.

'What do you want to do in your life, then? You're so certain about everything else.'

She was facing away from him so he could not see if his rude words had annoyed her. She said: 'Come down to the stream this afternoon and I'll show you. Do you want to?' and her personality suddenly moved close in to him like a substance, and took him by the elbow. 'Follow the path through the woods down to the ford.'

'What time this afternoon?' he asked unwillingly. He would be missing time with Susan.

'All the time.'

'Is this why we see so little of you; what you're always doing? Tell me.'

'I'm making the rain fall.' She smiled, and her dark eyes brightened. 'No, I'm not really making anything. But at least I'm doing something. I think it's what I'll always want to do.'

There was no one at the ford, but a quarter-mile away across the long grass he saw the greenhouse. Rowena's greenhouse, Susan had said. He trudged towards it in the drizzle. Rowena came out as he arrived, carrying a bucket of blackish earth.

Ernie looked up at the grey sky.

'Could you stop the rain for a little while. My feet are getting wet.'

She hesitated, uncertain of his mood; then smiled warmly. She looked very different when she neglected her expression of serious intent. She wore wellington boots and her muddy jersey had holes at both elbows.

'Come round to the back first,' she said. 'The rain's only light. And the path is firm.'

Behind the greenhouse were twenty little plots of earth about ten feet square. In half of them was a maize-like plant with large ears of corn standing between two and six feet high.

'What is this? Market gardening?'

She shook her head. 'I'm studying how certain things grow. It's nothing new, I know, I read it all in books but I like to try it out for myself. It's the only way to learn.' She said seriously: 'The books don't tell you the simple things.' She wiped her face, and left a theatrical muddy mark on her forehead.

He pointed to the maize plots. 'What is all this stuff?'

'Corn. In America it's a delicacy; here we feed it to cattle. In these first two plots it's corn, those next two are sorghum, and the next two are kaffircorn. Then there's two plots of durra and four plots of mealies.'

'It looks all the same to me.'

'It is, really. But it has different names according to where it's grown. And all these plots have the different types of earth where they grow.'

'You mean you've got earth from America and those other places?'

'No, I made it up myself, as near as possible. I try to repeat the conditions in which it grows, and then observe the results. This plot here has earth very like the Kenya highlands, while the one on the other side is like Rhodesia's.'

'Kenya seems to be more successful.'

'Yes, but there are other things involved. Come into the greenhouse.'

'Does all this belong to you?' Ernie followed her into the greenhouse and closed the door. It was warm and dry; a heavy insect blundered above their heads, knocking at the glass.

'Mr Raymond lets me use it. He rents the land from us, in fact, but he gives this bit back to me. He's quite interested himself,' she said defensively. She was beginning to read something in his face that made her conscious how small and unrelated her work was. 'The greenhouse is his, and all these boxes. Only this is mine,' and she pointed to a long ramp of earth supported on tightly-stretched wire fencing that ran the length of the greenhouse, inclined at forty-five degrees and covered with inch-high grass. The earth was very light and dusty.

'Three times a year I take a large watering pipe and drench this earth. I try to imitate the force of a tropical storm, about four inches of rain in an hour. You'd think all the earth would run to the bottom of the slope, wouldn't you? Well it doesn't. Some of it does, of course. It's a matter of soil consistency. See, the grass is all growing nicely.'

'It's interesting. But you can't eat grass.'

'Cattle can. And goats and sheep. For every square mile of eroded land in Africa you get a few dead cows. You know what that means.'

But did it make any difference, really? This girl versus the world's hunger? He had once seen a starving man in Delhi fall dead on the steps of the Jama Masjid. And people had stepped over him; he had lain there for an hour. Set this greenhouse and its mealie-plots down in the Deccan and see how long her enthusiasm would last. He recognized that his people were beyond the reach of good intentions.

But there was something impressive about Rowena's calm dedication, he stayed nearly an hour watching her at work.

Then he left to find Susan, but she had gone shopping with Mrs King in Swindon and didn't return until very late. So he had only ten minutes with her after breakfast next morning, for he had to return to college. He could think only of the missed opportunities of the last two weeks and blamed her miserably for his own failure. He didn't try to kiss her again. She held his hands and promised to write, and he went back to the university that morning, wondering if even happiness was worth the risk of disappointment.

The next time he went to the house it was high summer. There were seas of wheat rolling up against the grey stone house, and a stoat had run across the path as his taxi drew up at the front door. His visits were no longer an event, he noticed; the first time they had both met him off the train; last time it had been Robert alone. Now there was no one to welcome him even at the door except the housemaid shuffling down the steps in the warm sun. She stooped to pick up his brief-case, leaving the heavier case for him. He had always disliked her. She was never rude, but kept a different voice for the other guests. She reminded him of the taxi-driver on his first day in London; she had a damp grey face and an overworked expression.

'Where is Robert? And Mrs King; is anyone here?'

'They went to market. They expected to be back,' she added unwillingly. She smelled of soap and cheese and dust.

'All of them?'

She nodded. She had not turned her head, and having dropped the brief-case on the floor without bending more than an inch or two, she proceeded towards a door and closed it. A ball of temper moved in his chest; always there were ignorant people to remind him of his difference. How much difference?—he was more like Robert and his mother than that fat old servant would ever be.

It was three o'clock; he was suspended between meals and events. He looked into the library, for it was his favourite place, the old heavy table and chairs, the guns and swords on the wall. There was a Bechstein piano which Susan occasionally played. The rest of the house was veneered furniture, steel roof-beams and second-class surly servants, but here it offered a last resistance to the sadness of a style outgrown.

The sun slanted through the french windows and he walked out on to the lawn. On an impulse he started down towards the stream. As he entered the copse the chugging of a tractor came gently from fields far away; a large thrush was grubbing for worms in the ditch beside the path. He emerged from the woods and continued along the edge of a wheat field. The path grew narrower until the cow parsley and dandelion brushed his legs.

Down by the stream grew a line of elm trees with scruffy crows' nests in their highest branches. And he heard the wood-pigeon as a punctuation to his thought. He knew he would never go back to India to live. Too much he had learned to love was only here, the gentleness, the dignity and peace of everything. And he was not Indian, he felt no obligation to share the poverty and meanness he had left behind. He had come home.

There was the greenhouse with its plots of mealie cobs; and as he watched, Rowena came from behind it pushing a laden wheelbarrow. She was dressed in heavy boots and wide breeches, with a scarf enclosing her hair, and for one moment it was as if her upbringing faltered; she looked akin to the complaining housewoman who had dropped his case.

He stood still, unwilling to disturb her at that moment; but after she had already turned away and set the barrow down she straightened and turned back towards him, as if recollecting she had noticed something out of place in the scene. After a moment of recognition she started towards him.

She pulled off her scarf as she approached and shook out her dark hair; the breeches looked uncomfortably thick and he experienced again the heavy reluctance to disturb her.

'Ernie, fancy you coming like this. Nobody told me.'

He was vaguely affronted. 'Well, you are here to greet me, anyway. But I'm disturbing you.'

'No.' She pushed the scarf into her pocket and took his arm. They walked back up the path. 'Is no one here? They went to buy a horse in Bradford. It's bad of them not to be here. But you're not a visitor any more, are you? You just come when you like.' Her arm through his was a pleasure that seemed somehow familiar. 'They never remember to tell me anything.'

'You always use that word.'

'Which?'

' "They".'

She hesitated. 'I don't know why. I'm very close to my family. But in many ways I'm apart from them.'

'But,' said Ernie, sensing a new understanding, 'you're a rather lonely person, aren't you? I don't mean anything wrong, I'm lonely myself. You spend so much time by yourself, down here for instance.' His thoughts pointed to a meaning beyond his words. 'It's just that you're like me in that way.'

'I'm not lonely, Ernie. Loneliness isn't being by yourself. It takes people to make you feel lonely.'

Her eyes held him; and he felt his whole existence revealed in the simple words. They walked together up the stony path towards the copse. He had been lonely in India, at his house in Delhi, at school and often at university . . . but happiest always when alone with his books. But there were some things books never told you. They entered the woods.

'Rowena.' There was a deep need in him to speak to her. 'I've always been lonely.' Her arm was still in his and he wondered if she was as aware of it as he.

Rowena looked at him with her frank eyes. It was a very peaceful face.

'I like walking with you,' he said. 'You're quiet. You're part of the beauty of all this place.' He knew he was going too far; but why didn't he stop? Susan moved like a shaft of pale sunlight before his memory. The rafters of the forest arched over their path like the roof of a church, and pools of coloured light lay occasionally at their feet. 'I wouldn't be lonely, Rowena, if—if. . . .'

They came out into the sunlight and the grey house sat among the yellow fields a hundred yards away. The open driveway lay just in front of them. Ernie said: 'Let's sit here for a while. We'll wait for'—his thoughts raced—'the car.' And they sat down on the bank in the tall grass.

But the car returned at that moment. It travelled noisily up the drive and prescribed a neat half-circle to finish at the steps. They saw Robert jump out and run to the door. Susan and her mother pulled parcels from the boot, and then Robert came trotting down the steps again. They all looked at each other; it was like a mime in a pageant. Then they all went up into the house, and the next scene was Susan and Robert entering again at centre; they must have seen his suitcase in the hall.

Robert cupped his hands to his mouth. 'Ernie!' A bird started up from the path and alighted on the roof. Robert shaded his eyes, scanning the fields. 'Where is the beggar?' they both heard him say.

They started off to look in different directions; Robert towards the stables, Susan down the drive towards them. She gave an occasional skip, and her skirt lifted in the light breeze; she passed so close they could hear her humming. When she had passed out of sight they exchanged a swift, guilty look of humorous intrigue and put their arms round each other. Her calm, he would learn, was only the slow rise of the curtain, but he had now left the audience to take his place on the crowded stage.

Then his memory caught up with the present and he was back among the heavy furniture and flowered wallpaper. Her picture looked down at him from the wall, calm as always between the times of passion. His smile as he looked at the picture still had a quality of wonder; the sisters had been photographed together, but he had cut off the extraneous half of the portrait. The clumsy line of his scissors showed on the left-hand margin of the picture. It was a slice of all the years in India he had daringly thrown away.

They had arranged for his letters to go to Mr Raymond. Neither his newly-assumed confidence, nor her self-possession, were yet ready for their discovery to be shared by Robert.

He had come across them once while they were on one of their walks. A moment before, they had been embracing; the sudden distance between them as he appeared was an over-correction and they had seen a grim smile on his face as he stood before them. A sudden defiance of Robert's assumed authority spurted up in him, but he glanced at Rowena and saw her troubled eyes warning him. Could not even she—? but reluctantly he had obeyed. Afterwards she had partly explained: 'I don't really believe in challenging people.'

Recognition of his own weakness, her strength, made him reply angrily: 'Do you belong to him then? Am I to tilt for you, or whatever used to happen in your chivalrous days?'

Her reply, as always, calmed him with its wisdom. 'A part of me belongs to him. And brothers have the right to be jealous. Let him discover our love, and think about it, and then accept it because there's no reason not to. But why should we fight him? He's very strong when he's fighting.'

'But he knows already.'

'He doesn't really. He doesn't know either of us well enough to be sure about it. You see, my dear, he'll forget everything he might see, and the grocer in the High Street will know before he does. But when the announcement comes he'll re-member all the little signs and realize he knew all along. Then he'll be grateful to us for taking him into our confidence.'

'I wish I knew Robert as well as you do.'

'You do, Ernie my love. But we know different sides. Different truths, remember? Between us I think we know my brother pretty well.'

Halfway through term they met in London; he stood for a long time on the platform feeling her all against him in a long embrace. She wouldn't kiss him on the bus, and suddenly he was too shy to look directly at her. They squeezed hands, staring through the window at the streets which were bright with rain.

They left the bus in Oxford Street; neither of them knew where to go. He had borrowed an umbrella from a fellow lodger, but it had broken when he practised opening it in the train. With the rain coming down they peered in at the shops and small cinemas, crossed the wide road several times, dodging the looming red buses. Once he stepped ankle-deep in a puddle and gasped. . . . Rowena laughed at him, and so he went limping along the street as if the damp foot was heavier than the other, and they were both laughing and clinging to each other. Neither of them could stop laughing; it wasn't funny any more, but it needed only a glance to start them both off again. They hurried closely along the bright window fronts of Regent Street, running across the exposed space between awnings, the broken umbrella flapping against his leg. In Soho they found a small restaurant where they sat in the window and hung their raincoats over the chairs.

'I love you, Rowena.'

'Ssssshh!'

'No one heard.' He lowered his voice. 'I'm going to marry you. I'm going to get rich and in about three years we'll have a house and I'm going to marry you. I don't care about any-thing—but I'm not being romantic. I'm very serious.' He had never seen her laugh before their run through the rain.

She leaned forward, but the waiter arrived abruptly between them. They stretched apart and tried to look unconcerned, then closed again over the waiter's departure. Ernie moved his hand forward on the table and got his sleeve in the soup; he cleaned it thoroughly, wiping with a serviette, working with concentration. He had just told this girl he would marry her. He couldn't look at her . . . it was amazing.

He had thought of the cinema, but they all finished so late; their trains left within a few minutes of each other, just after ten. He didn't know London very well. They started walking again, and he tried to pick his way through Soho to the Indian hostel to show her where he had lived, but he came out in Charing Cross Road and then turned right instead of left. It had stopped raining now. They crossed Trafalgar Square, with the wind whipping the surface off the water in the brimming fountain basins, and walked under Admiralty Arch. He didn't know he was in the Mall. He never would know. They walked down to the lakeside and sat on one of the benches. It was very dark under the trees, and completely black on the water. The wind brought leaves up the path and turned them in a circle at their feet. It was cold, but very warm where their bodies touched. A few ducks paddled hopefully towards them, but after witnessing several moments of utter stillness moved away to search further up the bank, where the drooping branches almost touched the dark surface of the unmoving water.

There was a note from Robert:
'I shall be in Dublin for the first three weeks of the vac. There's a chap from Rawalpindi who's hot stuff on the Indus Valley religion, so he says. If he is, then he's the only one, but it's worth trying. He's more interested in revolution, that's why he's gone to Dublin. I'm going by boat and I'm looking up some rather dusty relatives while I'm there so I shan't be back until the 28th. Come down to the house any time after that. Not before, please. Give my ma a ring to say when. Cheerio.'

It was now a week till the end of term. The letter had been picked up from the doormat and he hadn't moved while reading it. From the crumpled paper his glance moved across to Rowena's picture, and already a seed of revolt was sprouting in the space between them. He couldn't wait three weeks. Even his work was suffering; he couldn't read about economics any more, he was sick of it, and he hated the dark and crowded room where he sat every evening of the week. It was horrible being apart from her for so long.

He telephoned Rowena in despair. She said: 'If you can't come down here, then I must come to you.'

It was so simple! Robert would be in Ireland, of course; but what about her mother. He said: 'How will you—?'

'We have an aunt in Oxford. She's Mother's aunt really, but I'm quite fond of her, no one will think it strange. . . .'

He showed her the grey-walled colleges, the tea-shops and strangely deserted cafés in town, the empty alleys where cycling students would suddenly appear like circus troupes at particular hours of the day. They took bus-rides to Abingdon and Stratford and walked through the flat, ploughed fields around the city. The Carfax Tower had never interested him until he took Rowena up there and showed her where the town ended and the long slopes of the farming land turned into woods on the horizon. The days were sunny, and on the third afternoon they took a boat and rowed as far as Sandford. There they moored, and found a tea-shop further along the bank, and ordered scones and toast and jam. The waitresses buzzed around, treating them as a couple. He felt a strange proprietary pleasure in his ownership of this young woman beside him, the old teashop with its polished wood tables and copper pans, the bottle-glass windows through which he could see the river and the boats. He knew he looked well in his tweed jacket and worsted trousers, and had forgotten any self-consciousness at the cravat he liked to wear.

A family of swans came galleying down the Thames and turned towards the tea garden. Robert had told him only a year ago that he would be more English than any of them, and he felt it truly now without a thought of irony. What knows he of England. . . ? And really, Robert and his family, Rowena, living in the seclusion of the high-walled cantonment, they had never really left England. Only he could see how beautiful it all was, like the desert traveller's heightened response to an oasis.

They took the last of their scones and walked down to the

bank. The swans turned with elegant attention and accepted the offerings without haste. Ernie was able to show Rowena the marks on their lower bill which showed that they belonged to the King. They found a wooden bench, and the swans came with them like attendants, but when the scone was finished they turned and continued their interrupted course, paddling their surprising whiteness along the current. The quiet of the afternoon settled like comfort into Ernie's soul, but looking at her beautiful face he felt the slow drip of despair that always accompanied his premonitions of happiness. 'I want us always like this,' he said, and they touched hands, and the swans sailed away downstream.

They rowed back down to Oxford and, in their loss of direction afterwards, walked slowly back through the hushed streets to his room. The yellow December daylight was fading quickly, and they quickened their pace against the evening cold. He sensed the inevitability of events as they climbed the stairs, in the closeness of the small room after the day on the river, the searching look she gave him at the close of the door, and the smile they exchanged made him feel nervous and happy. He made tea on the small gas ring and brought it to her; but then, the intervening period being the one they most feared, she put his cup gently aside.

'Ernie . . . my love. . . .'

The pale light from the window made all things one colour, the wall and furniture, their limbs, the ceiling and eventually the sky outside. Even in failure something is accomplished. When he turned his face away from her he saw her again on the wall, the enigmatic personality that had eluded him again. But if she loved him, and understood as she promised she did, then he would have everything he wanted, in time.

Ernie waited until ten minutes before the train left, then hurried downstairs with his suitcase bumping the banisters. As he opened the door a boy arrived on a bicycle.

'Telegram. Mr Maher in here?'

He slit the envelope slowly in fear, while the boy watched curiously, straddling his bike; you never knew when the 'Arriving Sunday Four-fifteen Love' sort of thing could give way to a message whose effect was worth observing.

In fact the boy was quite satisfied, but better knowledge would have made his simple mind feel cheated. 'Do not come down. Wait for another telegram. Rowena.'

'Any answer?' the boy demanded. Already his foot was on the pedal, poised for departure; no calamity was enough to delay news of the others.

Ernie said No and went inside, stumbling on the suitcase by the mat. He raced through all the possible reasons, anxiety heightened by the curtness of the message. Had Robert returned? But she would have said so. And why 'wait' and not 'please wait'; it was only another penny?

The second telegram did not come for three days. The same youth on the bike could observe the full effect of the wait on Ernie's drawn face.

'Trouble back home?' he enquired with vulgar sympathy; sometimes they liked to talk. But 'Please meet me in London Tuesday Victoria arriving from Brighton four o'clock' was no basis for an answer. It wasn't until the boy had cycled away that Ernie realized what he must have meant by his 'home'. The reminders of his difference were always going to come when he was least prepared.

Rowena stepped off the train and was one of the first through the barrier. She presented her cheek with a troubled abstracted air; it was as if she had handed in her self-assurance along with her ticket and now looked rather small and frightened and unhappy.

The evening rush hour was beginning and they walked against it up Victoria Street.

'This will do,' Rowena said suddenly, and he followed her unwillingly into a Lyons; this was the sort of place you ate in usually when alone. They were always crowded, no matter what time of day, with people of an uncertain existence, without regular working hours or mealtimes, who surely never had to catch trains home to suburban stations. A woman served boiled and fried meals, sweating with clockwork effort, and an African waiter pushed his trolley warily between the tables on an unwilling safari for dirty plates. Here at least there would be anonymity, they would have nothing in common with his problems. But what problems?

'Rowena.'

When she turned to him it was the first time he had noticed the expression in her eyes and he was struck with amazement. He did not know what he read in her face but it was not calmness. 'Is there any trouble, darling?'

Her voice also had changed. 'I don't know. It might be—'

She started to pull rather desperately at her gloves as if they had to be off her fingers before she could speak properly. Even her hand, he noticed, trembled as she put it down on the table.

A tray was settled beside them, nudging his arm, and a chair pulled back. He froze at the intrusion. But the diner must have sensed the strained atmosphere; the tray was lifted again and moved away.

'Rowena, please tell me what is wrong. I am so worried.'

'Don't you really know?'

'But how can I?'

She looked at him strangely; he felt like some sort of criminal and this girl was picking holes in his alibi. 'How can I know?' he protested. 'I've been in Oxford all the time.'

'Yes,' she said bitterly, 'so has Robert.'

Now what did she mean by that? It was terrible how things changed . . . three weeks ago this girl had made love to him and now he was a stranger. There was no reason; unless. . . .

'Oh God, Rowena, you don't mean . . . it's been discovered. . . ?'

She looked at him steadily. 'Yes—?'

'I mean,' he finished uncomfortably, 'Robert knowing about us, you know, in Oxford—in my room.'

She shook her head impatiently. 'No, not that. At least—' she corrected herself, 'he does know—now. But that doesn't matter.'

'What do you mean?' he whispered. '*Does* he know?'

'I told him.'

'Why—?' he felt himself veering steadily from sanity, like a climber on a long glissade. 'Why did you tell him?'

'It doesn't matter,' she said.

Someone came over and asked if they were eating. If they weren't eating they weren't allowed to have a table because tables were reserved for customers. He went to stand in the queue for two cups of tea and watch Rowena sitting forlornly at the table. A man with a loaded tray tried to join her, but something she said made him move away and sit further down. The serving woman dashed sweat vigorously from her forehead as she filled two cups with the brick-red mixture and when he got back to the table Rowena tried to smile at him.

'Let's drink our tea first,' she said. 'Then we'll start again. We were getting too complicated.'

But when they had drunk the final drops she still sat there turning her spoon in the cup until Ernie thought he couldn't stand it another moment. But of course we always can. He merely said: 'Rowena, tell me. It is Robert, isn't it?' A terrible idea occurred to him. 'You're not pregnant?'

She pushed back her chair and stood up. 'Don't be silly.' A smile passed across her face like a shadow. 'Let's go for a little walk. I hate it in here.'

'You chose it,' he muttered; it seemed important to establish something. Of course, she had chosen at random; she wouldn't have known what a Lyons was. He followed her outside and they were immediately engulfed by the crowd again. It was almost impossible to walk against them; but to go with them meant being swept back up the street to the station, and

perhaps through the barrier and on to a train and out to
Waddon or Wimbledon Chase. 'A bus,' Rowena said desperately, 'or a taxi.' He couldn't suppress a laugh; she knew as
much of London as she knew of India. Always the high wall
to separate her and her greenhouse from the crowded world.
They pushed along in the kerb between people and buses all
moving inexorably backwards like a high spring tide. Then
in front of them was a small open space and a great stone
façade stretching back. The road bent round it and suddenly
the red buses were not tall any more, dodging round the grey
wall like racing cars on a circuit.

They crossed the space and moved thankfully inside: a
church, a cathedral? Neither of them knew; but it was famous,
and recognition hovered just before them as they wandered
down the shadowy nave. They stared at heraldic inscriptions,
knights of stone lying close in under the walls. Regimental
flags hung heavily above them, rotten with age. There was a
little chapel with candles and a dozen Sunday School chairs,
and they stepped inside.

'Now?' whispered Ernie; but he was not surprised when
she said 'Not here,' and moved on again. There was an open
doorway on the right: a long covered passage of cloisters surrounding a chequered lawn, with the sky above. 'Please,' he
said.

A clergyman came out of one of the rooms and after
glancing once at them, passed by in experienced silence. Two
birds were hopping about on the squares of mown lawn like
knights on a chessboard, never making contact. 'I'm going to
be sick,' Ernie whispered, 'if you don't tell me what you have
come to say.'

'Do you,' she said, 'love me, Ernie?' He cleared his throat
to reply, but in her eyes he saw the long train of doubt begin,
whatever his answer.

'Do you have anything you want to—confess to me?'

At last he gave way to anger. 'I don't know what the hell
you are talking about. Confess what? Yes, I've told lies, I've

wet my pyjamas, I've done things I ought to have left undone. I've chalked a moustache on your photograph, I've cooked boiled eggs with my hat on. What is the matter with you now?'

Strangely, his answer seemed to give her some comfort. She patted his cheek and said: 'Well, perhaps . . .' and they moved back down the aisle. But by the time they emerged into the daylight the pain was back in her eyes, and she walked swiftly, without looking at him, back up Victoria Street with the last of the crowd.

'If you've fallen out of love with me,' Ernie said, 'I don't understand, but I think I'd rather be told. There must be a reason and you can tell me.'

He remembered what had happened in his Oxford digs, and said: 'But I must say it doesn't take much to change your mind.'

Suddenly he was crying; he couldn't stop, it was terrible. He hadn't really thought of it till he'd spoken, but now he contemplated the years without her, and shades of the lonely bed-sitter closed over his future.

But they couldn't talk while he was like this, and they walked in silence all the way back to the station. 'My train leaves in ten minutes,' Rowena said. 'I'm sorry, Ernie. I just don't know how to talk about it. Whether it's true or not. . . .'

'Yes?'

'It's too awful to ask.'

His was the bewilderment of a child with all the grownups turned suddenly hostile. 'But now that you are going,' he said, 'you must tell me.' But he saw in her eyes that she was not going to.

At last, when she was in her compartment and he stood on the platform outside, he said: 'Perhaps you had better write to me.' For a moment she looked grateful; but then as the whistle blew she said: 'Robert's told me something about you. If it's true—then you must know. . . . Now I can't say any

more,' and like a contrived stage cue a flag waved and her
unhappy face was borne away.

The next day he was capable of no coherent thought. He
considered all possibilities but without any controlled progression of reasoning, only the flotsam of dreamed memories, half-
digested ideas whilst frying his breakfast or walking along the
road. Race? No, she had already accepted him. Disappointment with—? But she had been happy afterwards, had made
plans for his visit in three days' time, and besides, although
he was very inexperienced with women, he knew they rated
performance low. It was to do with Robert, something he had
told her. . . . But any idea he embarked upon, before it corre-
lated with another to produce a train of thought, dispersed in
worry, despair, and the effort of looking up the timetable and
rehearsing his intent.

And the next day he went down to Turley for the last time.
There was only one way to clear it all up, or at least find out
the truth, even if it was something he didn't want to know.
Something to do with Robert. What. . . ? But again his reasoning lost direction at that particular point. He held it in reserve,
anyway, and watched the wintry fields with more than usual
interest, engaging all the unoccupied corners of his mind. Not
until his taxi turned into the drive between the isolated gateposts did he make the effort to gather himself for. . . ? He paid
the taxi off and turned to see Rowena.

'Well,' she said. 'I should have realized you would come.
But I've been all day writing you a letter.'

He had not realized before today, or perhaps before two
days ago, how much of her calm beauty had in fact been the
mask of her strength. Now her whole body looked exhausted,
and the beauty of her tranquillity had given way to a new
season. It gave him an instant of hope.

'I've come to see Robert,' he said. It was the best way.

She nodded. 'It was silly of me not to speak the other day.'

She was going to say something else, but Robert and about six others came round the corner from the library windows. They carried shotguns; half of them were dressed in self-conscious wellingtons and college scarves, walking a little strangely like actors at a first dress rehearsal. Robert looked startled only a moment; then he said something to the others and came striding towards the steps. The shooting party continued on round the house and down across the stubbled fields.

'I think we had better go into the library,' Robert commanded. 'Rowena, you stay away.'

As hard as he looked, he could see no discomfiture on Robert's face. Though, of course, he never had; Robert had only his own rules to break.

Robert closed the two glass doors and, to Ernie's amazement, turned on him instantly.

'Now I don't want any damn nonsense from you, coming down here like this. I know perfectly well you've had the bloody insolence to interfere with my sister.'

He had not only struck first but from a totally unexpected quarter.

'Yes, but—'

'You little bastard. After all we've done.'

'Wait a minute,' Ernie shouted; he raised his hand as if to stem the words physically. 'That is not the issue.' But for a moment of incomprehension he could not recollect what the issue was. 'You . . . it was all before. . . .'

'I'm listening,' Robert said calmly. So the anger had only been pretence. He had changed his position already, keeping his opponent bewildered, like the generals he most admired.

'You have told her something. God knows what, but it has made her hate me.'

'It was meant to make her despise you. I must throw in a few further details.'

'Details of what? What right had you—?'

'Did you think,' Robert said—the anger was rising again—

'did you think for even one moment that you could marry her? You stand there and talk of my rights!'

'What business—?'

'I was a friend to you. I've wet-nursed you through college, had you down to the house, but for God's sake there was a limit. Talk of the beggar on horseback! You're a wog! I don't care if you're only half a wog, you're not marrying her. You're not even touching her, do you hear? You won't even see her or come down here. Not again, anyway, you dirty coloured bastard.'

Somewhere in Ernie's crowded mind he was thinking: 'It is happening . . . I am here and this is happening now, to me.' His thoughts swam upward, and when Robert's face realigned in his vision he said: 'Rowena loved me. She knew all my weaknesses. I don't understand what you could have said to her, but I want to know.'

'It wasn't difficult,' Robert said. 'It was a pity but it was getting urgent. I told her you were a homosexual.'

'I don't believe you,' Ernie said. And laughed—he hadn't meant to. Nor had he meant his knees to shake. He had thought it a writer's convention, but they were shaking all right, and when he tried to stand straight he could feel them knocking gently together.

'You're wondering aren't you,' said Robert (and he was aware that Robert was enjoying himself), 'why she should have believed me?'

He could see, through the french windows, Rowena strolling slowly back and forth over the lawn. She bent to pick a blade of grass, and then went on again without looking up.

'But it's funny . . . she was believing it almost before I spoke. What happened between you?'

Ernie closed his eyes.

'And then I'm her brother. I'm a rather special brother. She couldn't believe I'd tell a lie like that, which dishonoured myself.'

Time stumbled forward, leaving him behind. 'Dishonour?'

'She asked me how I knew.' A look of surly triumph passed across his face. 'And I told her—oh, I can't remember the exact words but, you know . . . the only way a man can know.'

He couldn't go on any more. He stared and stared, aware of what a fool he must look. But he could not say anything at all.

'Do you think I enjoyed it?' Robert said. 'Telling that to Rowena, my sister. Christ, what a mess you've caused all round. How the hell—Rowena? But I'll never understand her. First you try it with Susan, and when that didn't satisfy you quick enough you turn to Rowena. What exactly were you up to? Why them? You bloody dirty Indian wog. And I have to disgrace myself to get her out of it. I'm finished with her, but let me tell you you're finished too, for good. You've completely finished with all of us and there's an end of you playing British. I was a fool to pretend you were anything but what you are, but I'm paying for it now all right. I should have left you in the jungle. You married to my sister! My god! Well she'd rather marry the gardener now and it serves you damn well right.'

Ernie's voice sounded unnatural even to himself. 'Why— why did you do it?'

'Why? Look, you little fool, you know what it's all about. You weren't asking much! What a sheer bloody nerve! And you didn't even have the intelligence or decency to hide it. The housekeeper saw it, people in the village saw it. And I saw it—plus anyone who happened to call at your room, apparently. The photo on the wall. Perhaps you meant me to see it. It's not enough for you, is it, to feel superior. You have to hang it on the wall and canter it through Turley and parade it in the streets of London Town.'

'But why—tell her we were—what rotten satisfaction did you get from that?'

'I'll leave you to think that one out, you're so damn clever.'

At last he managed to say: 'It's ridiculous . . . I will just go and tell her the truth.'

Robert immediately went to the french windows and threw them open. 'Go on out there,' he said.

Ernie walked out of the room and across the grass to where Rowena was waiting. As she turned, a first thin layer of pain settled into its familiar place in his head. She looked pale and cold and he knew he would never learn to bear the memory of that look on her face.

'Is it true, Ernie?'

Oh God! He looked at her, trembling, his whole mind held down by incomprehension and pain. If only there was a suggestion of hope in her eyes.

'I don't understand, Ernie. I just don't.' She looked helpless, like a lost child. 'Perhaps you thought—but I don't want to guess. I just don't understand. Robert has been my father for the last four years. And you . . . I thought you loved me. . . .'

'Rowena!' His voice was unnaturally loud, and he controlled it so that he nearly whispered: 'I did love—'

'But how can you say that now? Ernie, I'm very ignorant— I'm not even sure I fully understand what I've been told. How could I? But it's not love, is it? When I think that we have made love together,' and she started to cry; 'I can only feel— disgust. . . .'

Anything he might have thought of saying was stifled by another jolt of pain.

'And now I understand why you couldn't—'

The tears were falling on his face. He saw her with bright eyes and cheeks flushed by the cold air, utterly miserable, and there was nothing he could do.

'I thought,' she said, 'there was no difference between God's people. It never mattered to me that you were Indian—at least I thought it didn't. . . .'

Whatever happened now, he could not face the memory of it; and in his mind a large, wide door swung softly open and he was being drawn into the darkness beyond it. He closed his eyes, for the pain had begun to frighten him. When they

opened a moment later he was dimly aware of Rowena running away from him across the grass before the darkness came
down again, heavier and blacker, and it was his turn to go
running, away from her towards the dark woods, because he
knew that what he had been holding off for the last ten
minutes was now going to happen and he wanted to reach
cover before he was helpless.

He was soaking wet and cold when he woke, or whatever
it was he did; it had not been sleep, for he had always been
aware of the pain and disgust and Rowena running away
across the lawn. And sleep is something which gives rest.
When he stood up from the long grass his legs were shaking.

From the woods he heard the deep thumping of gunshots,
and the crows were starting up out of the elms to gather in a
dark ragged cloud on the far side of the river. He started out
in that direction, and after a moment he started to run. The
stubble and winter hedges and bare-armed trees rushed back
past him. He reached the edge of the copse and plunged into it,
tearing his face and hands on the bushes. There was a path
but he was blind to it. He ran in the straightest line he could
manage to where he remembered the shots, but came breaking out five minutes later at the bottom of the woods, soaking
his trousers and shoes in the long grass of a ditch.

Away across the meadow he could see the greenhouse by
the river, its outline softened by the rising mist. He couldn't
bear to look at it. There were more shots; two pigeons came
whirring past him in haste and he turned along the line of
trees and then plunged in again. But the gunshots had ceased.
On the way back he lost his direction and came out into the
meadow again, several hundred yards further down the ditch.
But now he recognized a path he had walked on with Rowena.
He ran back towards the house roof showing above the top
of the trees, and as he cleared the woods he could see the
scarved and booted figures disappearing through the front door.

But he had to give up running. He walked back, and climbed the front steps one at a time.

The library door stood open, and on the polished table Robert's gun and a pair of binoculars lay on top of his coat. A pair of wellington boots stood aggressively upright on the carpet. Someone had lit a fire, and the draught from the open door brought the smoke out in a rosy cloud to catch the last of the winter sun coming through the window. A man in his stockinged feet came in through the door.

'I say, hullo.'

Ernie knew him; one of the crowd always around Robert. They had once drunk beer together on a pub-crawl in Abingdon.

'What have you done to your face? Nasty!'

He could feel his ear bleeding from a deep scratch; when he wiped the blood away he left a muddy smear down his cheek.

'I say, have you seen *Punch*. I left it on this table.' His face was extraordinarily youthful and empty, and Ernie could see the tidemark of suntan stopping short at the place where he usually wore his college scarf.

Ernie said: 'Where is Robert?'

'He hasn't got it—oh, I see. I don't know. In the kitchen.'

'Please fetch him.'

'Well actually, can't you find him yourself? Somebody else might have bagged *Punch* and—'

'Fetch Robert!' Ernie screamed. He heard the man say, after a moment's fright: 'No control, these fellows,' and then the door closed and he was alone. He picked up Robert's rifle and cocked it—and then the overwhelming silliness of it all came home to him. He knew what he should do: go and find Rowena. Speak to her and make her understand. His head was clearer now, and suddenly it all seemed easier. Perhaps she wouldn't listen now, but there would be other opportunities, there was nothing irrevocable . . . he loved her still, and beside that Robert was unimportant.

A solid brass Buddha sat hunched on the mantelshelf, and he leaned the rifle against a chair and picked it up. It used to be in the Kings' sitting room in the cantonment, together with a Gurkha kukri and a pilgrim's pot of Ganges water. He and Robert had often played with the kukri, knife versus bayonet in the saddles of the walnut chairs. He could speak to Rowena if he tried. She was sensible, and had been knocked off balance by emotion. He could explain. It would be something, then, to be free of Robert's spell.

'I thought you had gone,' Robert said as he entered, and Ernie put the Buddha back on the mantelpiece.

'I'm here to speak to Rowena.'

'She's in her room. She won't come out for anyone. And it would do no good,' Robert said, coming closer. 'Look, I want you to know something . . . that I've got nothing against you personally.'

'No?'

'No,' Robert said. 'We've been friends, I don't deny it. This is all very upsetting. . . .'

Ernie breathed deeply. 'And so. . . ?'

'I like you,' Robert said. 'I admire you. All that nonsense about, well, back to the jungle and everything, it was in the heat of the moment. I lost my temper. I have a great regard for you, it's just that married to Rowena . . . you do understand, don't you?'

Ernie looked at him.

'The reason it's impossible,' Robert said patiently, 'is that you are Indian and she is white. Now that's nothing against you personally, but there are some ways that, quite naturally, you would never be accepted by—ordinary people.'

It seemed to Ernie that every time he took a definite decision a wind hurried up to blow him back the opposite way.

'I like you,' Robert insisted. 'And you know that, don't you? But for Rowena to marry you, well, I settled for my dishonour rather than hers. Not dishonour, you know what I mean.'

'All right,' Ernie said, and picked up the gun. He thought he had painstakingly planned the future and then click! and the picture was changed.

'Ernie! Understand—none of this is my fault.'

'No.'

Robert frowned at the gun. 'It was for Rowena's sake. My sister. Put that thing down. I like you—I'm telling the truth,' he said grimly.

'Yes, I believe you,' Ernie said.

Only half-understanding the danger, Robert took another step towards it.

'Don't you understand what I've been saying. I like you as a friend, I've nothing against you at all. But I had no choice. You know how impossible it would have been, old chap,' and Ernie pointed the gun at his chest.

'Ernie, for Christ's sake, I love you,' Robert cried, and Ernie levelled the gun clumsily and shot him.

Mountains

Dark clouds built up behind the mountain's peak and Ernie smiled up at them, confident even in the face of a storm. For half an hour he went on down and across the hillside, following the suggestion of a path between the pine groves. The spears of rain struck on his shoulders and he felt light-headed and eager.

Now he was near the end of his quest, begun with the Minister in the dark, airless room. He did not question too closely his other motives for continuing the pursuit. He didn't hate Robert, he didn't love him, he did not want his humiliation or pain. He just wished to finish his job and settle the debt.

It was good to be free again. Robert was truly on the run and was not leaving signs to guide him now. Of course, he was no longer armed; the rifle had been lying in Ernie's sleeping bag and Robert had left without it.

At midday he could still look back and see the square black shape of the temple against the grey snow. But soon afterwards the clouds settled lower and twilight crept into the afternoon. The storm was breaking on the north face of the peak; he was on its lee side, though there was plenty of rain left over for him. Nevertheless, he smiled up through it, the raindrops glistening on his face, happier than he could remember feeling for years.

By mid-afternoon he had left the permanent snow behind. The mule's hoofs were squelching in mud and the rain was cutting dark holes in the soft snow beside the path. Where was Robert? Not far ahead: the tracks of the mule showed at intervals in the mud, and once he found himself walking in Robert's own footprints, lengthening his steps to accommodate Robert's stride. It was the feeling from the hockey field of years ago, driving in towards the goal, knowing there was nothing anyone could do to stop him.

With a feeling of astonishment he saw a goat standing before him on the path. For many days the world had contained only himself and Robert; and the snow. Now a goat shared it. He gave a shout and watched it scrambling up the bank among some wild cherry trees. He walked on round the bend and saw three others with their heads down in the stony grass.

The village lay just below. It was built of mud bricks; dirty white smoke issued from doorways. The path between the huts had become a river with goats and dogs lapping it. It was a gujer village. The gujers were nomads, moving up and down the mountain as the summers came and went. A dozen men and women stood on the path, sewn into their thick clothes, their dark Mongolian faces heavy with suspicion. The sight of an Indian Army battledress tunic on one of them caused Ernie to loosen the strap of his riflecase. The gujers obeyed only their own laws and a suit of clothes was probably worth a killing or two.

He hastened forward to give them salaam. He could not remember what their sect would be; Robert would have known, of course. He asked for food; and then, as he looked into the faces before him, he knew that, of course, Robert had been here before him, many times, and would be their friend.

'What is your name?'

The one in the army tunic had stepped forward. Ernie could see a sergeant's chevrons and an old campaign ribbon of the north-west frontier showing beneath the grey dirt. It seemed to invest the man with some vicarious authority, for he was not the oldest there but did most of the talking.

'My name . . .' Ernie said; he wondered how much Robert had told them. He had been travelling this way for years and they would certainly have been bribed. Several of the men wore watches, and half hidden under a goat's foot, pressed into the mud, was the silver wrapping from a bar of chocolate. Robert had come through within the last few hours . . . might even still be here.

'Tell us your name.'

'Iqbal,' he said. That could be anything; Hindu, Sikh or Muslim. He searched over their shoulders for a sign of Robert.

'You are speaking lies.' The man in the tunic had an angry red face and tufts of black hair growing from his ears.

'I am a friend of Robert King,' Ernie said. 'He has come through here today.'

The group seemed to contract as they all moved closer together. The man in the tunic said: 'No person has been here. We do not like strangers.'

'Never mind,' he said impatiently, 'I'm not here to bother you. Just a little food, please.' He was about to say he would pay well for the food, but decided not to.

'There is no food for you.' The man seemed to speak with awkward restraint, as if he would much rather have used the rifle. 'No food,' he insisted and the others nodded in support.

Ernie stared, and the man repeated: 'No food and no water.'

He seemed to be reciting words learned by rote, and Ernie chuckled as he looked up into the sky. A white mist hung over the hut roofs and the rain beat down on their heads and shoulders. Steam was rising from the mud and goat droppings. He sucked the moisture from his lips and said: 'Allah will provide the water. The food I can manage without. I will search for Muslim hospitality elsewhere.'

His new confidence took another flight upward. Robert had engineered this, trying to delay him. He was drawing nearer to his quarry, nearer to final peace.

He climbed on to the mule's back, wishing to make a nobler exit than stumbling through the mud. Whispering broke out among the group and the leader's face flushed darker as he stood in indecision.

'No, you must stay,' the man said suddenly; but the rifle

stayed on his shoulder and the voice lacked conviction. Ernie pretended not to hear, knowing he must leave quickly while these slow-thinking nomads still hesitated between action and doubt.

'Thank you,' he said, and did a small namaste. 'The yellow-haired gunrunner will not be coming here again.'

He kicked the mule to a walk and left the gujers to think it out from there.

From the corner of his eye he saw the man make an angry gesture to his companions. One of them shouted for him to stop. A dog ran barking at his heels and further down the path a youth stepped in his way and pointed with sullen nervousness back up the path. But he knew his only chance was to keep moving, to keep the initiative against their indecision. He ached to look back or to break into a trot, but with all his moral strength he kept an even pace, looking straight ahead. Twenty yards more and he would be past the last house and round the corner . . . but suddenly he became aware of a swift scampering noise and a dozen running figures overtook him and dragged the mule to a halt. His hand reached quickly for the rifle butt but someone had pulled it away a second before.

The man in the tunic pointed his gun at Ernie's face.

'We will give you food tomorrow. Tonight you stay here.'

Were they still pleading? He answered with a summoned firmness: 'No, I am leaving now. Get out of my way.'

Behind him they were searching the saddlebags. One of the flaps was thrown back, and he twisted round in the saddle.

'Stop it!'

But the man pushed his knee forward out of the way and dragged out a blanket.

'You will be our guest,' the man with the rifle said. 'You are invited to breakfast,' and laughed with a strange high falsetto voice.

'Now get down.'

They were pulling out his clothes on the ground, exclaiming

in pleasure and surprise. He watched his spare boots disappear under someone's coat. A woman picked up a small mirror and stared curiously into its revealing depths.

'You are Government?'

'No,' he said quickly; then cursed at the relief in all their faces. They were laughing happily now, nervousness buried under the comfort of joint action.

In a series of commanding jerks the rifle directed him to the only hut with a door. As he stepped inside he saw sacks of buckwheat grain and rice and several open baskets of green pears. Two men carried in his depleted saddlebags and dropped them on the earthen floor, while children peered between their legs, pointing in curiosity.

'You are our guest for breakfast.' The falsetto laugh shrilled out again and all the children joined in at the same pitch. 'Sleep in here, we will bring blankets.'

Although the hut was a food store it smelled horribly of goat dung. Branches of a large tree were scraping the corrugated iron roof as they moved slightly in the wind. The only light entered through a few chinks between walls and roof. He tripped over the bags as he stumbled about in the near-dark, then suddenly remembered his pistol.

Was it possible. . . ? One of the bags was half-empty, but the other appeared untouched. He loosened the buckle and pushed his hand down against the canvas wall.

Then a shaft of light fell like a floodlamp from the opened door. The red-faced man dropped two greasy blankets and walked over.

'What are you doing?'

Ernie's hand closed round a knife. Thinking swiftly, he allowed a look of sheepish guilt to appear on his face . . . then he held the knife out and dropped it on the floor. The man laughed and picked it up, turning it in the beam of light from the doorway.

'You were going to kill me with this, eh?'

Ernie smiled and looked at the floor.

'And I walked in and discovered you.'

He made a few admiring passes, exaggerated gestures of aggression, then stuck it in his belt and swaggered out after a covetous glance at Ernie's wrist-watch. The wooden door was pulled across and he could hear it being bound tight with a rope.

'We will send in food,' the man shouted.

When the shadow had disappeared from the door-frame he waited for two full minutes, then cautiously moved back to the bags. It was incredible they had not searched. He found the pistol where he had placed it at the temple, wrapped in cloth. He felt the weight of it in his hand for a moment, then pushed it down inside his trousers, into the crotch. It was fully loaded; he dare not keep spare bullets for they might search him yet. He took the bullets from his pocket and pushed them through a slit in one of the grain sacks.

He had never fired a pistol or killed anyone. It might not be necessary. If they were going to keep him only till next morning, as they said—but that was unlikely. Obviously Robert had demanded a good start; they would keep him prisoner two days at least.

They brought him food an hour after dark, a mixture of rice and meat cooked in oil. It tasted delicious; he scooped it up with chapatties still warm from the charcoal. Then he was given tea with knobs of butter floating on the surface. The village was filling up as the herds were brought in at dusk and he saw an occasional curious pair of eyes peering at him through the door-chink. Now he knew where the dung smell came from : the goats were being corralled within thorn fences around the tree outside and he could hear them coughing in the cold air and scratching their coats against the wall of his prison.

In the dark he took out the gun again. It felt heavy and ugly in his grasp and he wondered again if he could shoot with it, if he had to. He had never used a gun before—except that one time. And even then there had been the last-second indecision that had turned the aim from Robert's chest, from Robert's anguished cry that had been the one cowardly act of his life.

Rowena was married now. It would have been strange how little he cared, if he could ever remember his reasons for loving her, the well-bred English young woman whom he could not even touch without feeling humiliation. And Susan? He had also loved Susan . . . well, perhaps; she too had something of Robert in her. But memory rarely gives a true picture, our wishes distort the image, and that is why old photographs look so odd. He no longer knew what he had felt for Rowena or Susan, he could not compass the quantity of change in himself.

He coughed, felt the weight in his hand, and came back to his present situation.

He coughed again. The air had turned smoky, and for the first time he noticed a pink, flickering light against the corrugated iron roof in one corner. He walked over, the gun hanging in his hand. There was a two-inch gap between roof and mud wall, and against the metal overhang outside the reflection of a fire glowed redly. He reached up to the roof and pushed cautiously . . . he felt the corrugated iron give, and lifted it. The red light glowed stronger, and then he could peer under the roof to the soft outline of the tree, and a few stars in the violet sky.

The roof was probably lashed to the beams only in a few places; for the rest they relied on the weight of boulders to hold it down on the walls. If he were to heave strongly up at this weak corner he could perhaps make a gap large enough to crawl through.

It would be dangerous. The village would certainly have a guard at night to protect the herd. In the dark they might shoot him, but he had taken many risks on this journey and now he had to take another. Most of his life was routine and he had grown resigned to it; but there had to be moments that made the routine worth suffering, and if Robert got away

now he would have wasted perhaps the last good moment of
his life.

He waited for hours, until the fireglow was too dim to read
his watch. The grainsacks were heavy as he dragged them one
by one across the floor and built up a platform against the
wall. He retrieved the bullets from their hiding place among
the grain and loaded all his remaining kit into one of the
panniers. They were welcome to the other; a gift from the
Indian Government.

Then he climbed on top of the grainsacks and put a cautious
shoulder against the metal roof.

It moved up easily for twelve inches; then would not budge.
It was nearly enough. He peered down to the last embers of
the fire ten yards away. He could see no movement, and there
was utter stillness but for the restless movement of the goats
and the growl of half-digested food in their bellies. He pushed
up again with desperate strength : there was a horrible crack
as the binding parted and the opening gaped wide.

No one came. He waited ten minutes, then pushed his bag
through the gap and dropped it on to the goats' backs. He
hesitated one moment as he lay against the overhang, suspended between the stars and the dark earth. With a small shock
he recognized a feeling of exhilaration. Then he dropped away
and slid through the long hairy bodies into the dirty mud.
The chase was on again.

He had not thought how unpleasant the ground would be
and the ammonia stink made him retch. But he kept his head
down as he crawled between the rough backs, past the surprised
faces. A nanny belched warm air in his face and trod bruisingly
on his hand. He pulled his bag through the mud behind him
and then he reached what he had forgotten, the thornbush
fence.

It was shoulder high, and rustled noisily when he pushed,
trying to find a weak place. He stabbed his hand in two deep
places and felt the blood oozing into the dirt. No leopard could
get in, but no goat or prisoner could escape.

He heaved his bag over the fence and crawled back to the base of the tree. Already an idea had risen to the surface of his memory like a bubble from deep water. He scrambled up the trunk, keeping in the shadows of the hut. . . . It had been long ago, the sadness of childhood dragged on his limbs. He moved out cautiously along a branch, six feet above the moving backs. Where had it been? Nervous faces stared up as they had done before. He inched out over the thornbush and felt the sway of the tapering branch. It dipped down beyond the corral. He let go . . . and as he swung and dropped the knowledge burst in his brain so that he nearly cried out Robert's name. The ground knocked the breath from him and he lay on his back looking up, not at the stars, but the branches of a banyan tree with its roots in the Delhi cantonment.

He had found the mule, still saddled, twenty yards from the hut. It had been so easy he even felt a moment of disappointment, as with a goal in hockey when the goalkeeper was unprepared. No one had accosted him; there had been no sleeping dangerous forms to step over, dogs to knife before they barked. He had been wrong about the village guard; the thorn fence was apparently considered enough. Now dawn was coming up out of Tibet and he was six or seven miles from the village. Robert could not be far away.

Robert had been perhaps four hours ahead of him all the previous day. He had wasted two hours of daylight at the gujers' prison, so that made six hours. Now he had been travelling through the night for six hours, and although progress was slow in the dark Robert could not be far; believing Ernie a prisoner, he would be in no hurry. He was going to get a shock. Ernie had lost his rifle but he still had the pistol. Robert had nothing; he had only to be found.

It had stopped raining at last, but looking back he could see the storm raging in the mountains. The sun came up on his left hand, lighting all the valleys down towards the Jhelum.

He was riding the mule now, urging it with dangerous haste through the slippery mud.

At midday he stopped for a rest, and to eat the food he had been too excited to touch at dawn. Twice he had seen Robert's mule-tracks pressed into the ground, swollen with muddy rain, like a broken copper necklace. All morning he had heard the river roaring a mile away but now ravine and path had edged towards each other and he sat with his food on the bank and watched the flood carrying tree trunks, birds' nests, broken parts of a footbridge, and two goats drifting within five minutes of each other, down the stream with their heads unnaturally high above water.

There could be no more than twenty miles now to the border; perhaps two days. He watched the refuse curve round the bend of the river and wondered anxiously if Robert could yet escape. He had a pistol, but Robert had so much else: courage, experience, the habit of winning. And the stronger motive: a prison in Delhi waited on his failure.

Fearing Robert's escape, he swallowed the last of his food and turned to the mule. He stared. He had tied the animal to a tree ten feet from the bank. Now the water had crept up the sloping ground and was lapping at the mule's hoofs. The river was swift, but did not seem enough for this; it flowed with a smooth fullness, almost in silence. All the energy of the flood was hidden far back in the mountains, in cloudbursts and torrents on the peaks.

With his elbows leaning on the saddle, boots in the shallow water, he paused to reflect on his anticipation of triumph. Conviction had drained from him with his passage down the hillside, obliterating Robert's prints with his own. He was unused to the role of pursuer, and he caught a sudden, backward-glancing anticipation for the foolishness of the victor.

What Robert had done to him ten years ago certainly deserved this at the time. But he was a different person, Robert was a different person, and Rowena, and it was all just a mess of coincidence correlating at that one time into a tragedy that no longer made sense. If they had met for the first time that week, if Rowena had not existed, or if. . . .

But it was no good. From the flotsam of human experience you could grasp those few things that mattered, but in the end you were alone. Against the fear of solitude we invest our friends and lovers with more than they have, but in the end we are alone. It was stupid to think otherwise. He felt the brown water lapping at his boots, climbed painfully to the saddle, and turned the mule south, downhill, towards the sorrow that the past demanded.

He found Robert in the late afternoon of the next day, stacking brushwood on his mule's back on the high bank of the river. The water flowed in a deep ravine five miles above the confluence with the Jhelum and the flood carried under a narrow bridge with swift and near-silent force. On the far side of the bridge Robert had almost finished disguising his baggage with the firewood. He had changed his clothes too, and looked like any villager of the Jhelum Valley. His jacket and trousers were heavily patched with oddments of material, and his blond hair was concealed beneath a safa.

Ernie stiffened as he saw Robert walking back across the river. It was a crude suspension bridge with only two stanchions either side of the forty-foot distance between the banks. There was a single handrail for half its length; the rest was missing, probably stolen by a villager for his hut.

He faded hastily back into the bushes. He wasn't ready, he wanted to prepare himself, to have the right words ready to say. . . .

It had been an exhausting twenty-four hours. Without food, he had skirted two more villages for fear that Robert had warned them too. He was terribly hungry, and the night had been too cold to sleep more than an hour. All the fatigues of the journey, put off from day to day on the high mountains, had now overtaken him : he was tired and ill; there was a tic in one eye, and his thighs and stomach ached with the pain of riding downhill. He was dirty and unshaven and utterly weary, his face splashed with mud, his clothes grimy with sweat.

Robert passed within twenty yards of him, unlooping the binoculars from his neck. He looked strong and relaxed, the journey's end only a few hours away. He was whistling, loud and tuneless in the way that irritated Ernie so much at Oxford, the way it engaged a room: but as if remembering his peasant role the tune broke off in mid-note and Robert turned off the path into a clump of bamboo. Ernie listened to his crackling progress dying slowly away and minutes later saw him appear in a patch of bare ground, moving across the slope above the bamboo scrub.

At the top of the hill he stood for a moment with the binoculars to his face, staring southwards to a place Ernie could not see. He would be looking for Indian patrols. On the other side of the bridge the mule whinneyed impatiently and Robert stared down at it for a second before turning to drop from Ernie's sight down the far slope. Beyond the hill was a larger one. Robert would be climbing it and he had perhaps ten minutes before the bridge would again be in his view.

He came out of his hiding place and dragged his protesting mule across the flimsy bridge. He could feel it swaying beneath their movement and one of the stanchions groaned as if in pain. He had thought of laying an ambush farther down the valley but half-way across the bridge he had another idea.

The mules laid their ears back at each other but Ernie dragged his into the trees at the ravine's edge. He tied it to a tree and ran back to lie hidden in the nearest cover to the bridge. He would wait till Robert was half-way across and helpless.

He felt his heart bumping against the hard pistol clutched to his chest. Capture was so near . . . vengeance that had been waiting since a day which, as he tried to contemplate it, receded steadily into his past: since the night at the temple, since the interview with the Minister, since the day in Turley, since. . . .

Now he no longer desired it, but that was irrelevant. He tried to relive the humiliation of ten years ago, but emotion had drained away down the years and the event had happened to someone else, a youth at Oxford burdened by inferiority, desire and doubt. The Minister had tried to reawaken the anger, but since then he had crossed a mountain and now Robert was a cornered animal at the end of his pistol barrel.

He heard the tuneless whistling again and with a sudden shock saw Robert walk out of the bamboo. He seemed almost to burst upon the scene in the time Ernie adjusted his thoughts to the moment. The blood hammered in his head and the pistol shook. Now Robert had taken his first grasp of the handrail, there was no more time. On quivering legs, his shadow preceding him like some ungainly animal, he ran on to the bridge.

Robert had been walking with his eyes on the river below, his thoughts somewhere else. Shock flushed his face at the sound of Ernie's feet. His body performed a series of momentary jerks, paralyzed gestures of search for a weapon, escape, anything. An amazed cry was arrested before release. His feet, turning to run, stopped before they moved.

Then Ernie could watch all the nervous energy drain painfully out until Robert seemed to have shrunk slightly within his clothes. His shoulders drooped; at last he summoned a small bitter smile of defeat.

'You win,' he said softly.

And then began his first experience of learning to live beneath his pride; he would be accepting justifications and doubts, with shame ever rubbing at the edge of memory, and curious questions turned down paths of irrelevance. From the conqueror's table he stole a crumb; straightening his shoulders he stared frankly into Ernie's face.

'I am your prisoner,' he conceded.

They stood so long in stillness that a bird flew undisturbed through the space between them. As in a filmy mirror Ernie was recognizing in Robert's face his own inadequacy for the greatness of the moment . . . the sick face splashed with mud, dirty fingernails curved uncertainly around the pistol, the five-day beard a feeble growth of thin black hairs on his cheeks. His eyes were bright with tiredness.

'You can go,' Ernie said at last.

Joy at the sudden decision made his voice lift as if singing. 'I don't hate you, Robert. I won't take you back to Delhi. I—I'd be ashamed of myself if I did.'

Nothing had yet registered on the pale face before him, and he went on: 'I needed to catch you, but now . . . now you can go free, back to Pakistan or England if you wish. Remember our friendship—'

'You little bastard!'

'What!'

For a moment he thought it was a blurted exclamation of relief and love. 'Robert, I never really wanted—'

But his sentence tailed away. Robert's face was like a thundercloud.

'You condescending little bastard!' Robert cried.

So at last it all fell into place. Understanding bloomed like a flower on accelerated film.

And with his enemy already running at him, he let the floodgates open and hate came pouring in at last. The looming pistol filled half his vision and Robert's desperate angry face lay at the end of his sights. But, as the face grew quickly larger and the bridge shook beneath the running feet, he refused the mercy of release that only death could give.

Instead, at the last moment before impact, he jerked his arm and sent the gun arcing into the water. Then hands were on his throat and Robert fought like a tiger in darkness.

His face was smashed against Robert's upthrust skull, a knee jerked pain into his groin and he was flung across the handrail of the bridge. Stiff fingers were in his eyes, he felt his spine bending over the rail and then the fear rising like sickness. Aware that his puny strength on Robert would be spent like a hammer on its anvil, he fell swiftly back, ducked under the rail, and pulled Robert over and past.

Flung on his back, one foot hanging between sky and water, he saw Robert dropping down the edge of his vision till the river closed over his retreat.

Gasping, he turned to peer down at the exposed rocks beneath the bridge, the swirl of deep blackness. For minutes he sought a constant form in the tossing channels, but the first evidence, like oil from a shipwreck, was the water's discoloration from Robert's blood.

When the body did appear, marked by the trailing scarf of the safa, it was far downstream, already started on its last journey down to Pakistan.

He lay on the bridge, feeling as little pain yet as at the moment of injury, staring interminably at the sullen flow of dark water as the sun dipped into the hills. For it was already the last time he would have to consider it accurately, to have his knowledge in harmony with the event. Never again would the experience be like this, before time edged in as always to accommodate the desire. And before the barriers could start forming before him one by one, to make life possible to live, he saw his future mirrored in the past, and groping for what happiness it had ever offered he found, by the dusty green and the goalposts, with the blond boy running on the grass, a bench in Delhi. And sat down.